THE OFFICIAL True Beauty COLORING BOOK

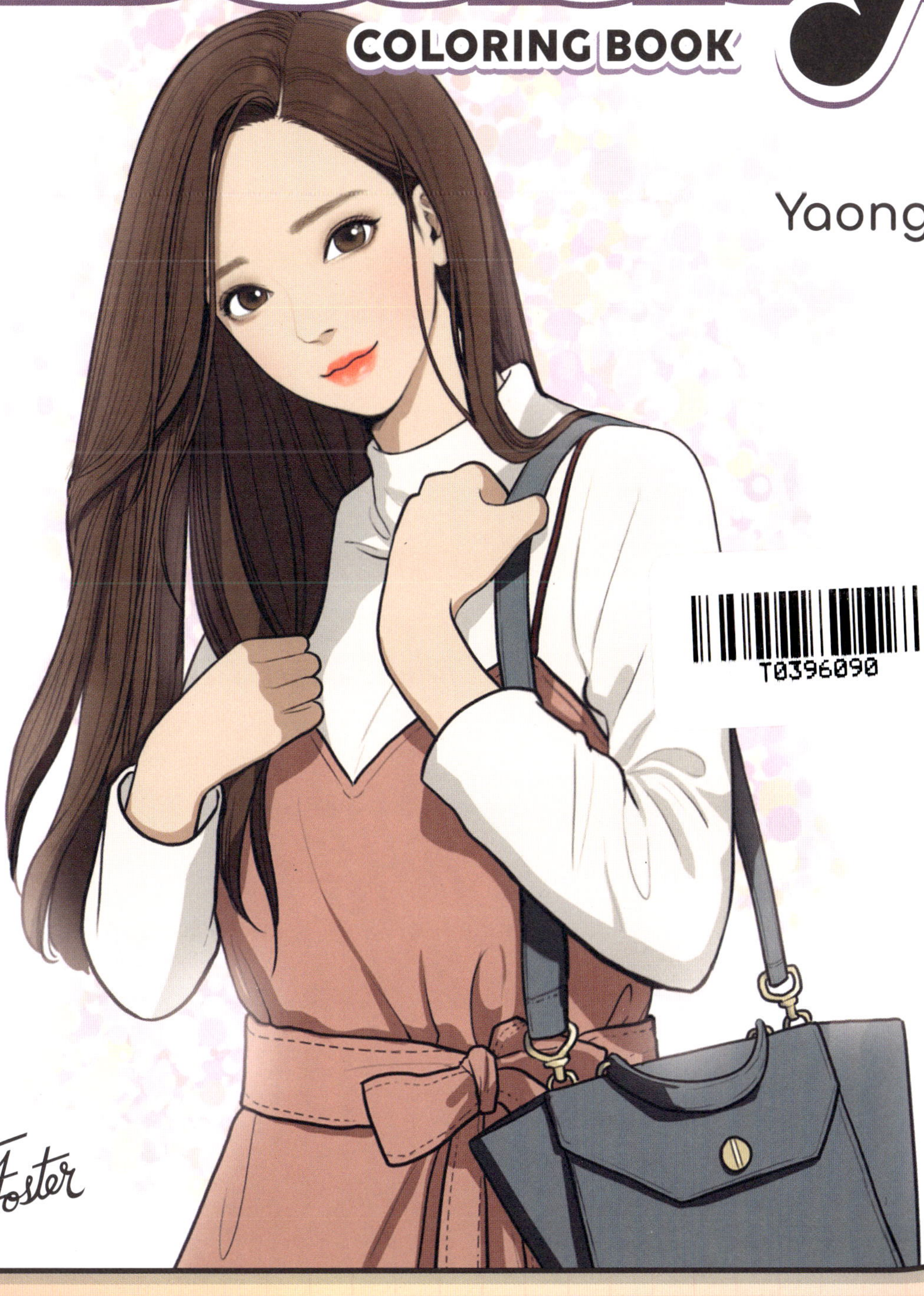

Yaongyi

Walter Foster

INTRODUCTION

Beauty isn't always easy.

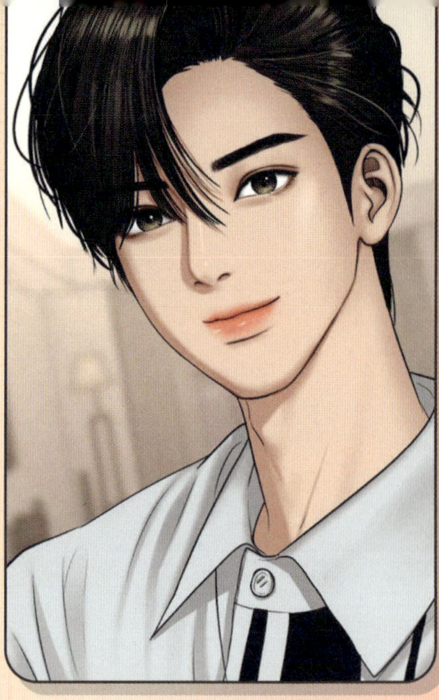

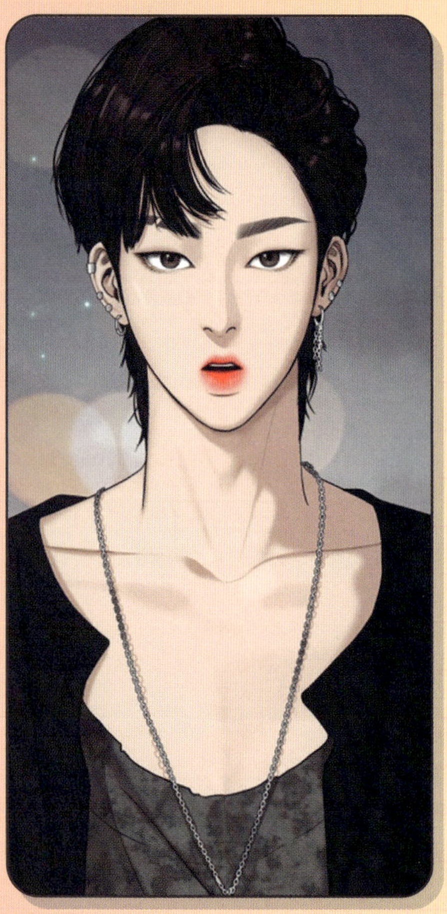

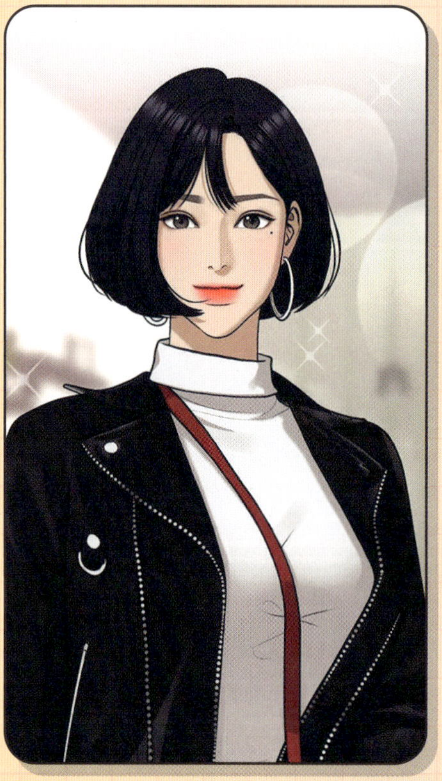

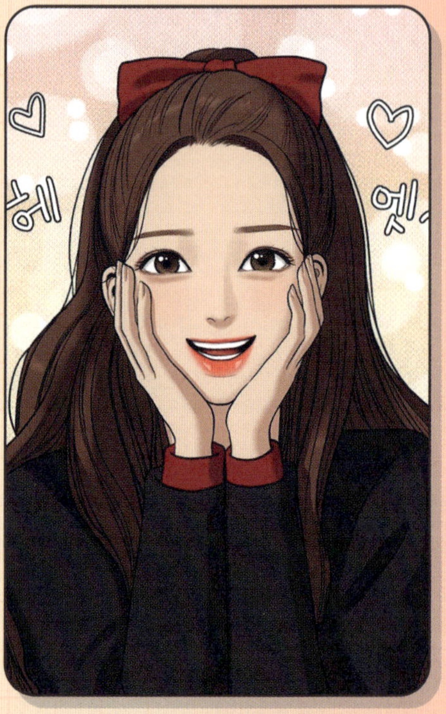

Get ready to immerse yourself in the world of the WEBTOON Originals series True Beauty, a webcomic about a young girl learning self-esteem and self-acceptance while navigating high school romance.

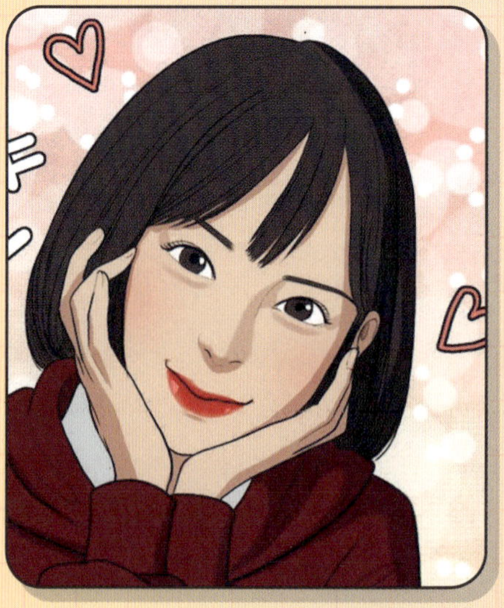

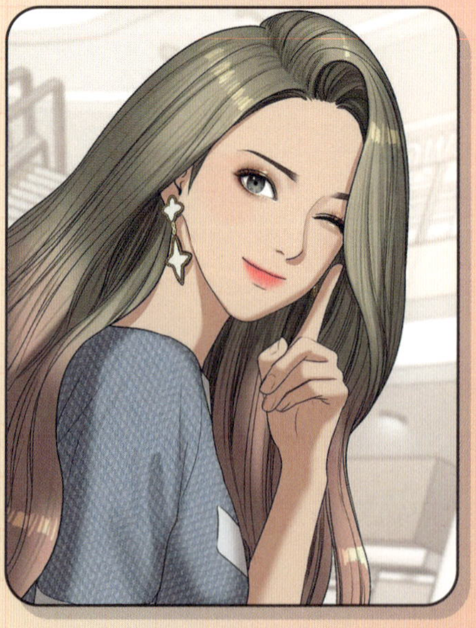

What Is True Beauty?

After binge-watching beauty videos online, a shy comic book fan masters the art of makeup and sees her social standing skyrocket as she becomes her school's prettiest pretty girl overnight. But will her elite status be short-lived? How long can she keep her real self a secret? And what about that cute boy who knows what she's hiding?

Check out the latest episode of the hit WEBTOON series!

SYNOPSIS

Jugyeong has been bullied and made fun of throughout high school. That all changes when she learns how to use makeup. Suddenly, she's the most popular girl at school. She quickly becomes close with the two most handsome boys: former best friends Suho and Seo-jun. The three create a love triangle, putting Jugyeong in a tough situation.

True Beauty follows Jugyeong's high school and adult years, highlighting her rise to makeup tutorial fame and the struggles—good and bad—that come with popularity. Follow along as she navigates the intricate labyrinth of high school life as well as a riveting love triangle. Who can resist both a mystery man and a bad boy?

About WEBTOON

WEBTOON is the world's largest digital comics platform, home to some of the biggest artists, IP, and fandoms in comics. As the global leader and pioneer of the mobile webcomic format, WEBTOON has revolutionized the comics industry for comic fans and creators. Today, a diverse new generation of international comic artists have found a home on WEBTOON, where the company's storytelling technology allows anyone to become a creator and build a global audience for their stories. The WEBTOON app is free to download on Android and iOS devices.

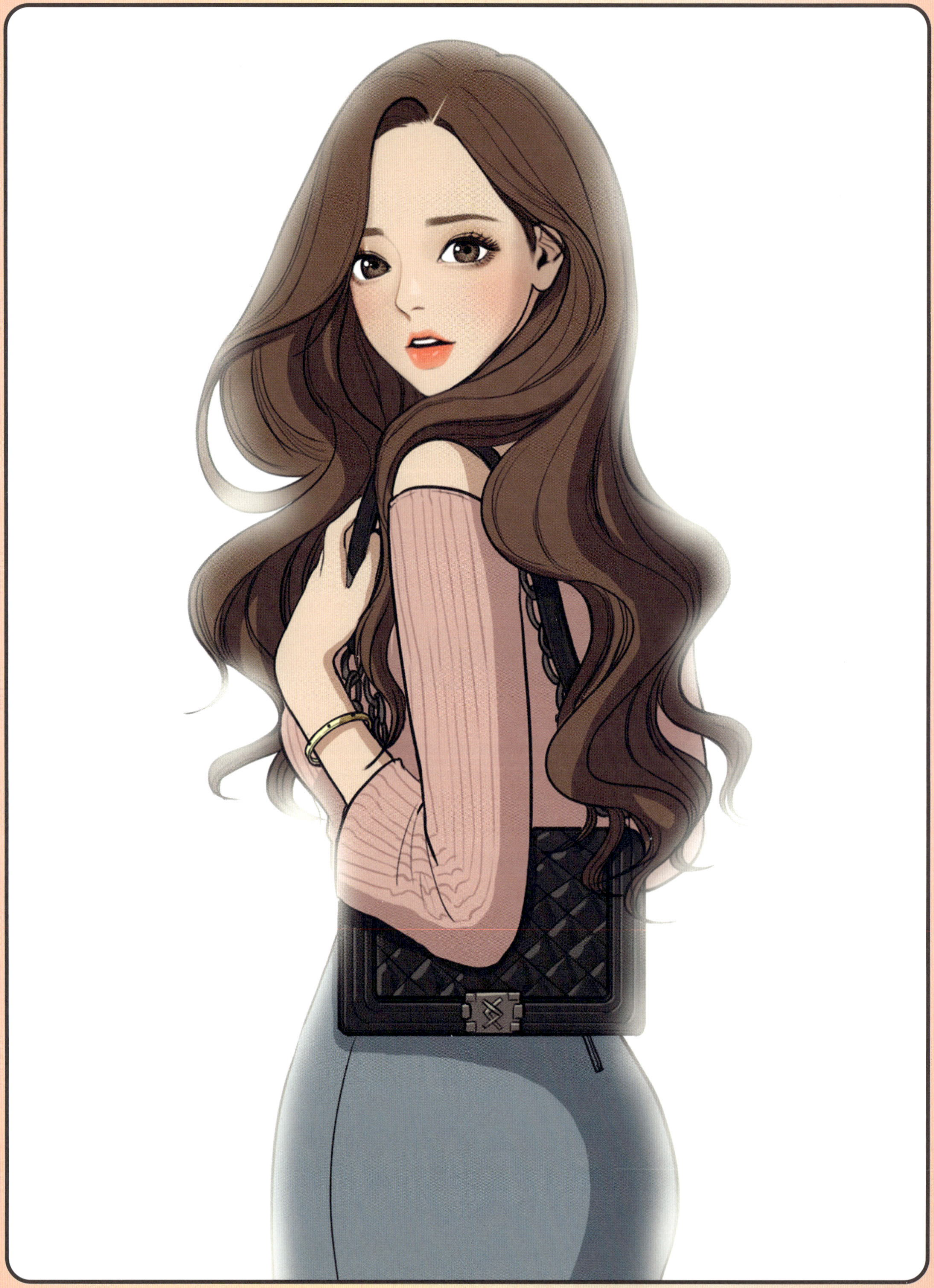

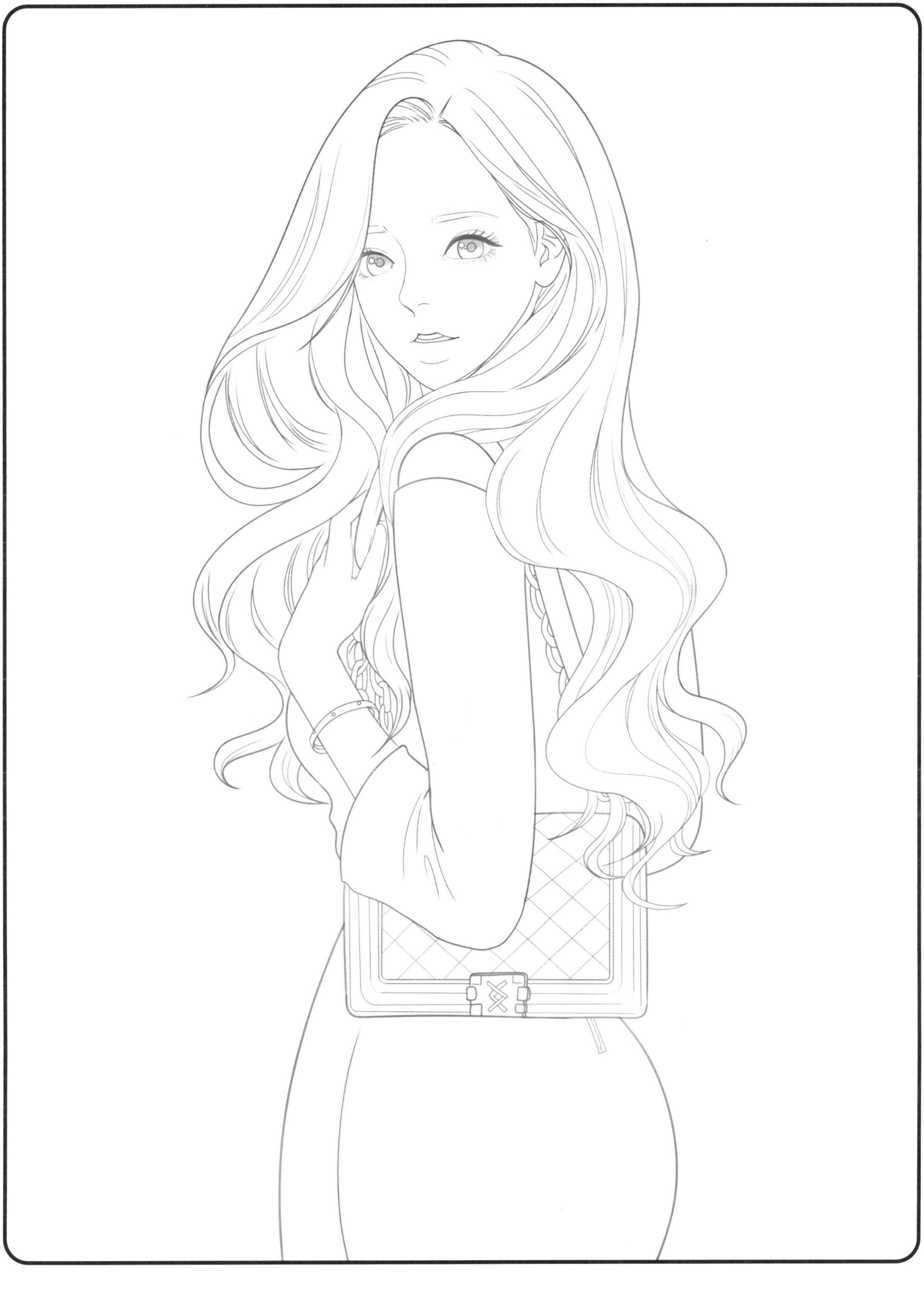

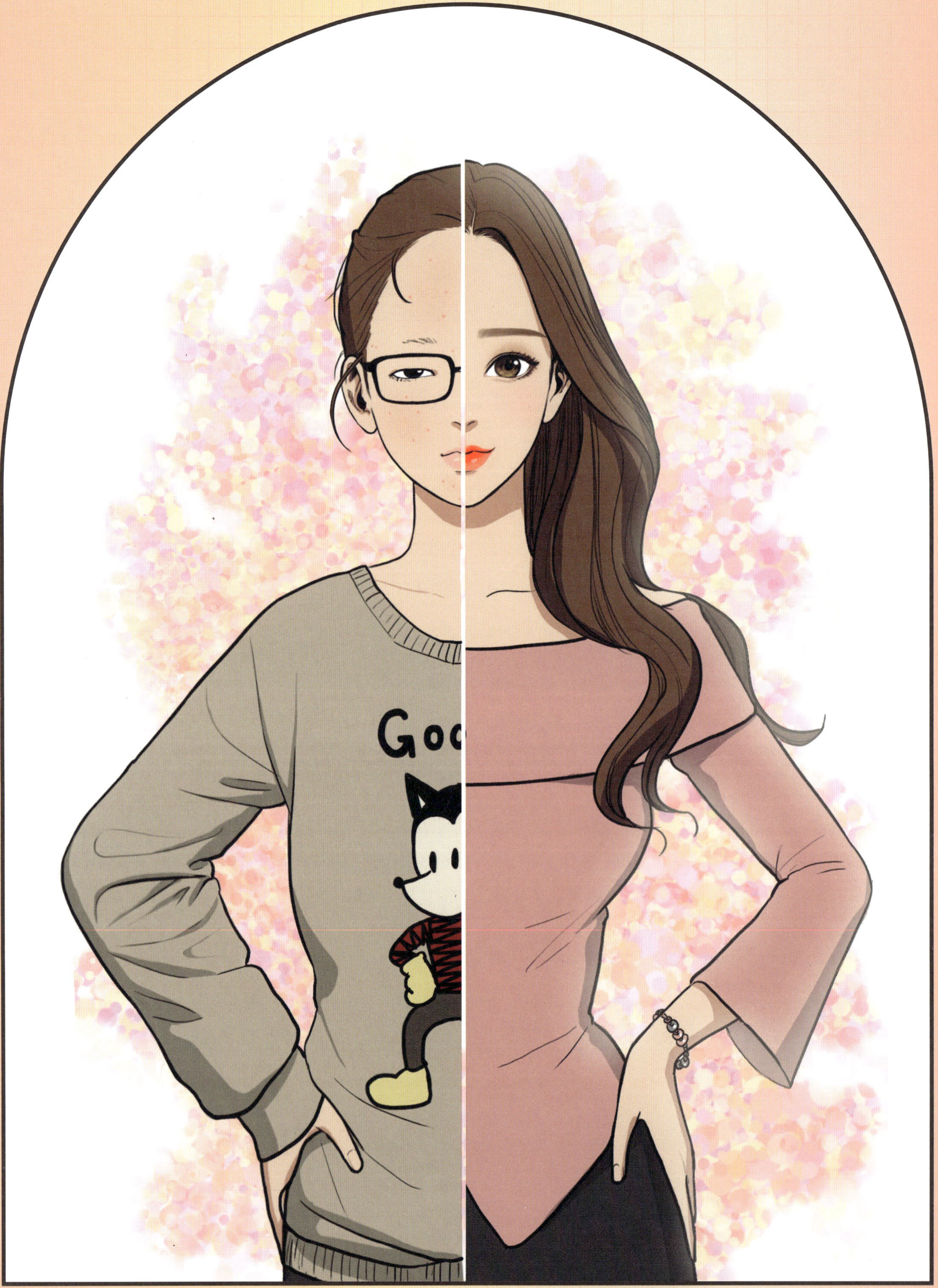
Goo

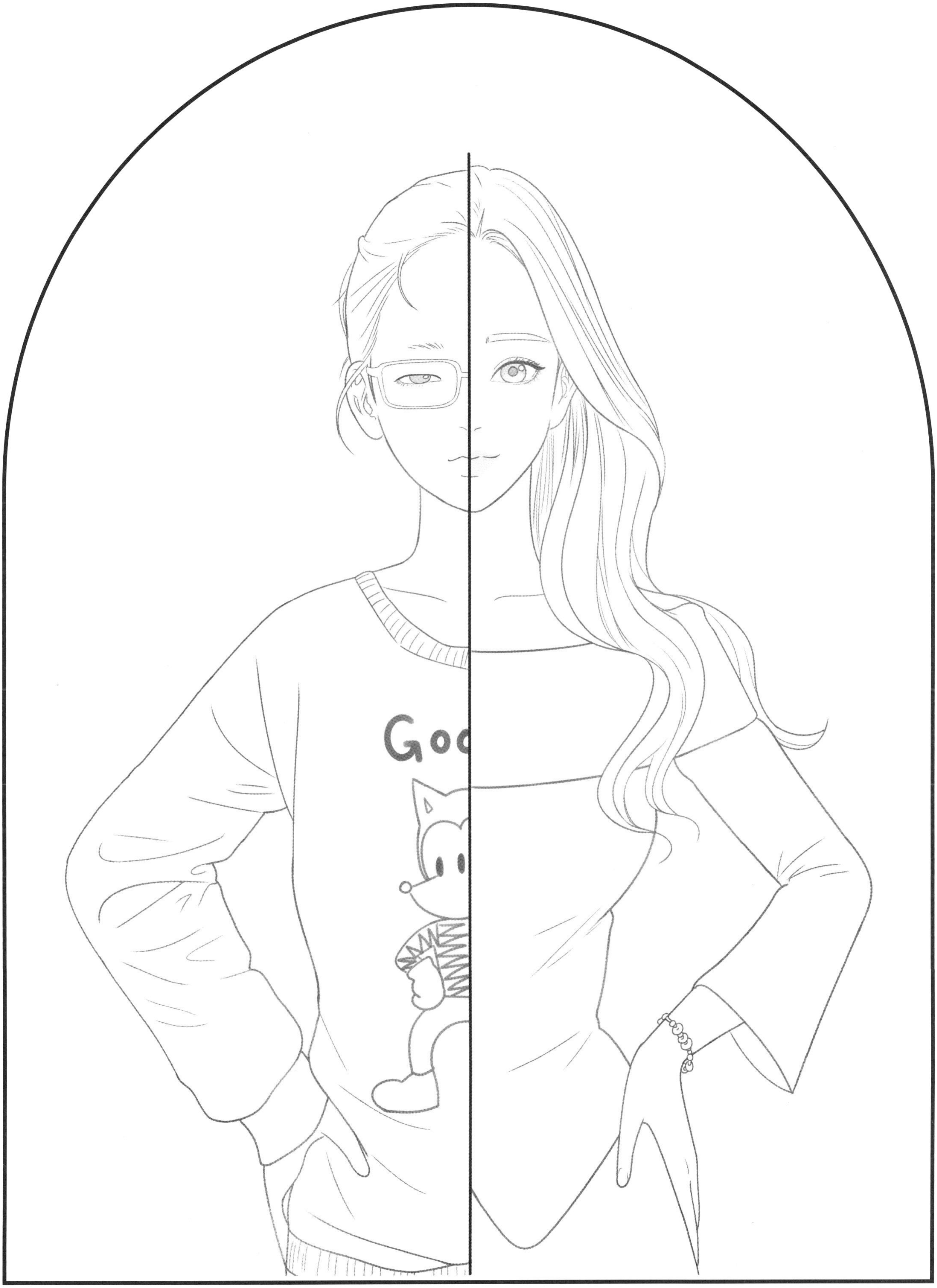
Goo

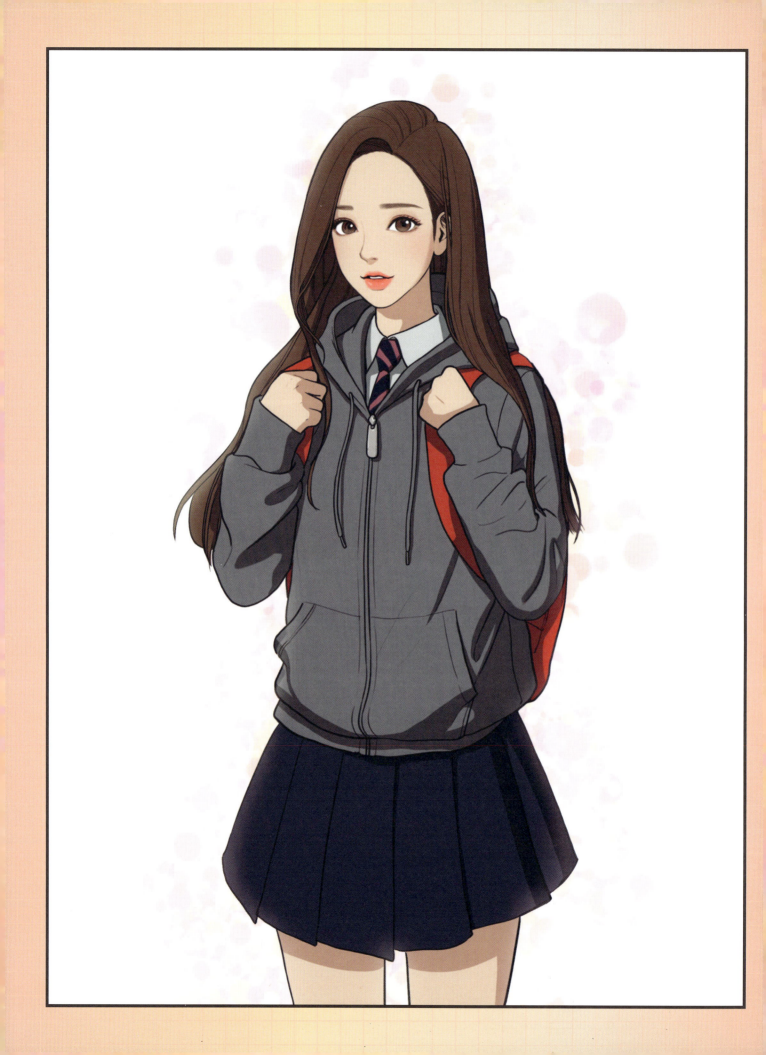

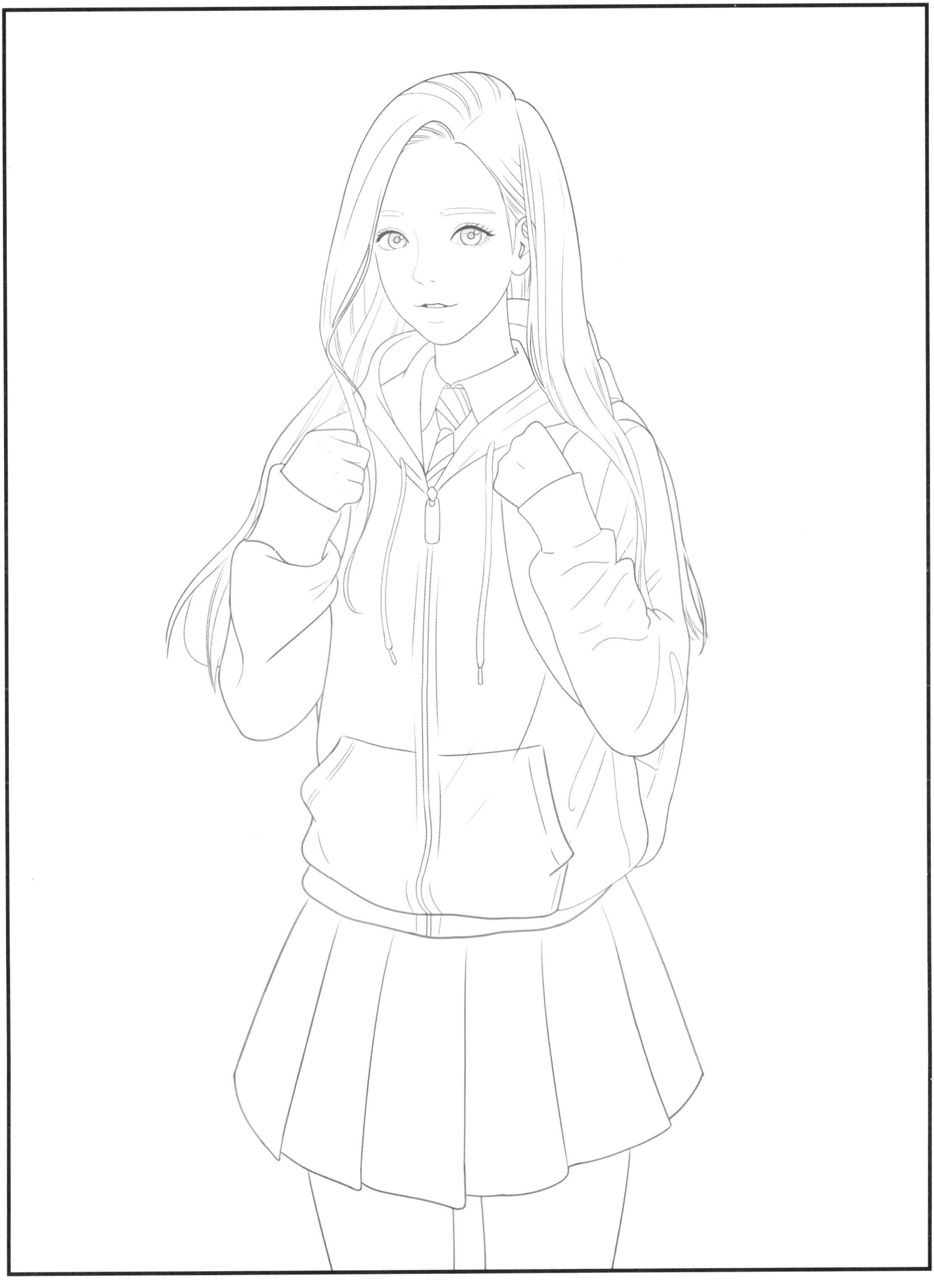

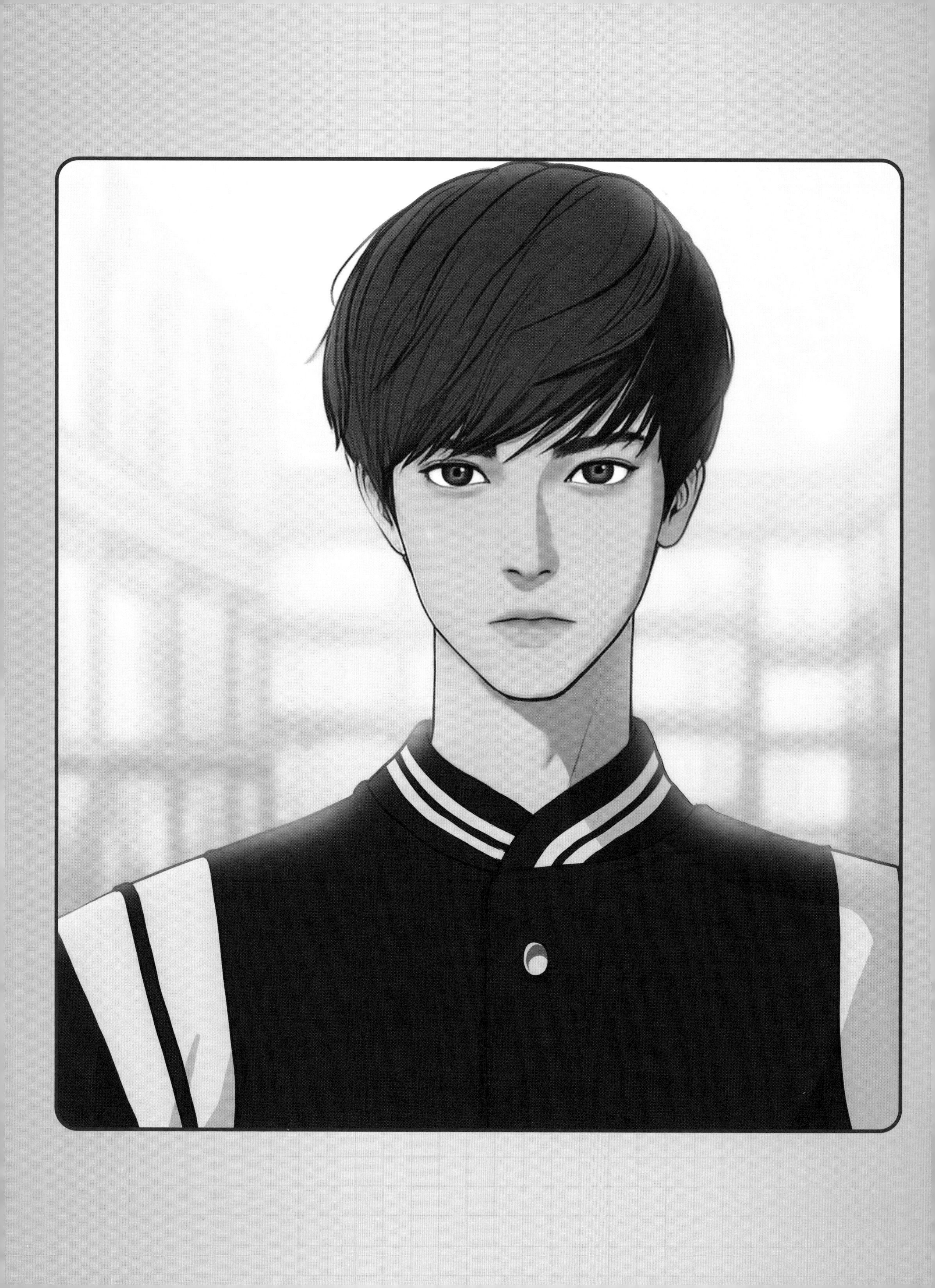

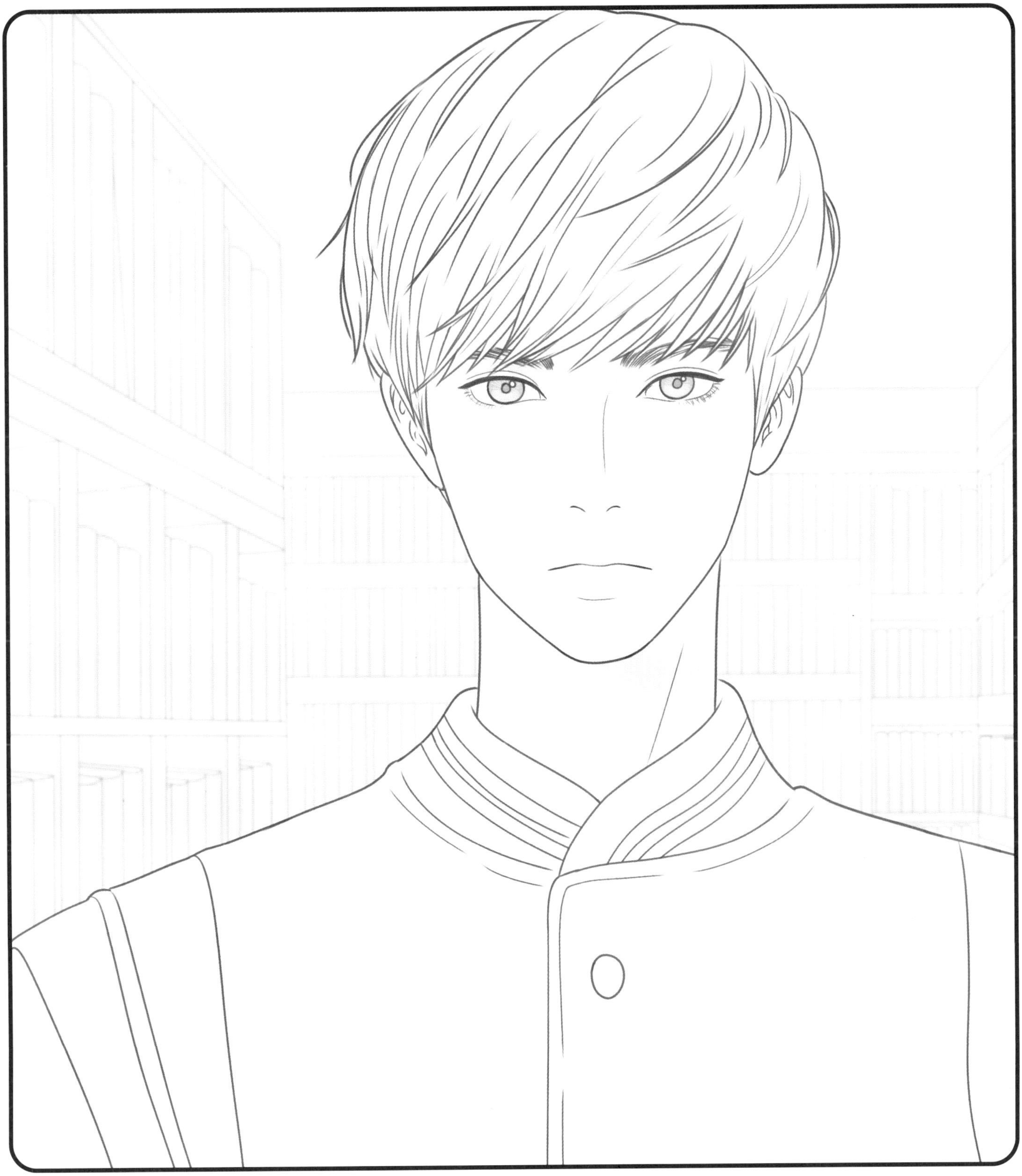

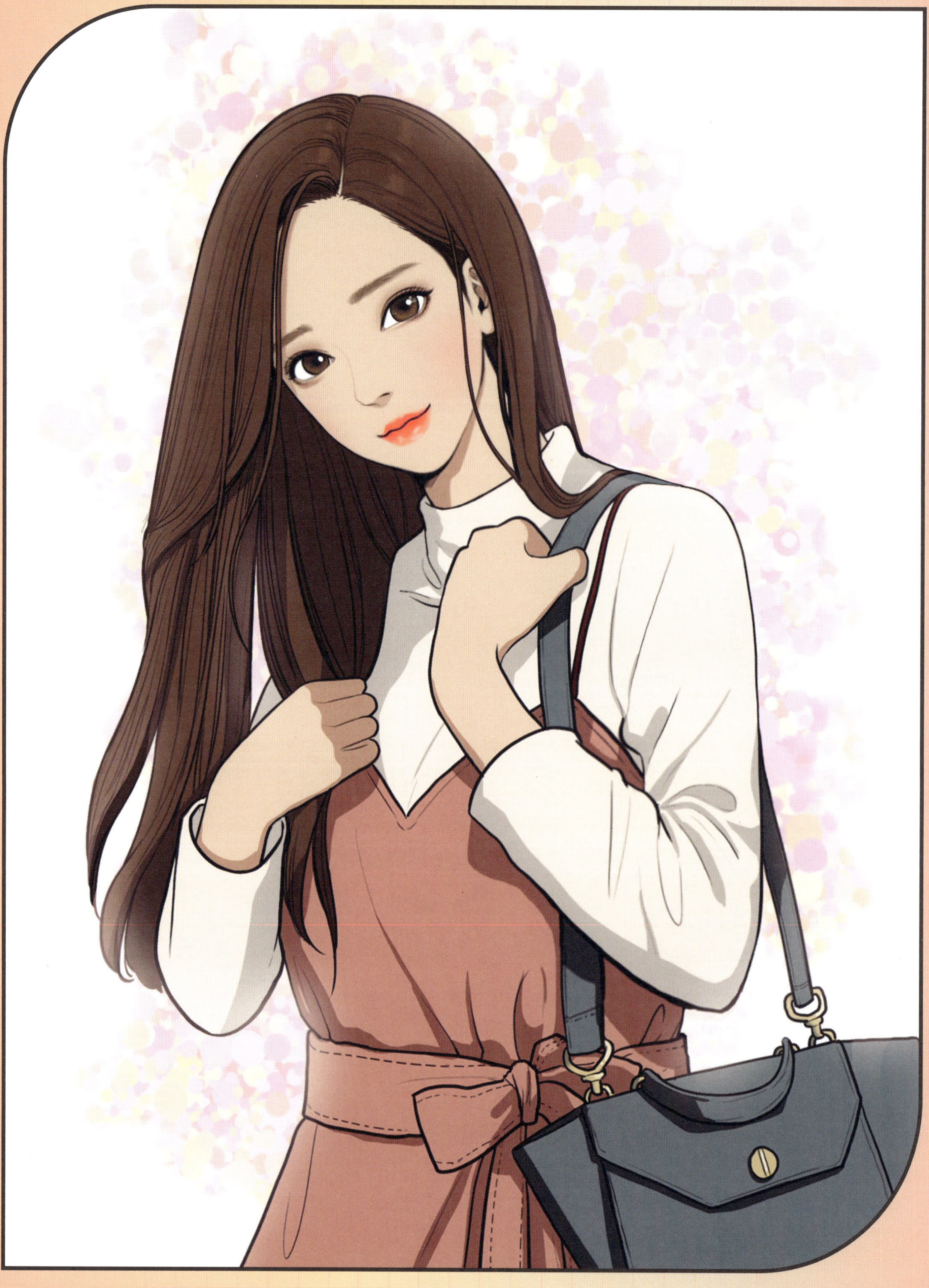

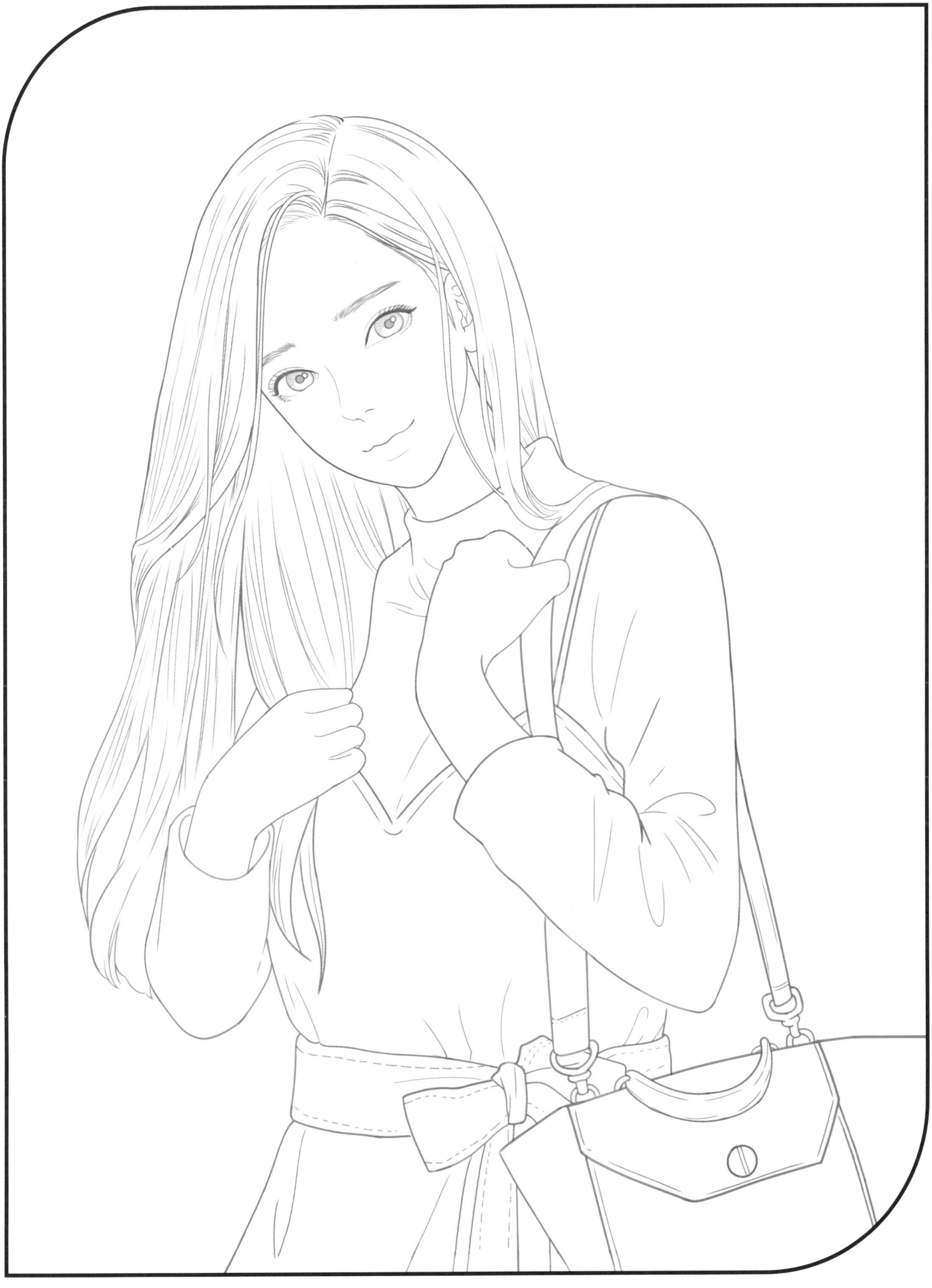

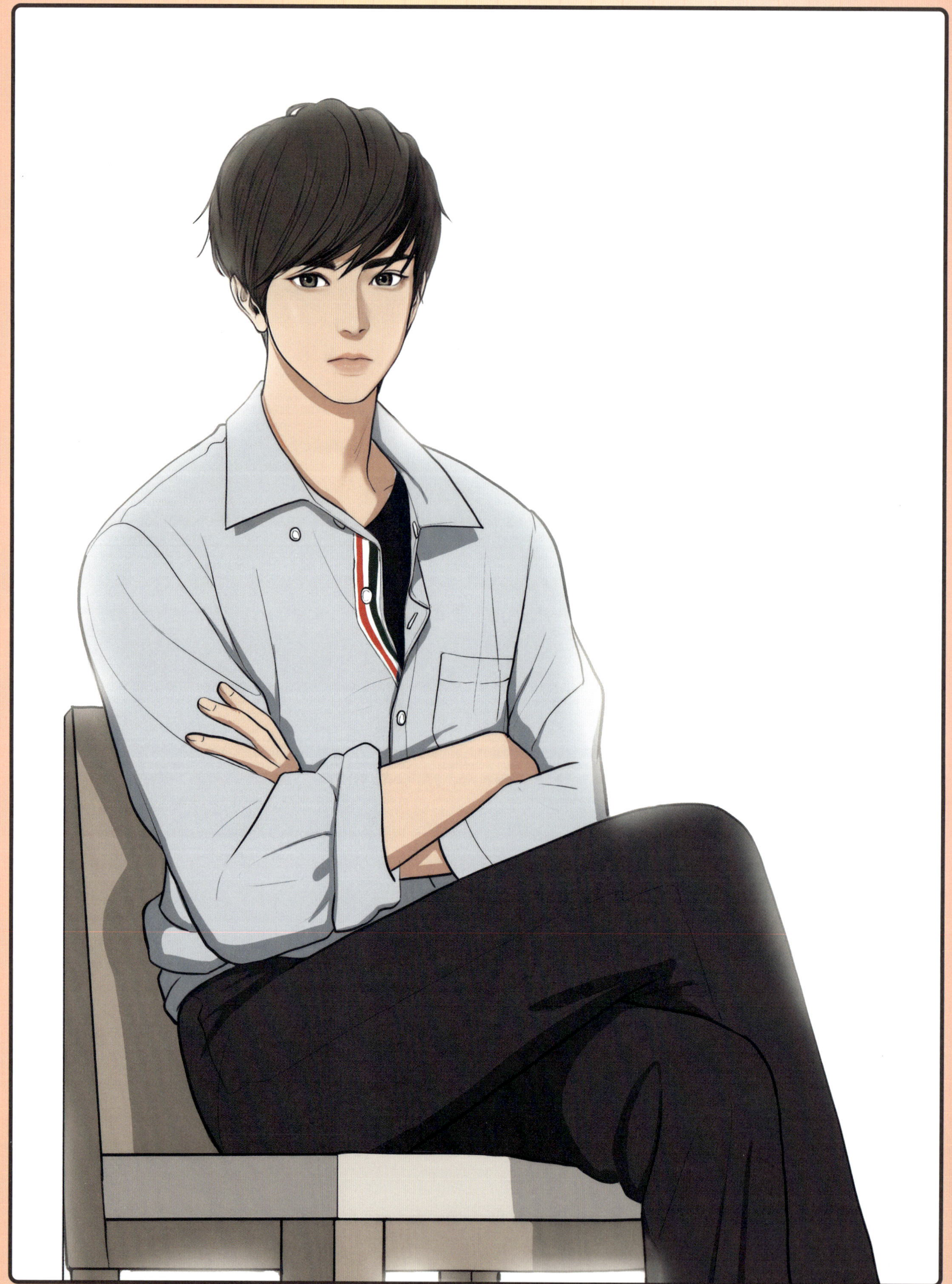

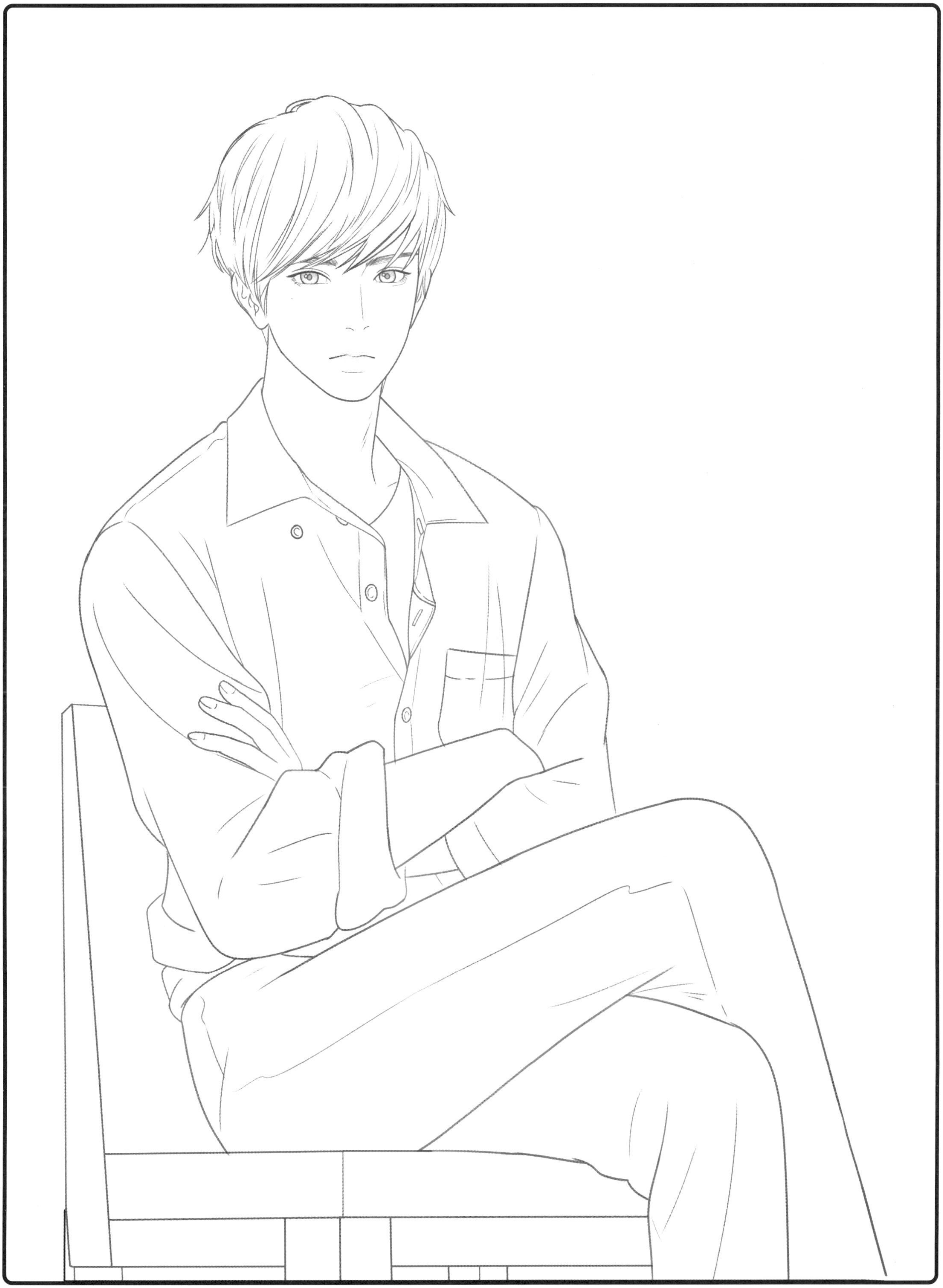

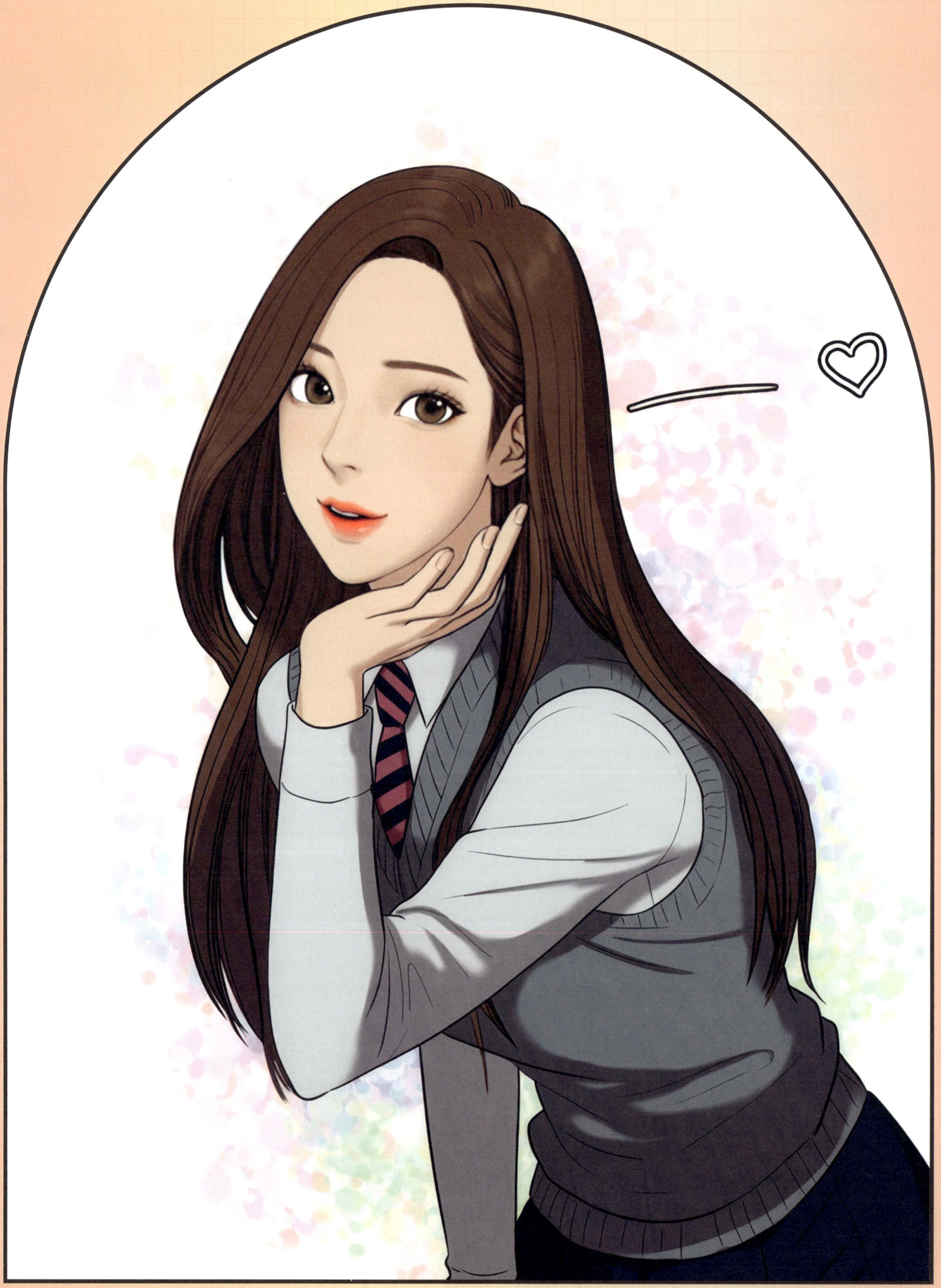

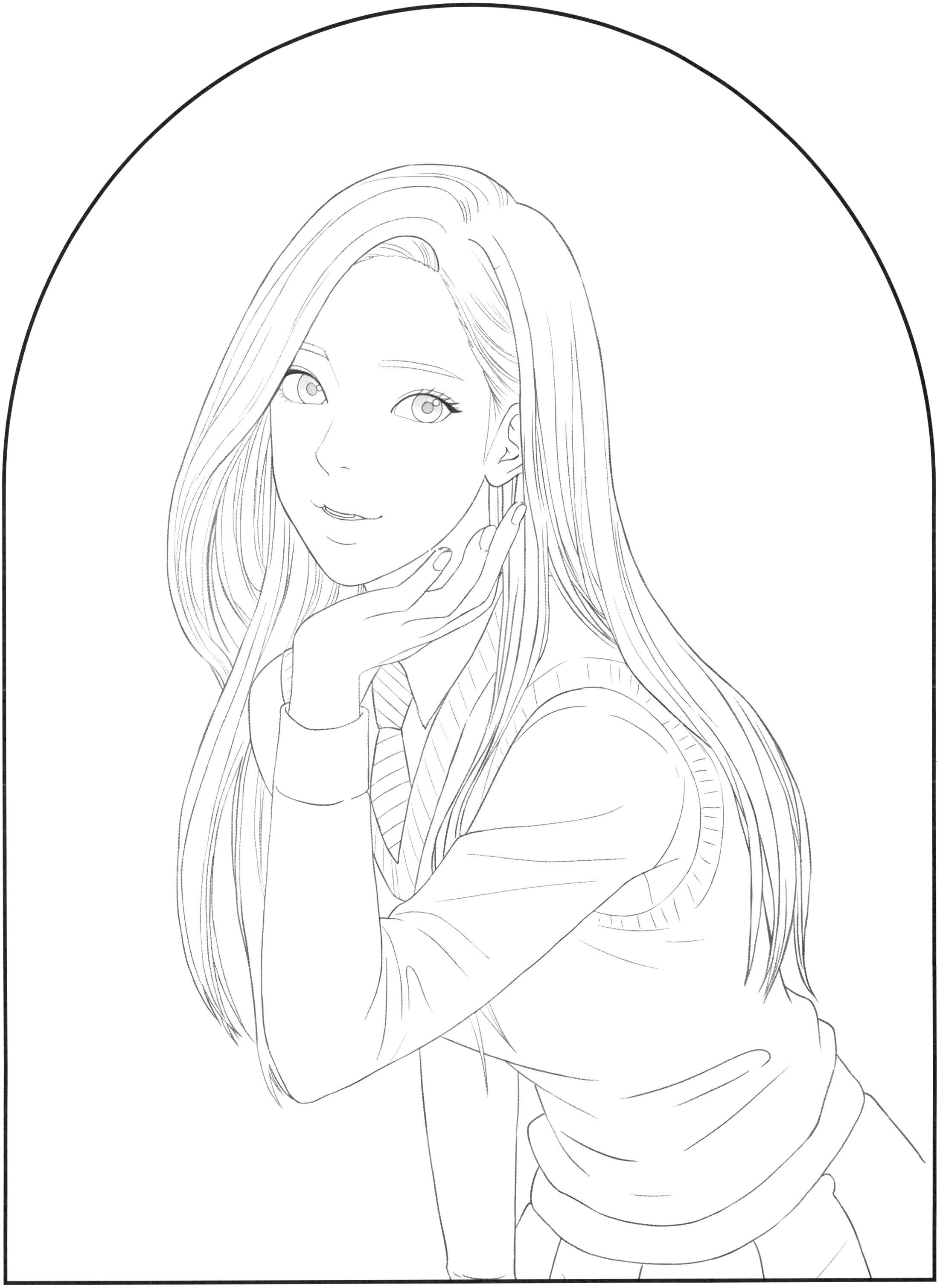

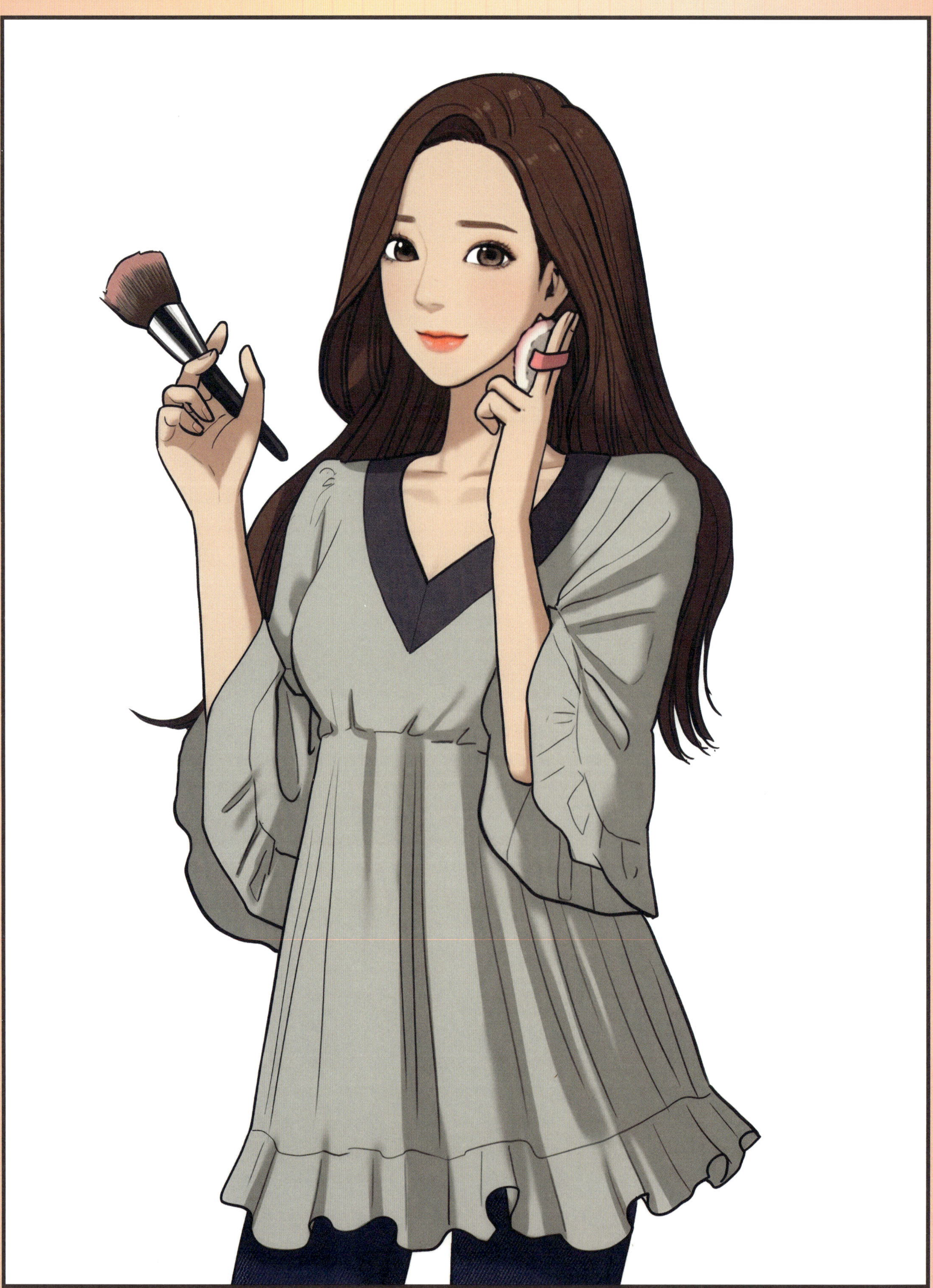

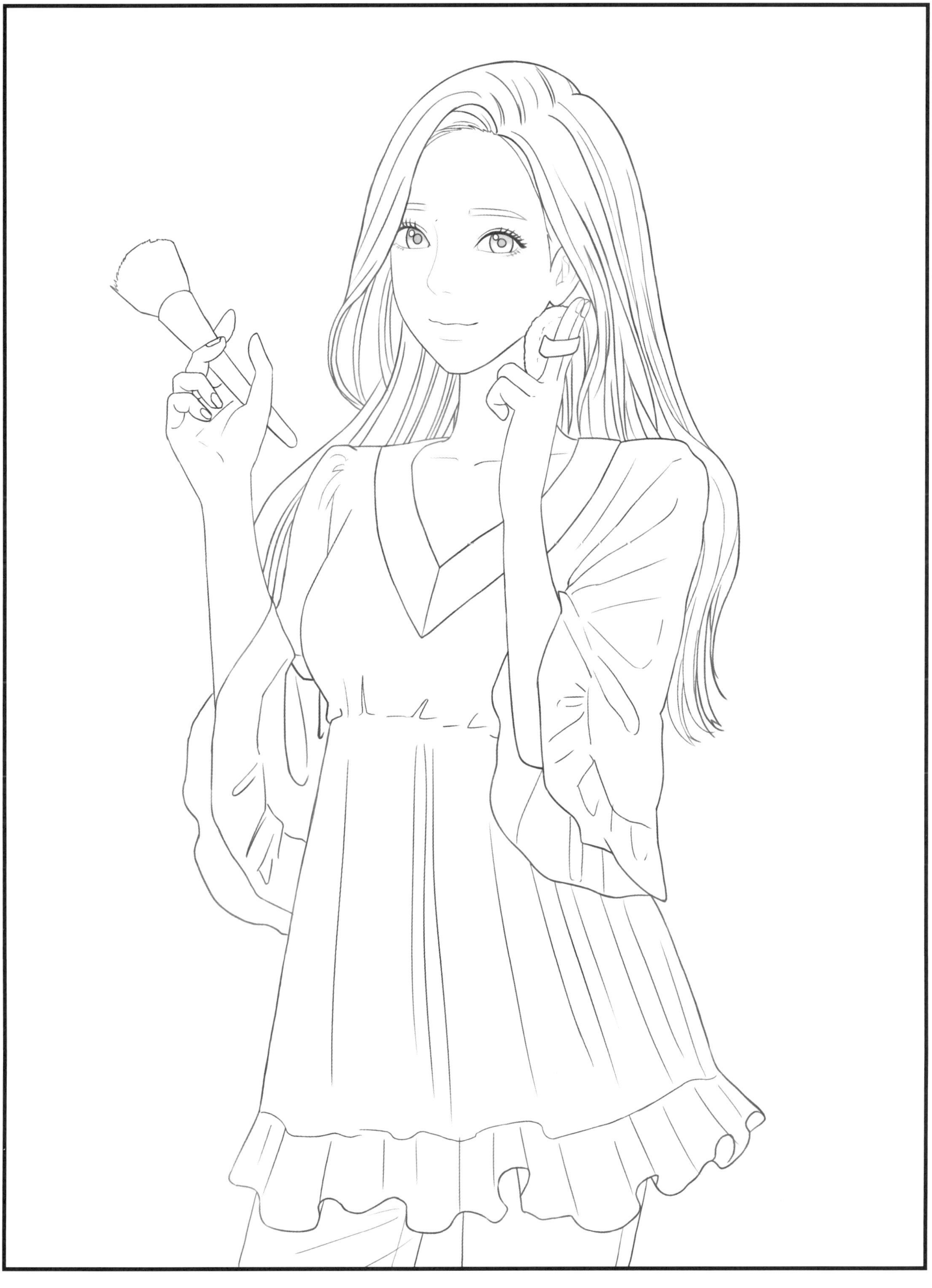

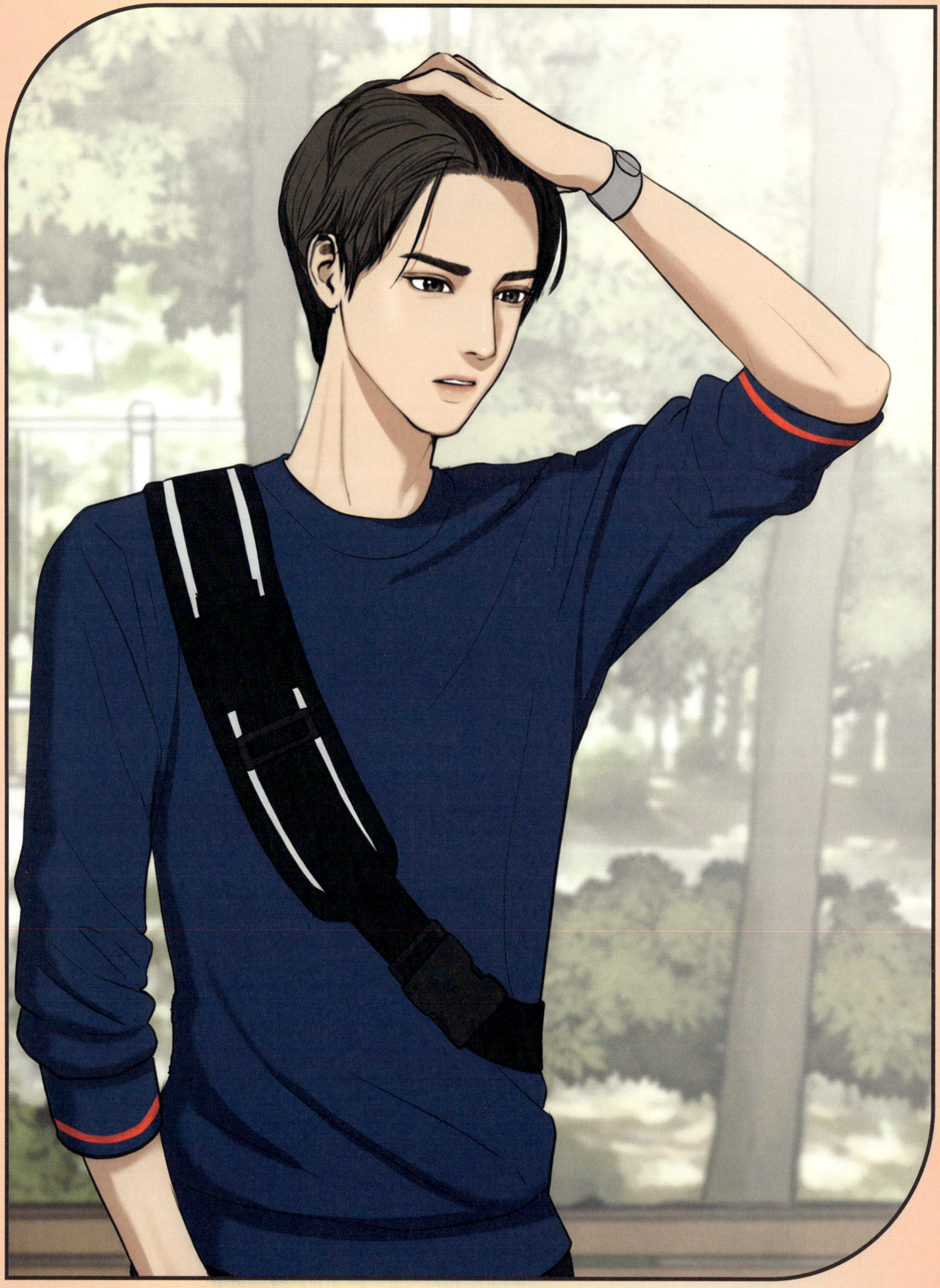

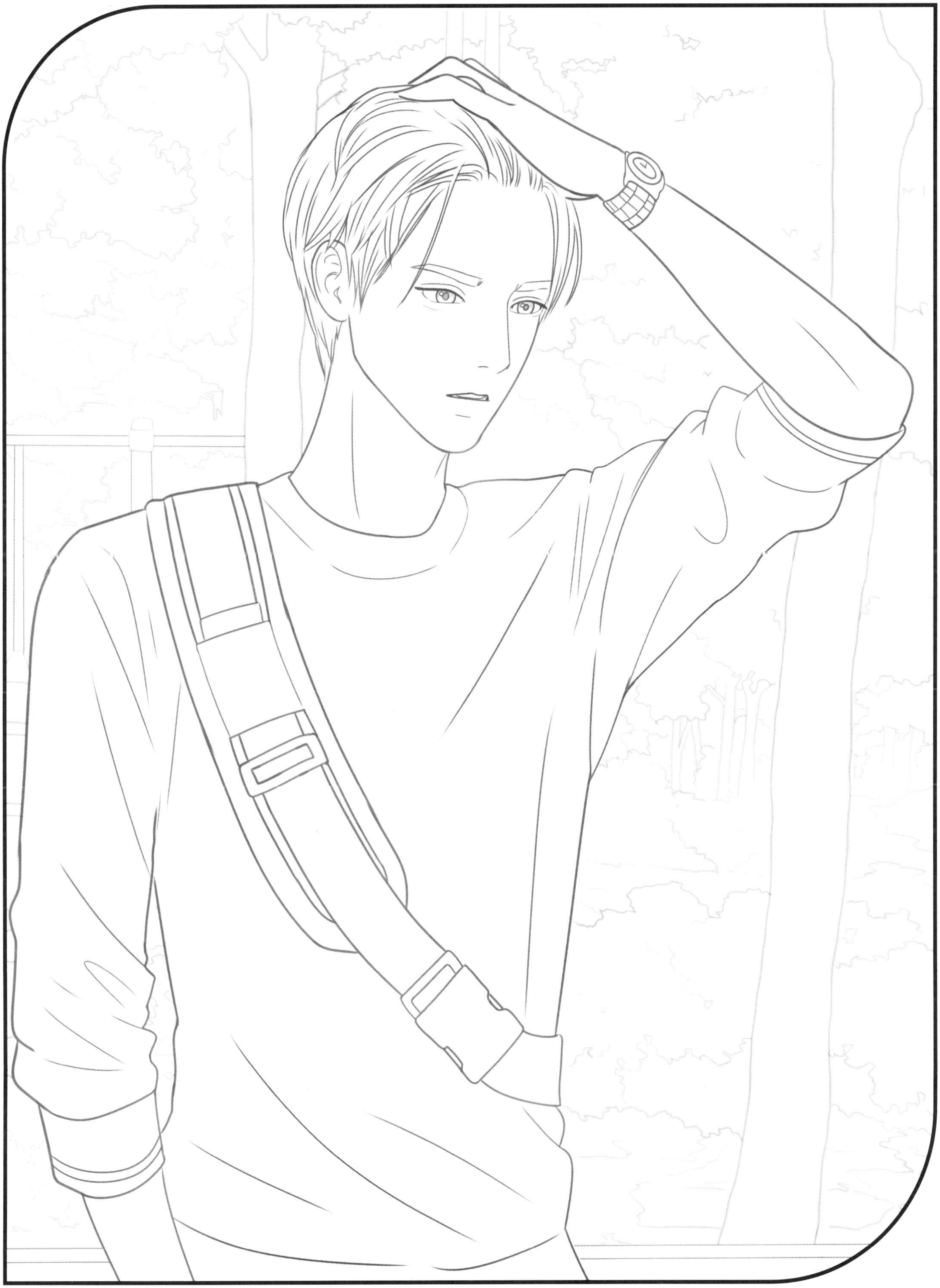

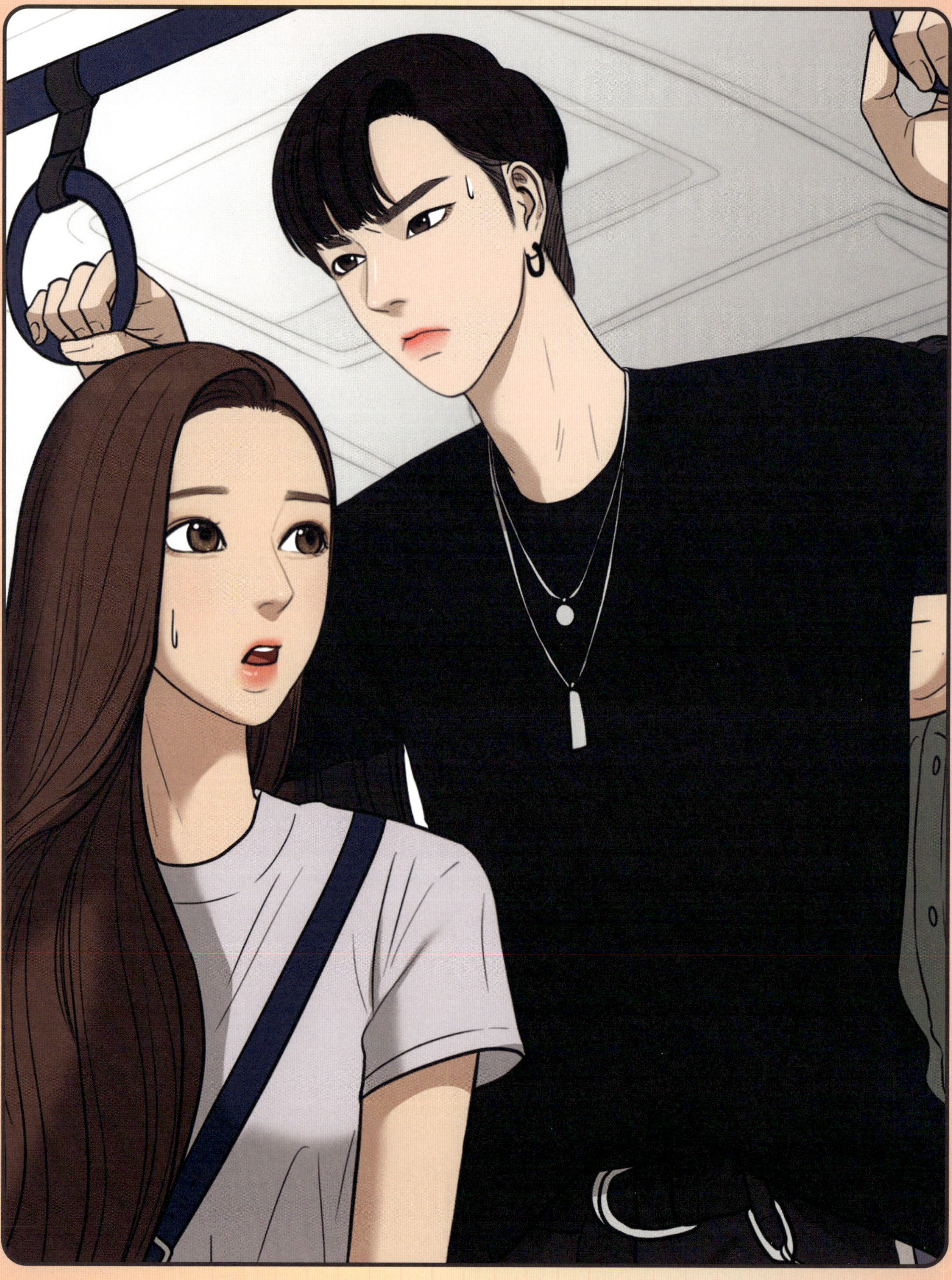

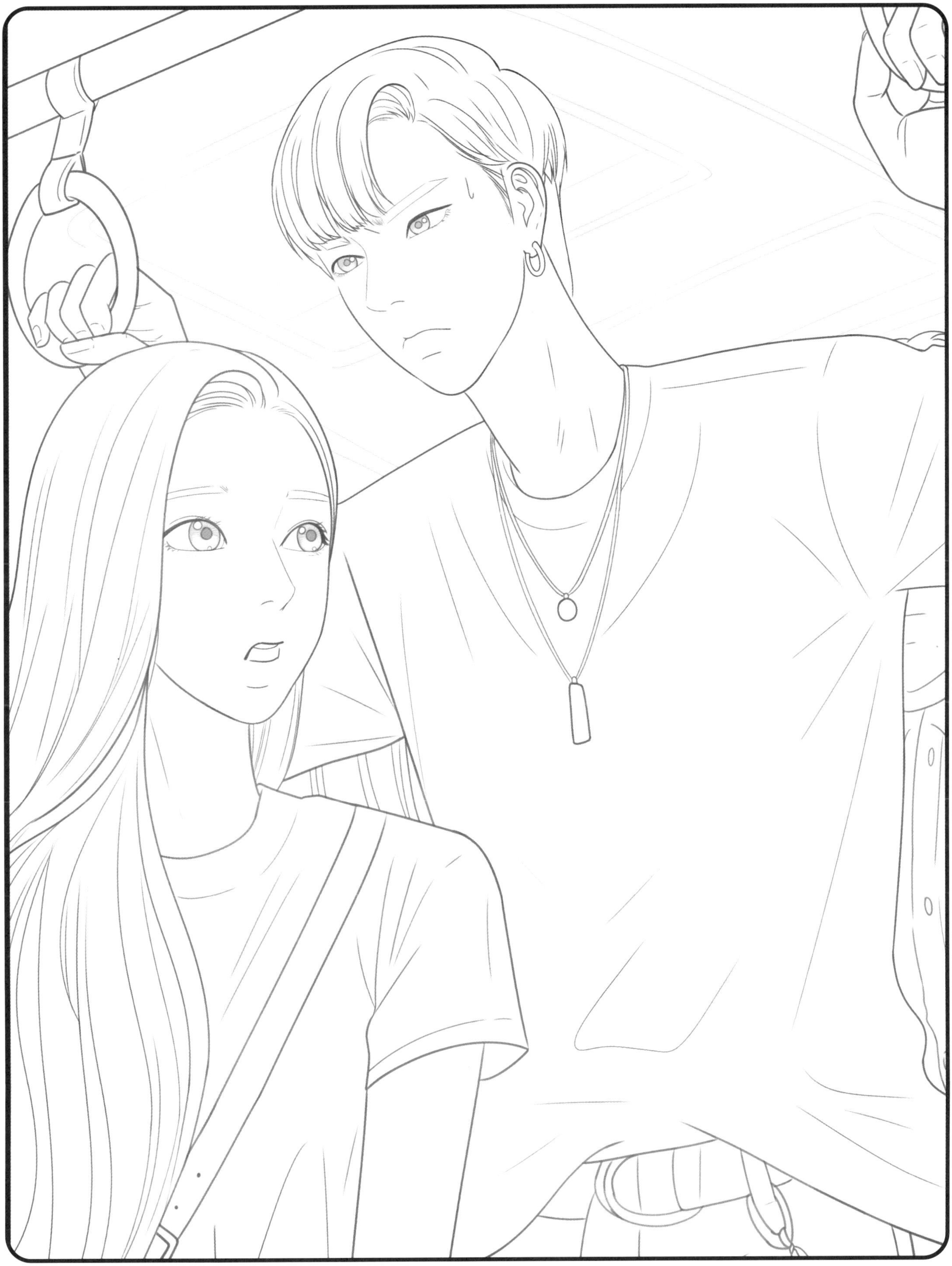

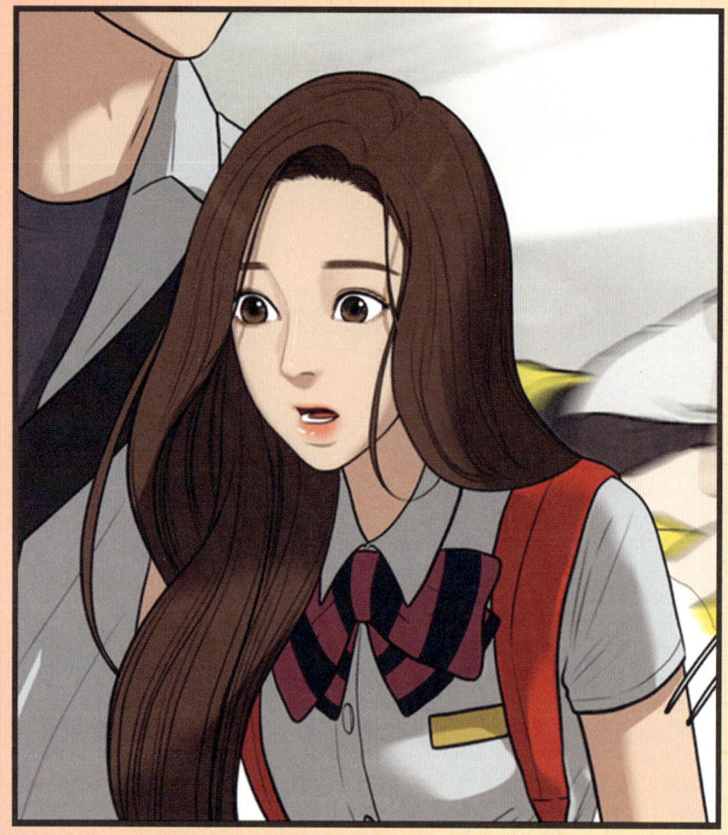

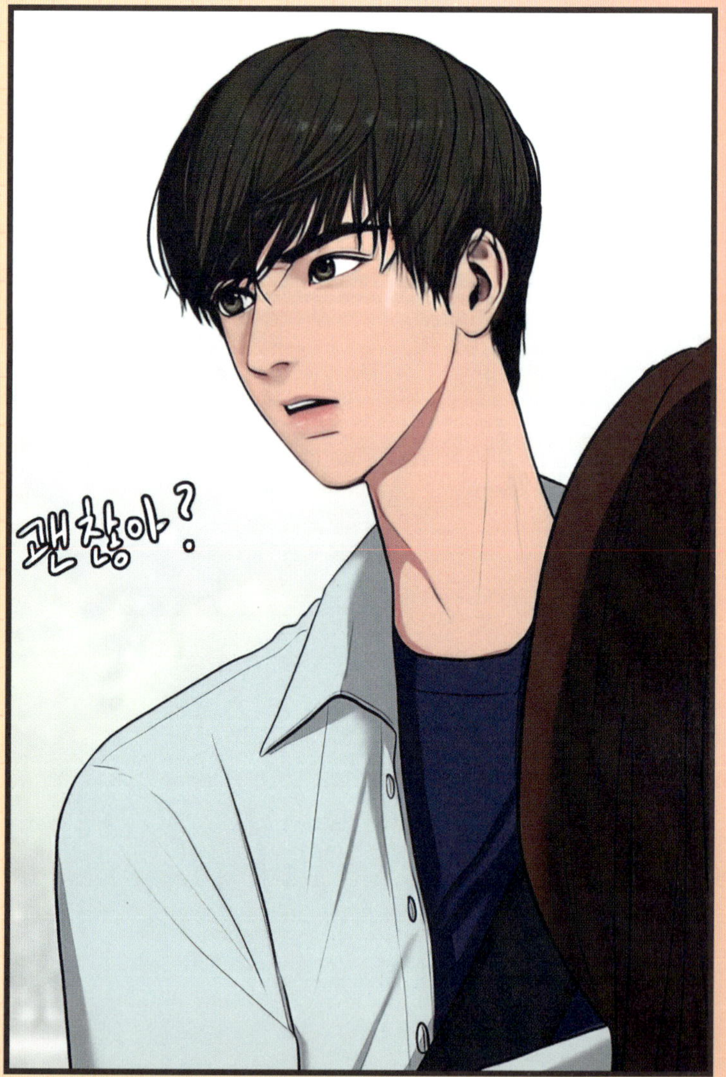
괜찮아?

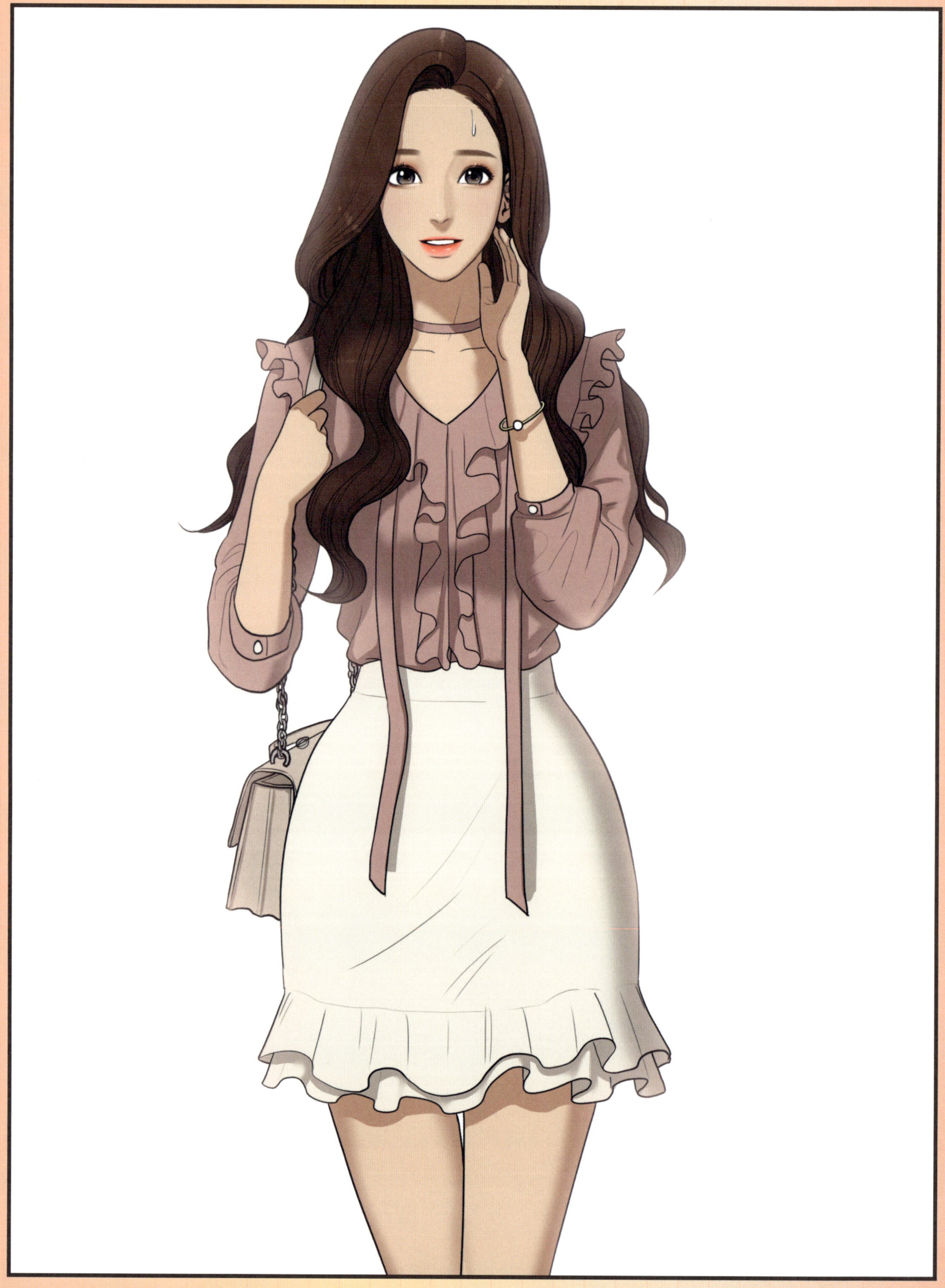

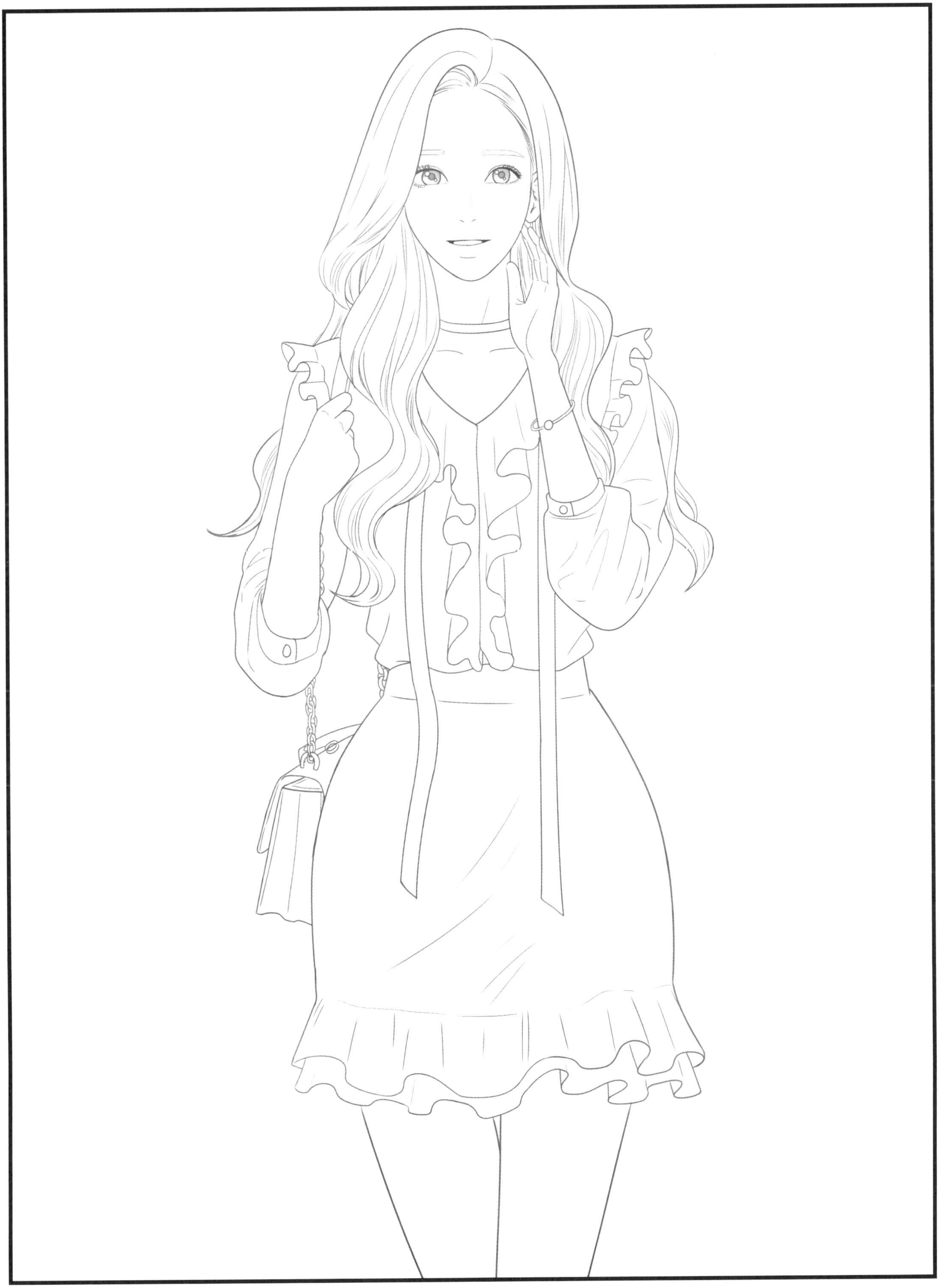

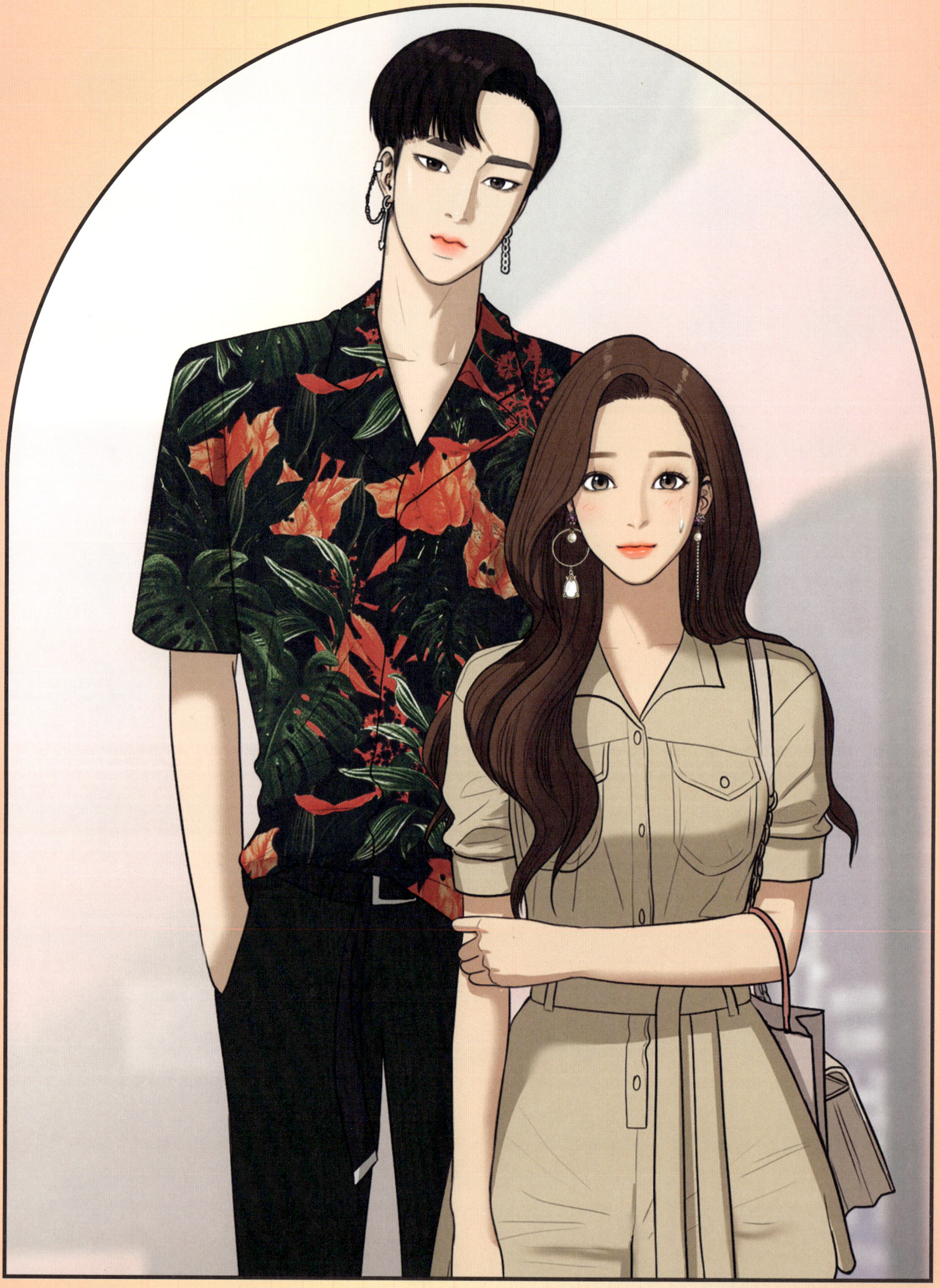

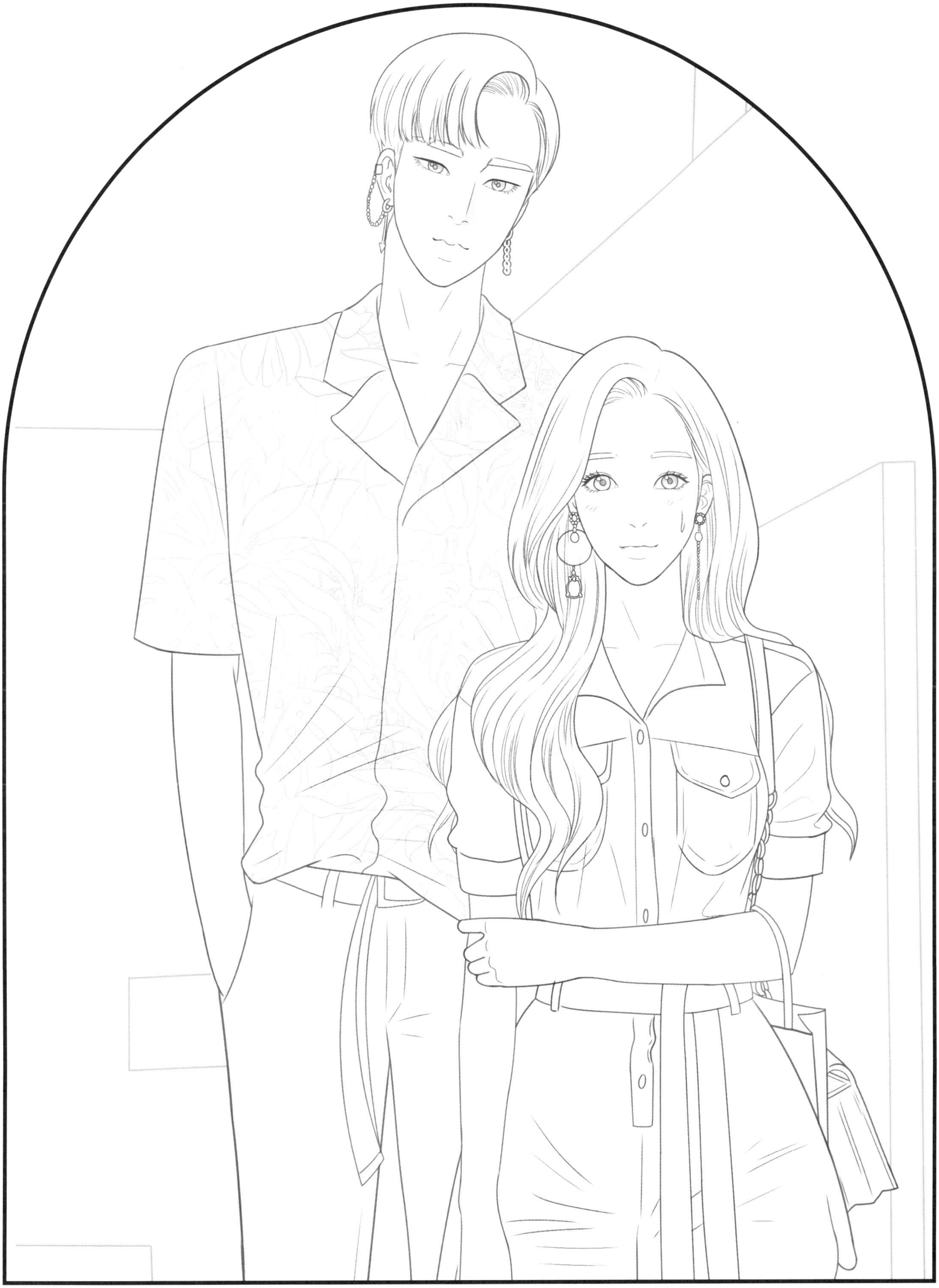

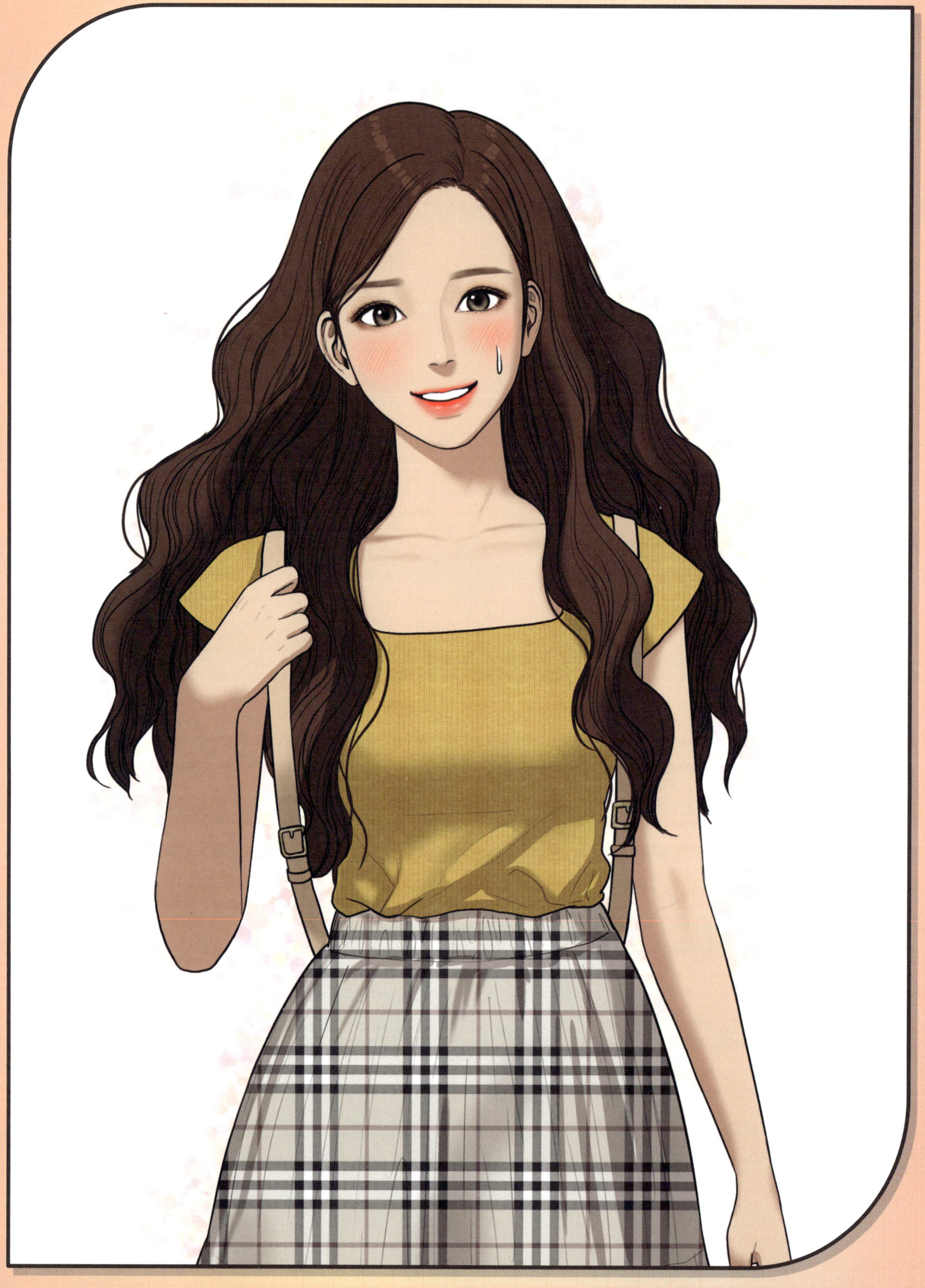

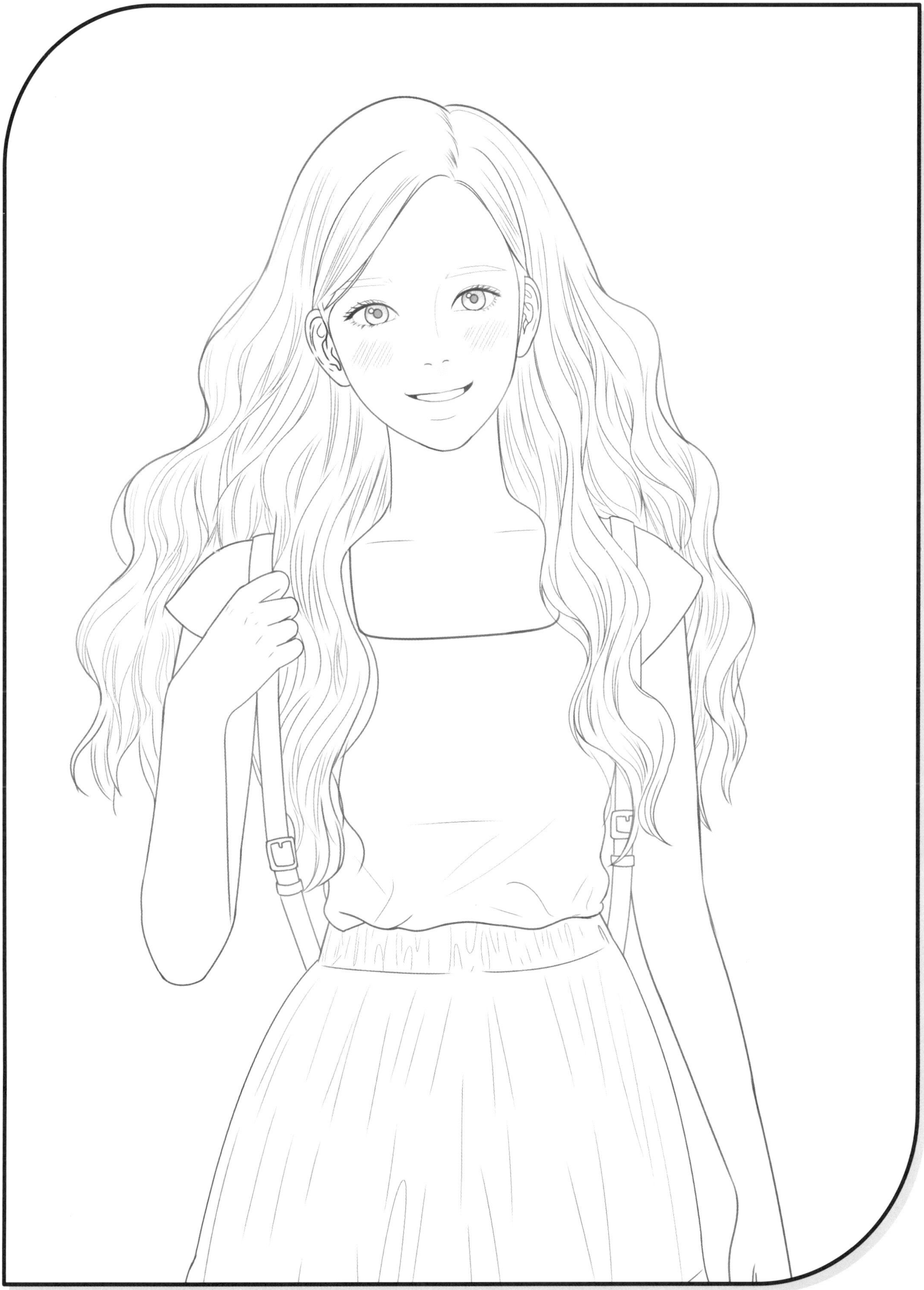

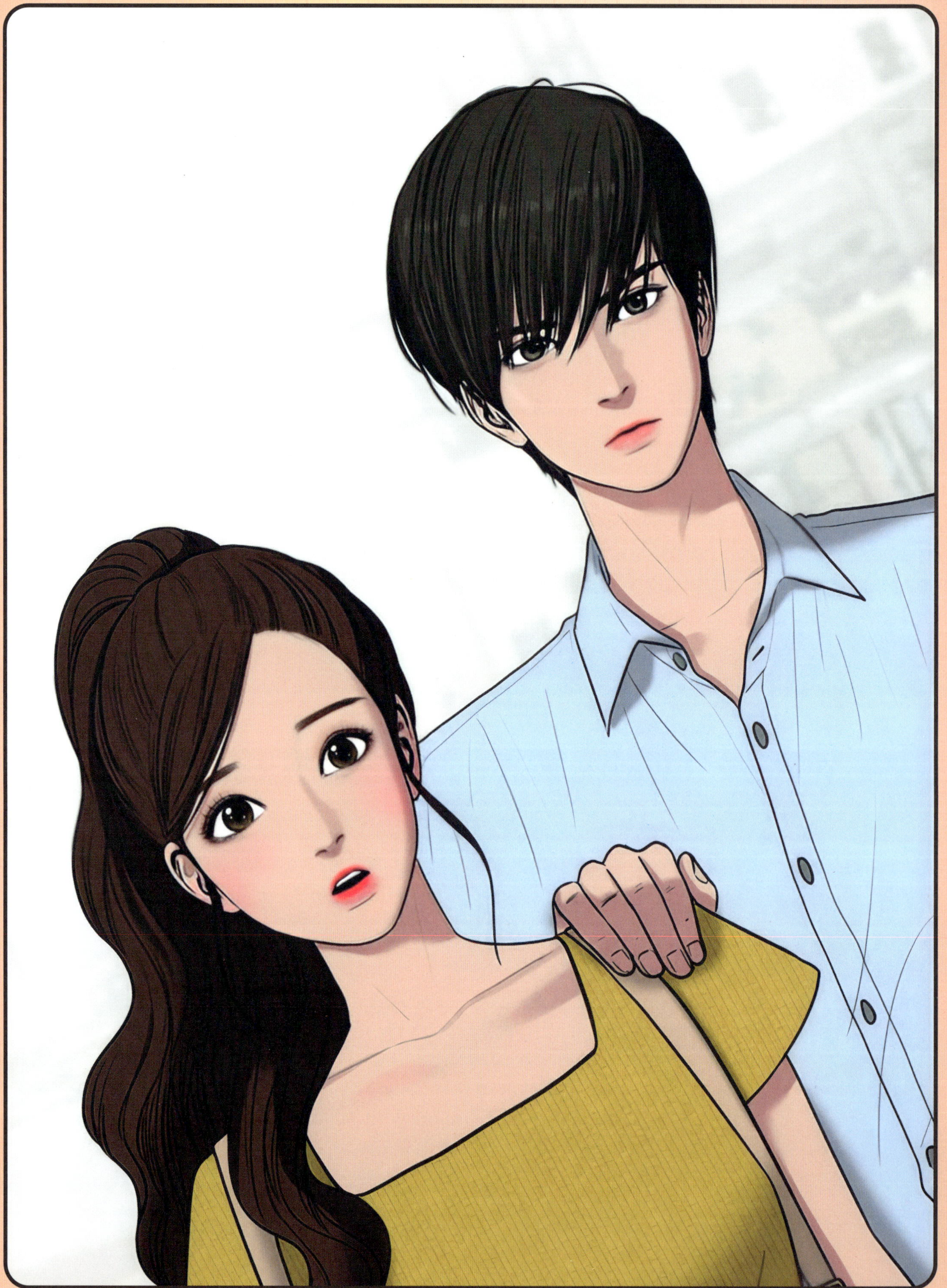

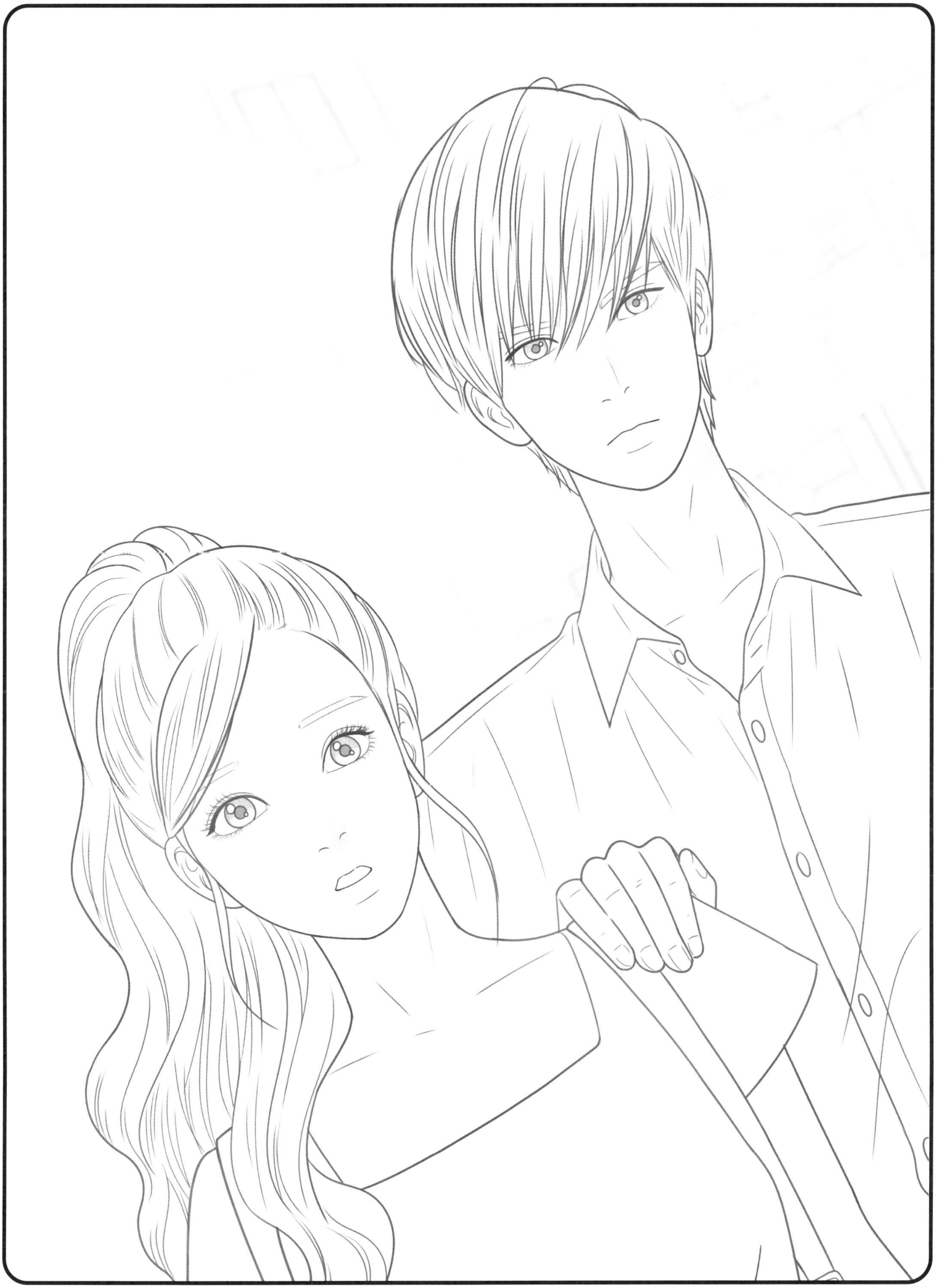

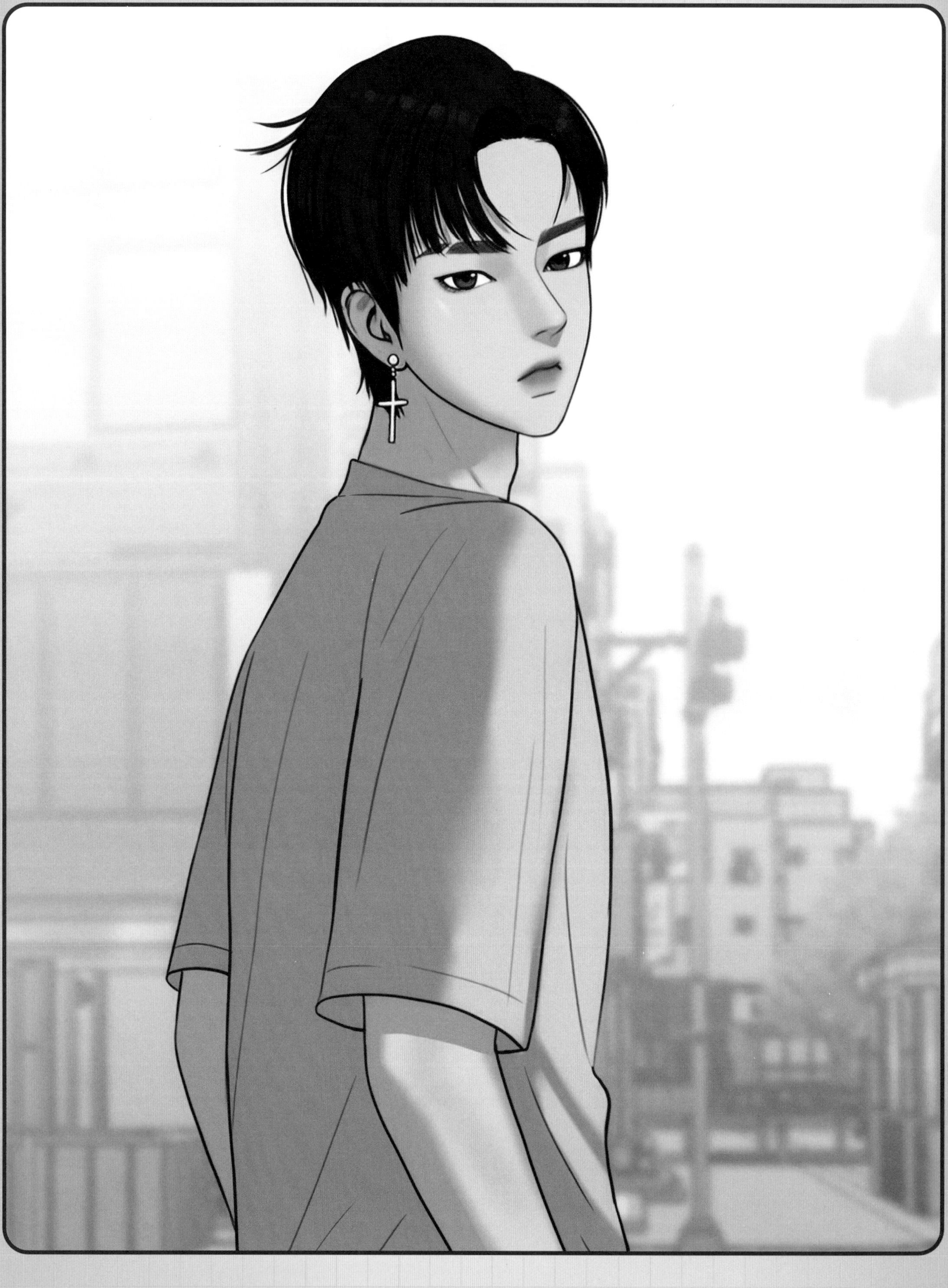

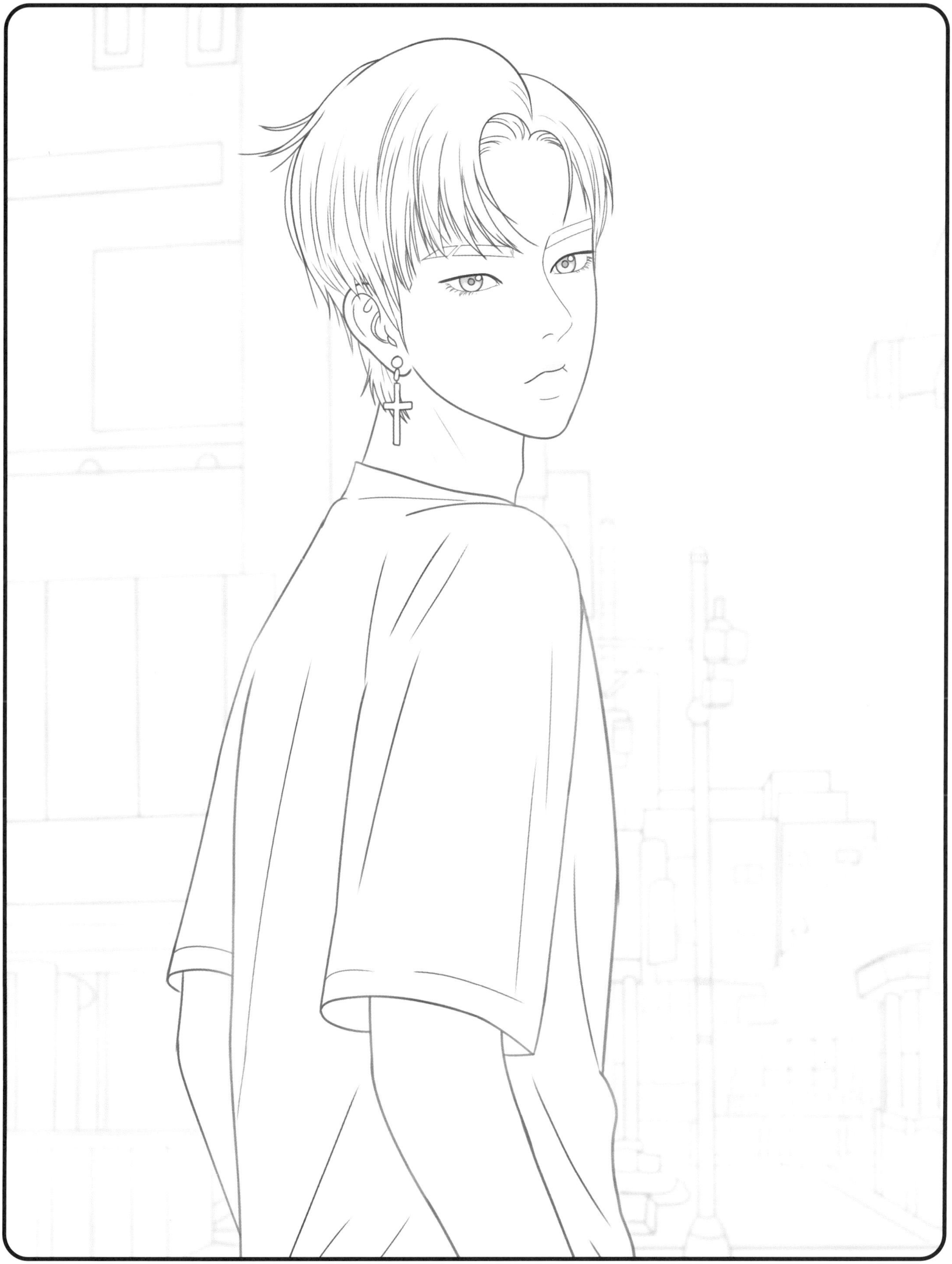

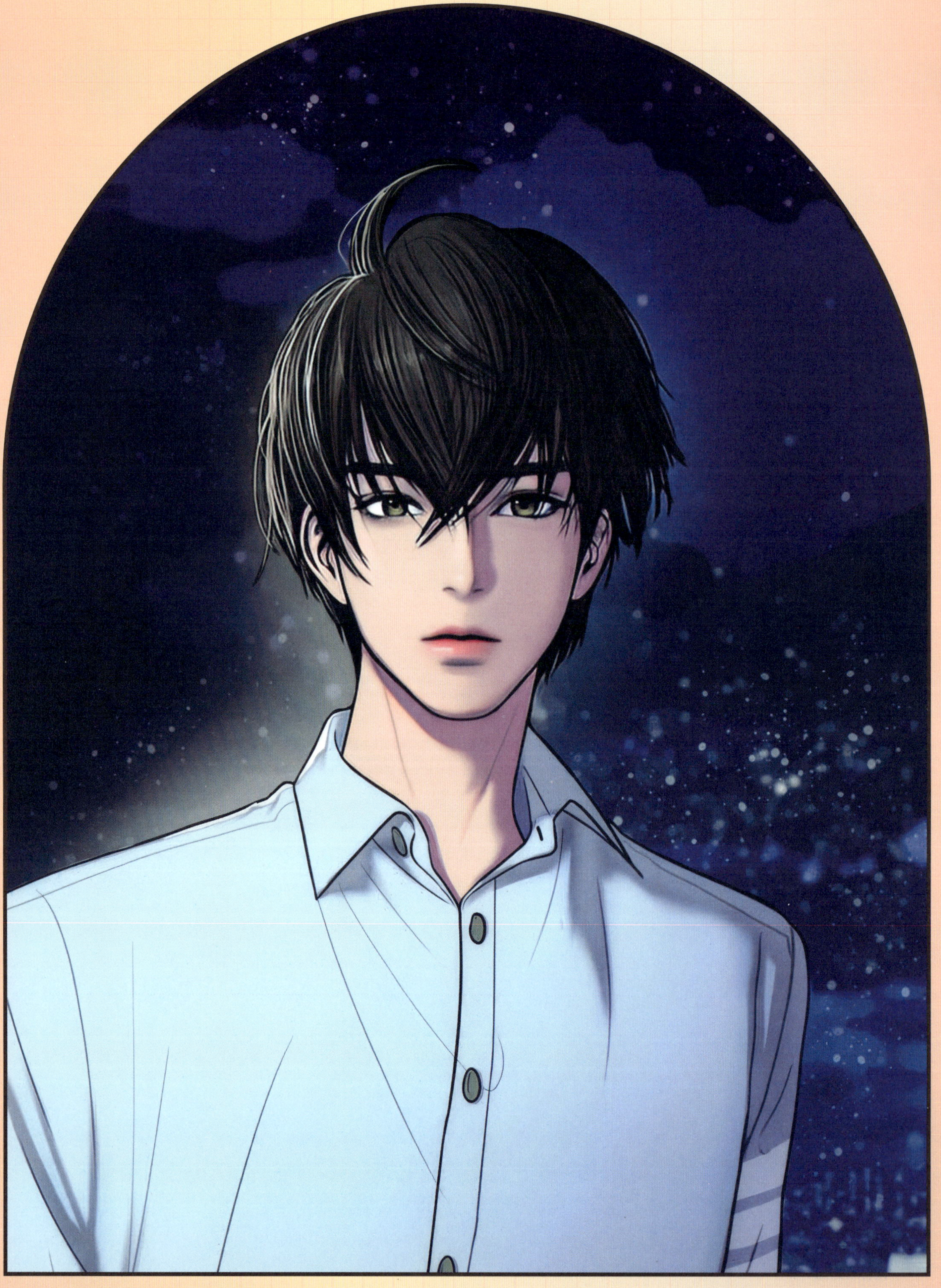

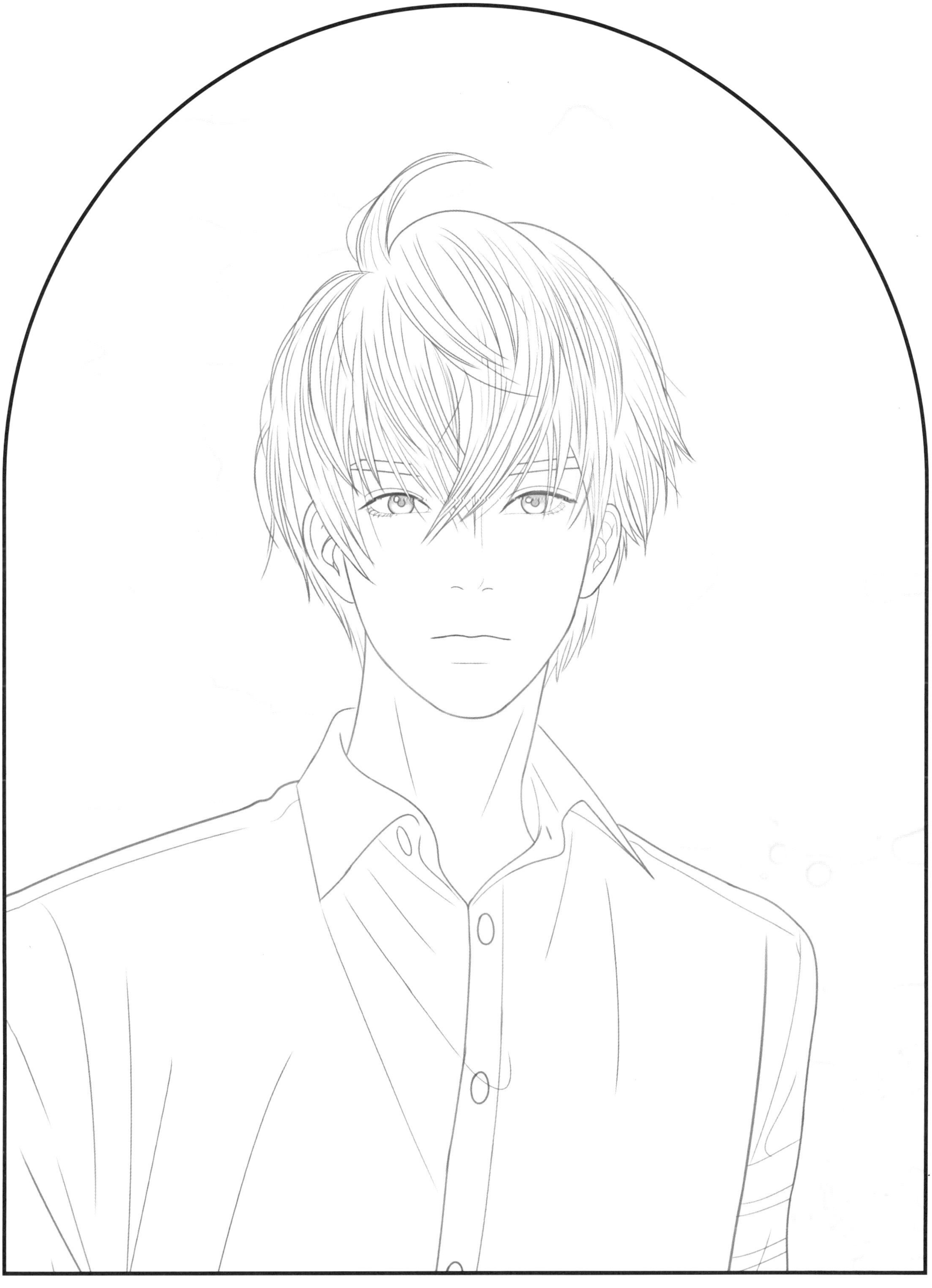

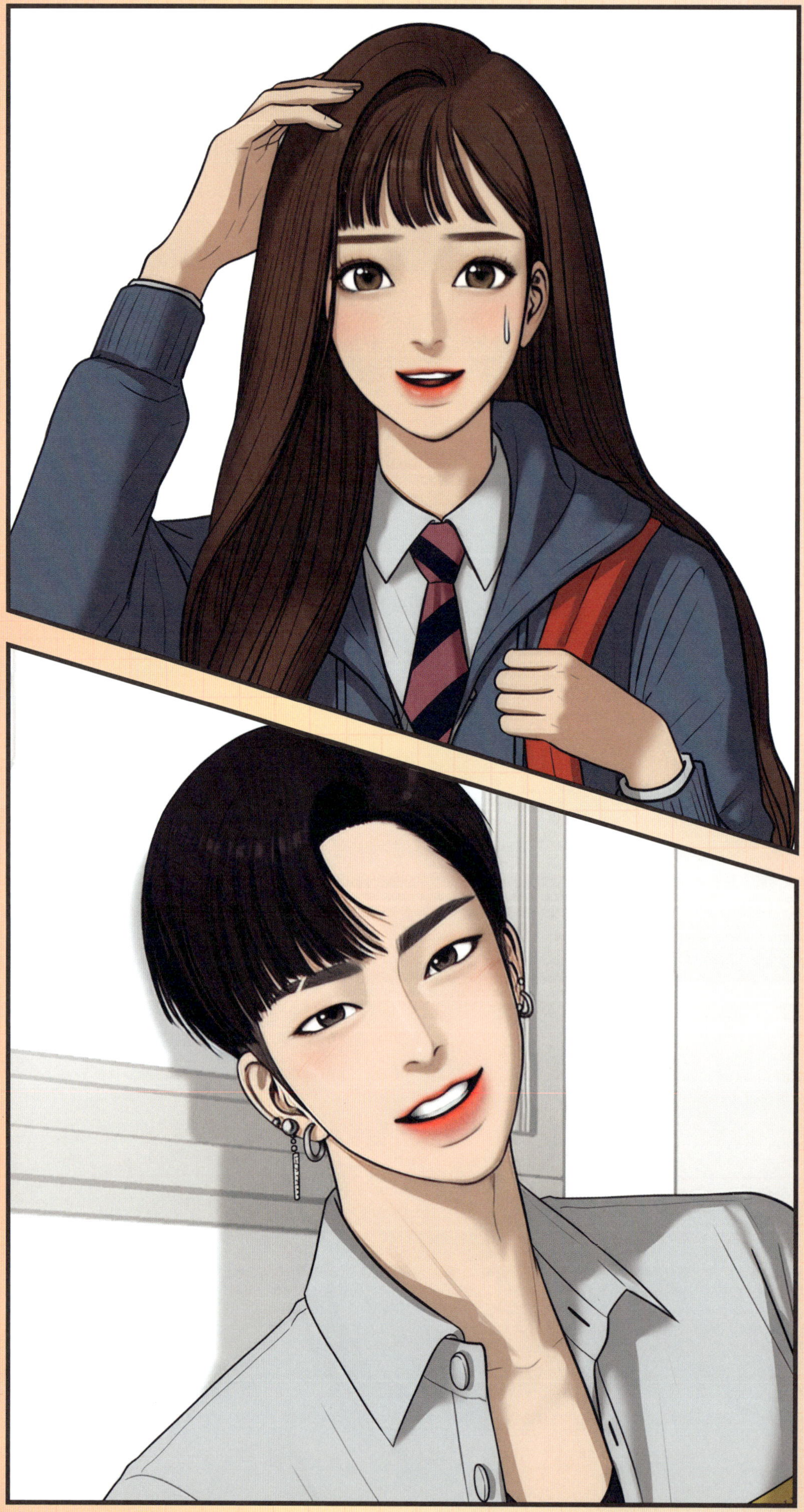

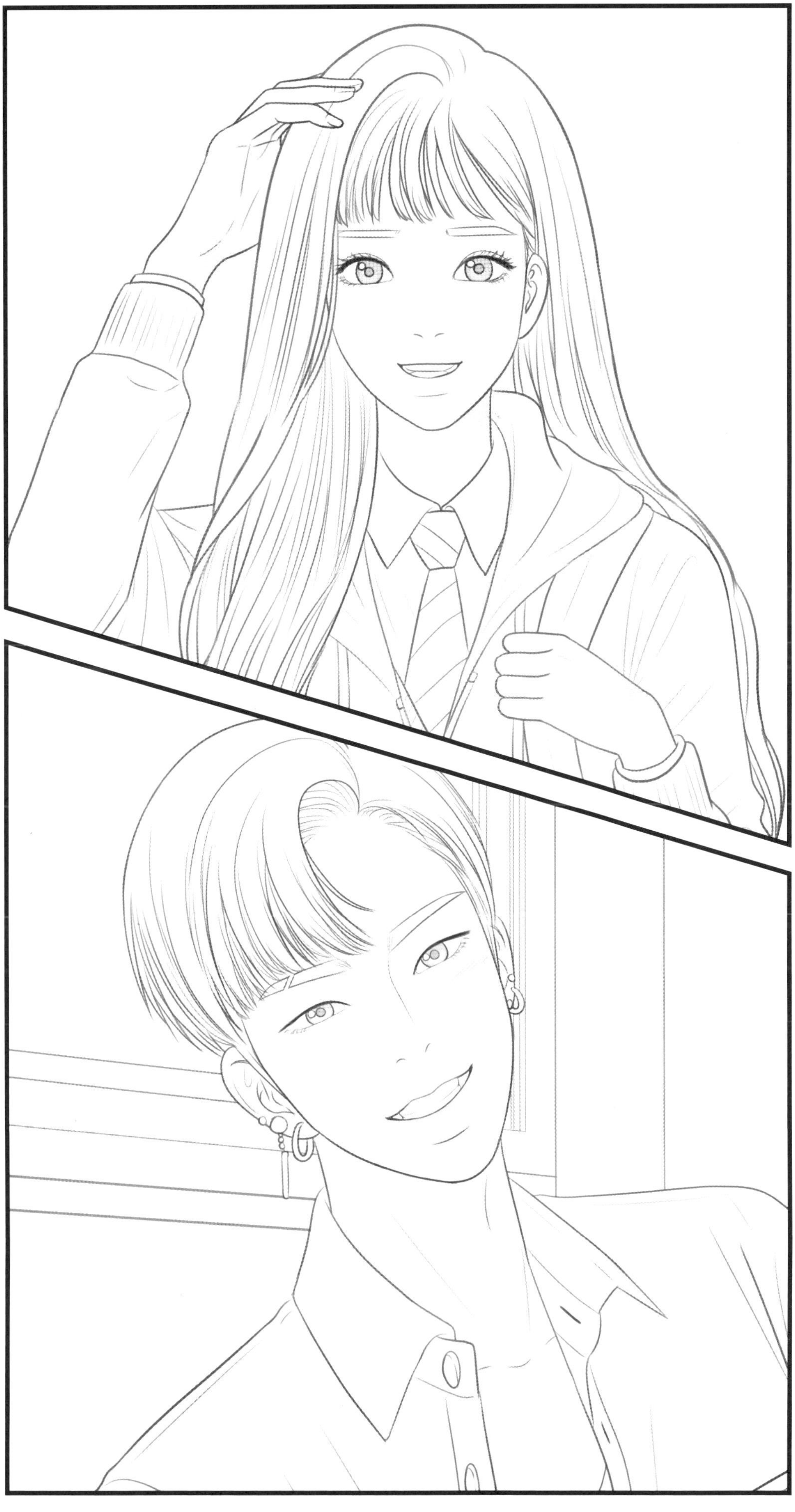

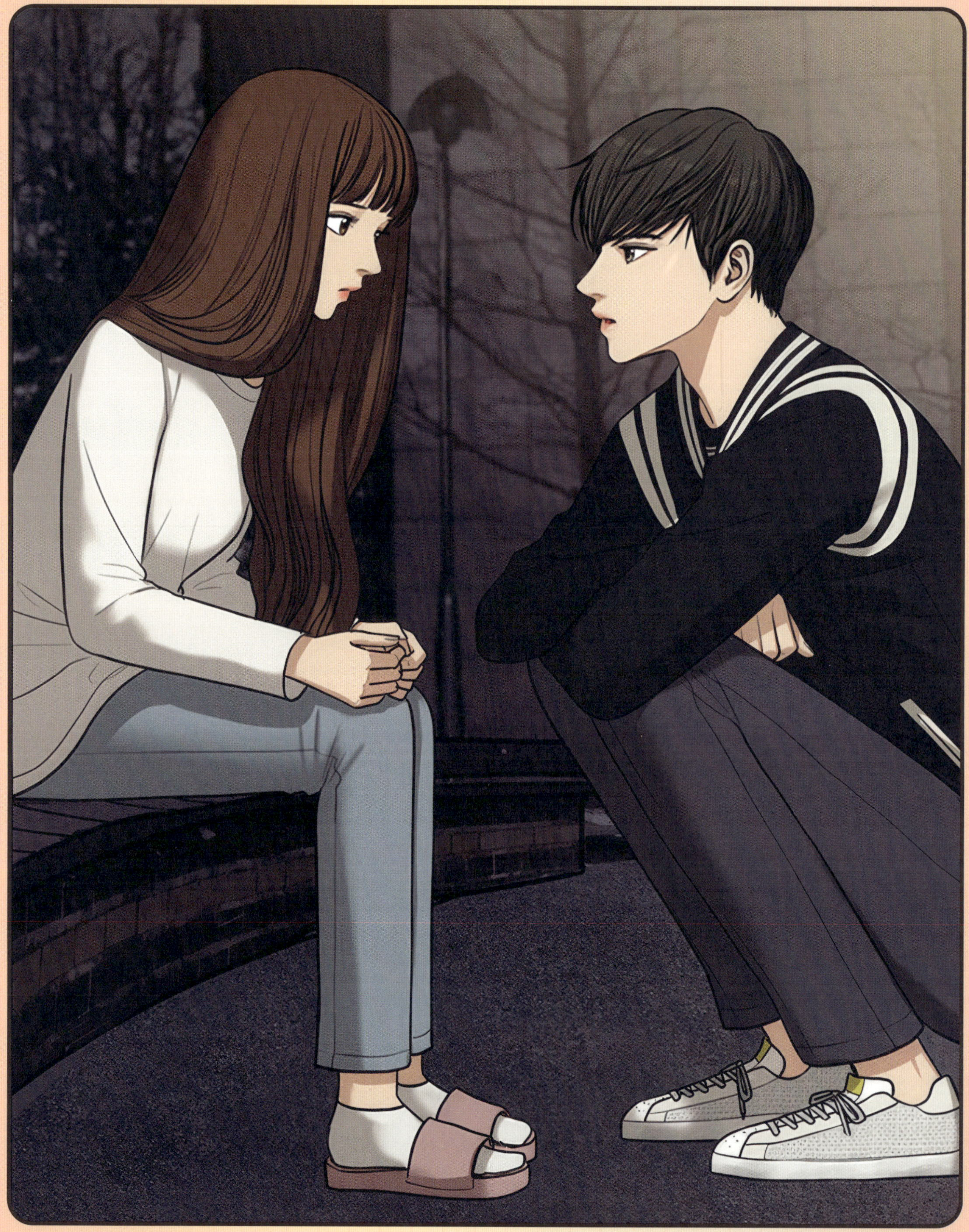

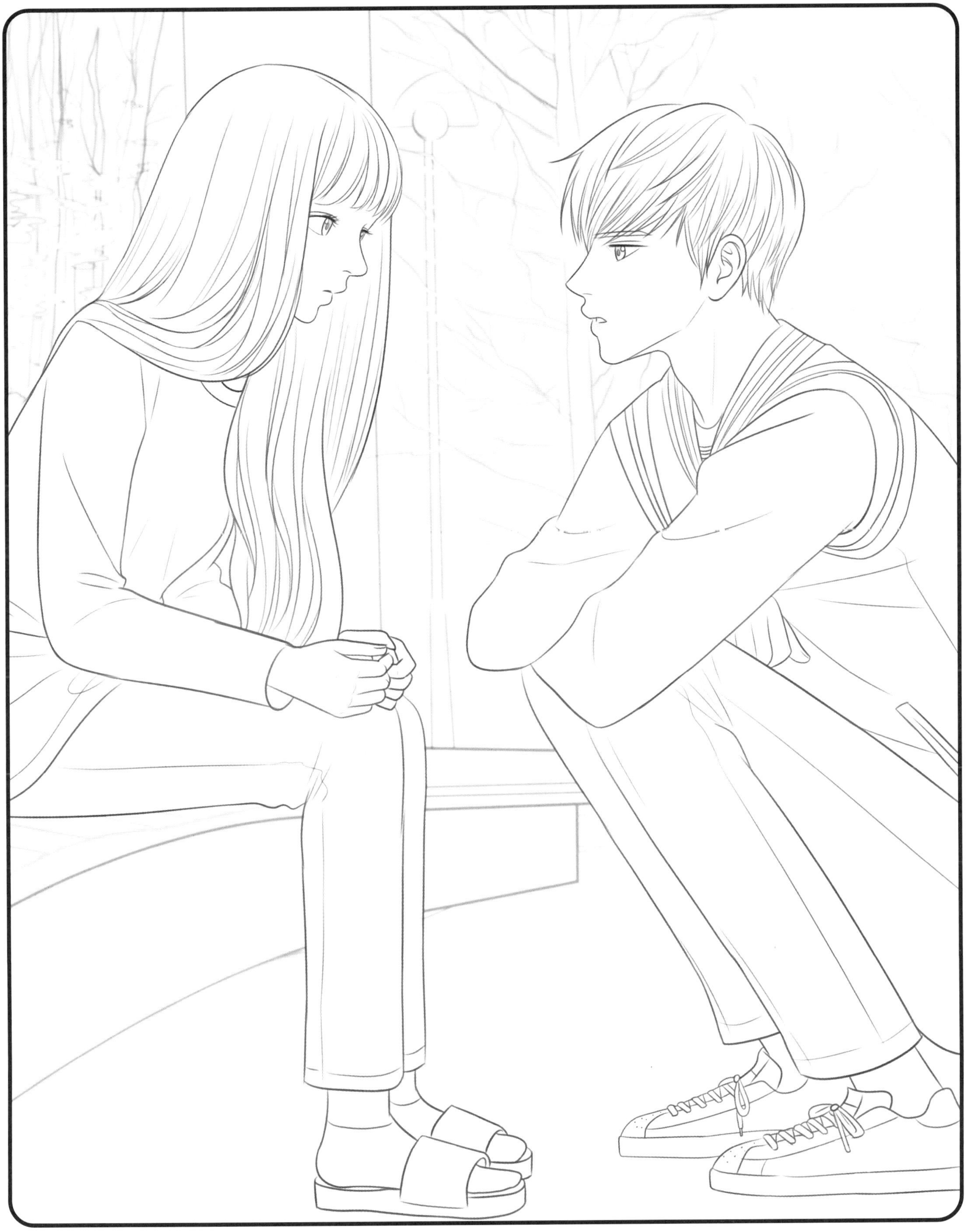

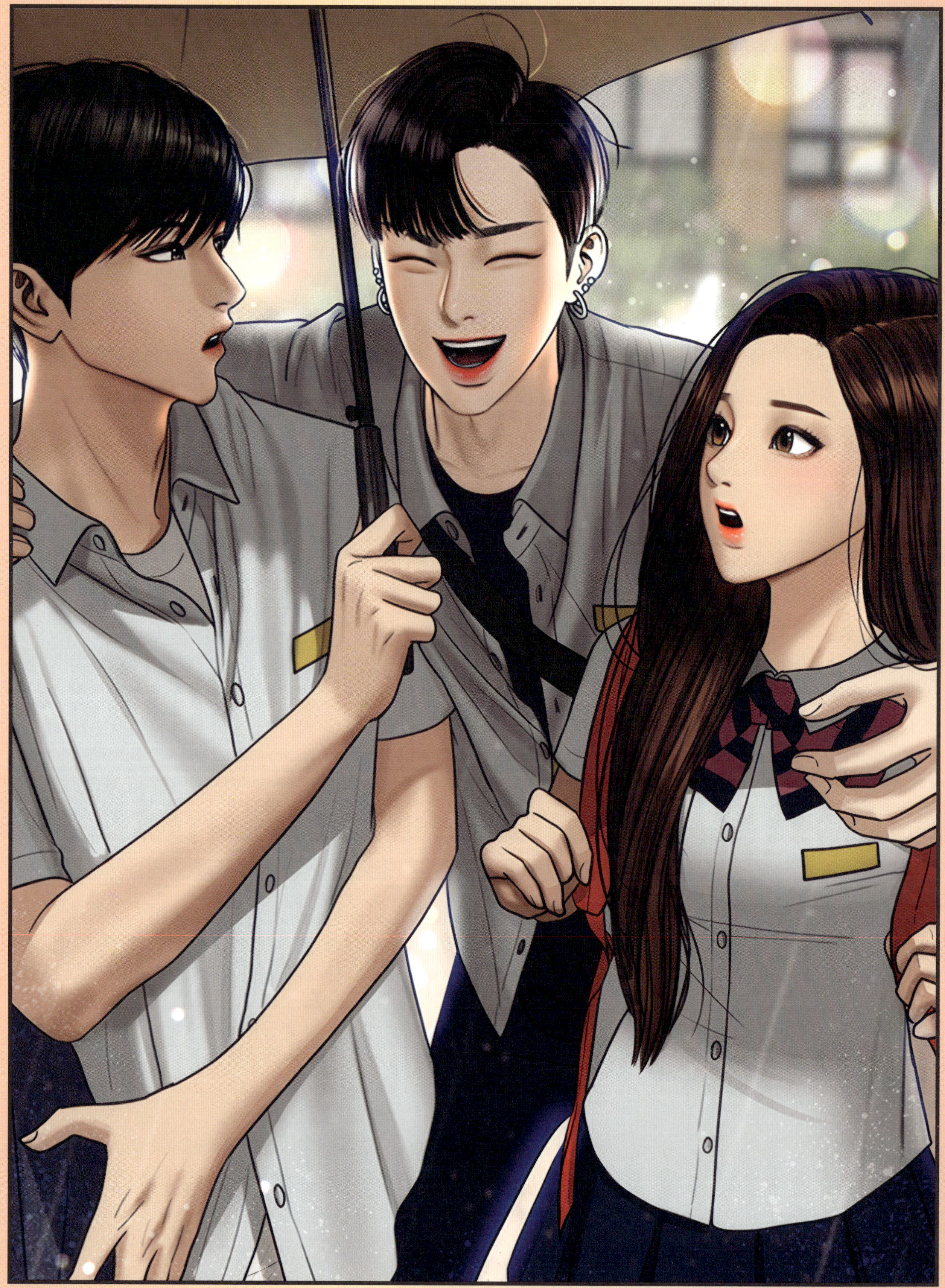

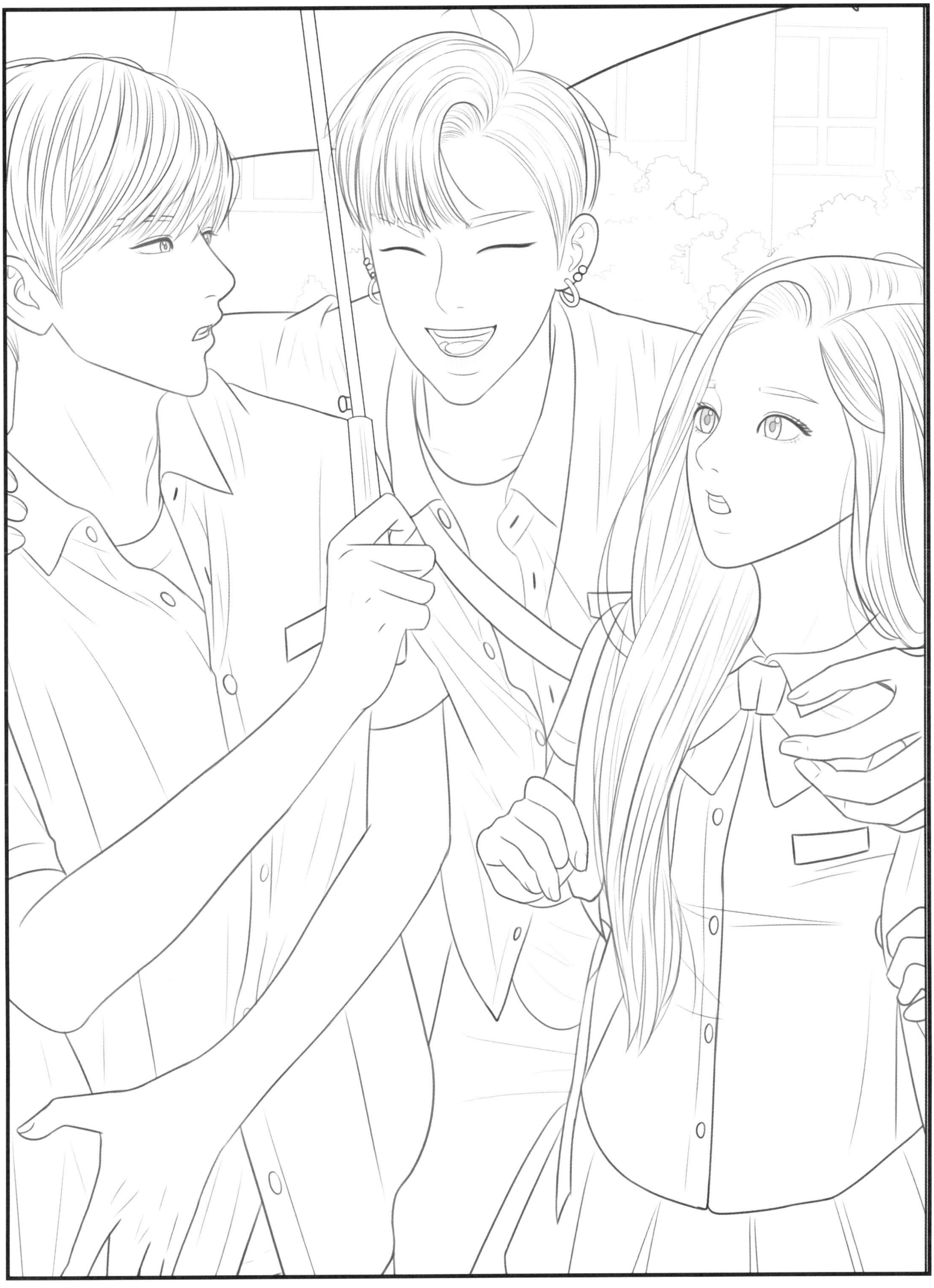

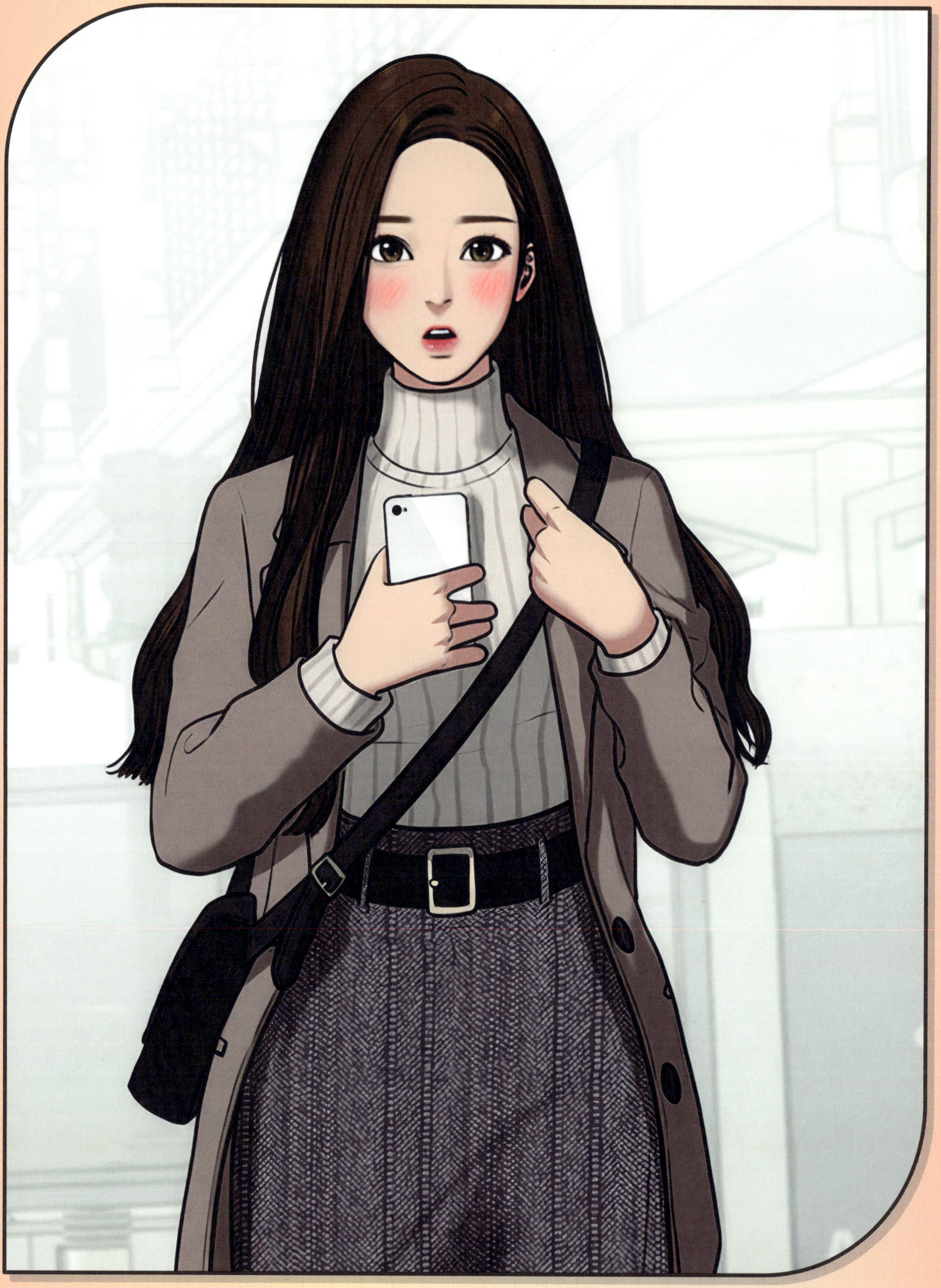

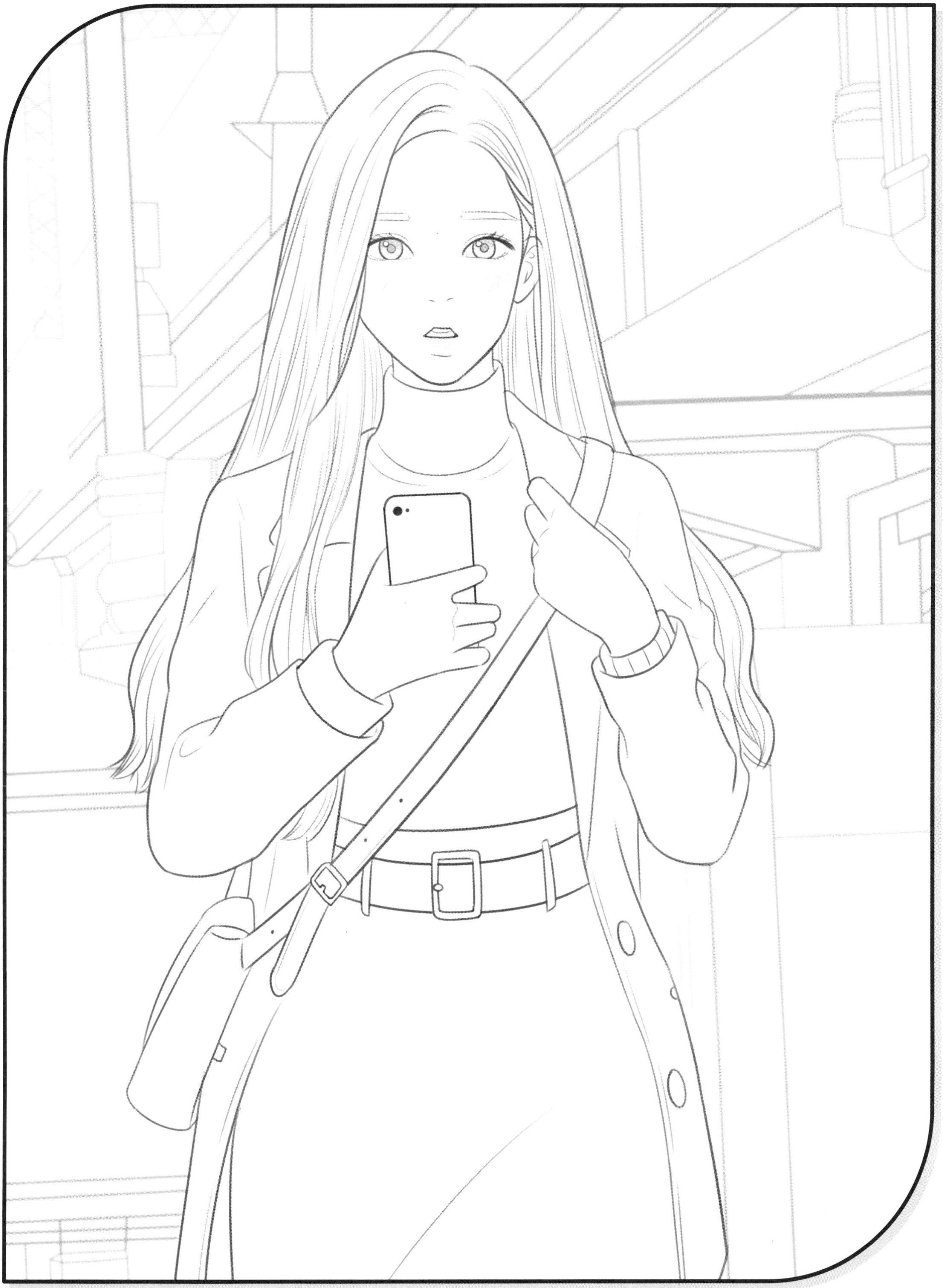

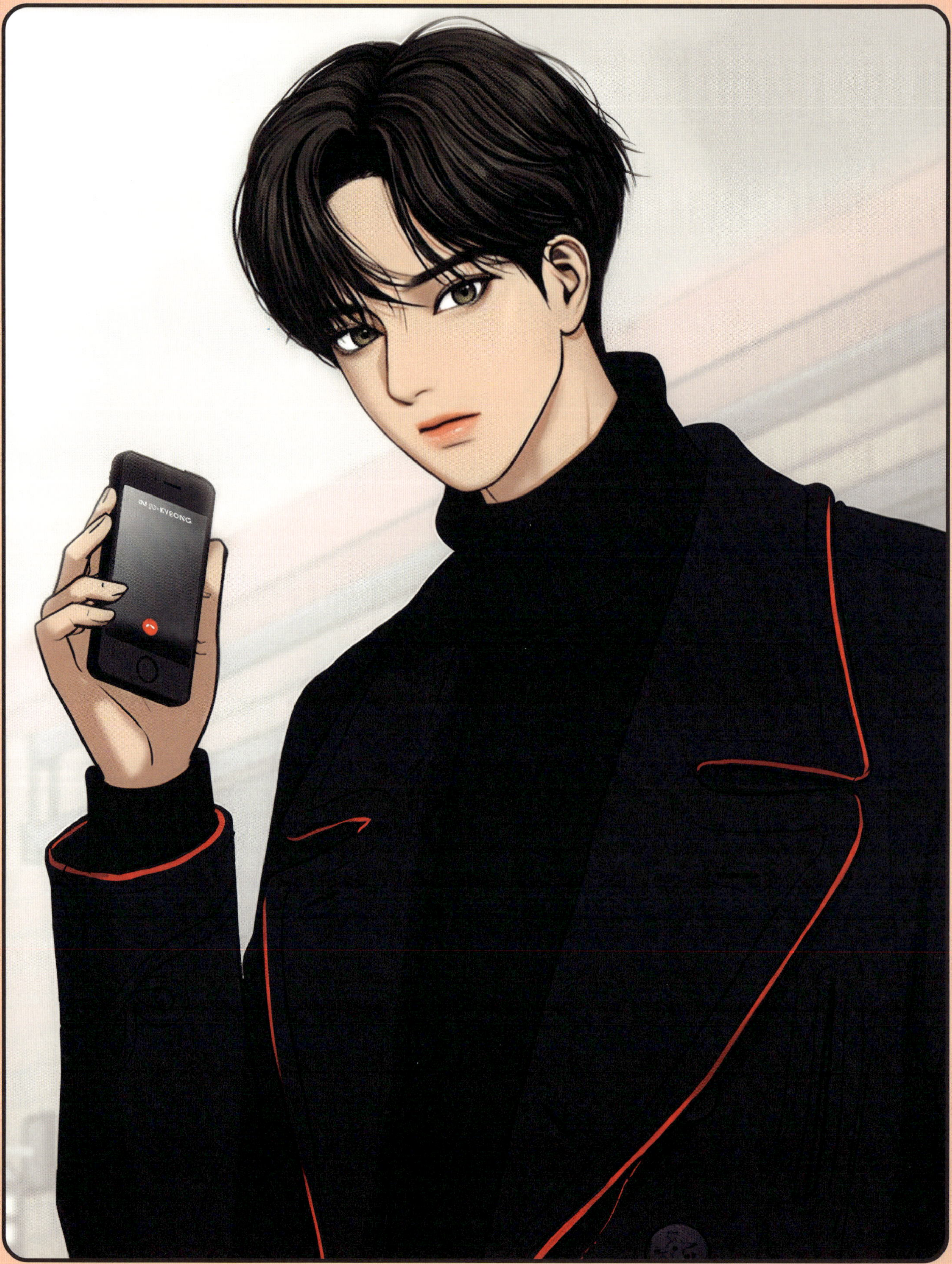

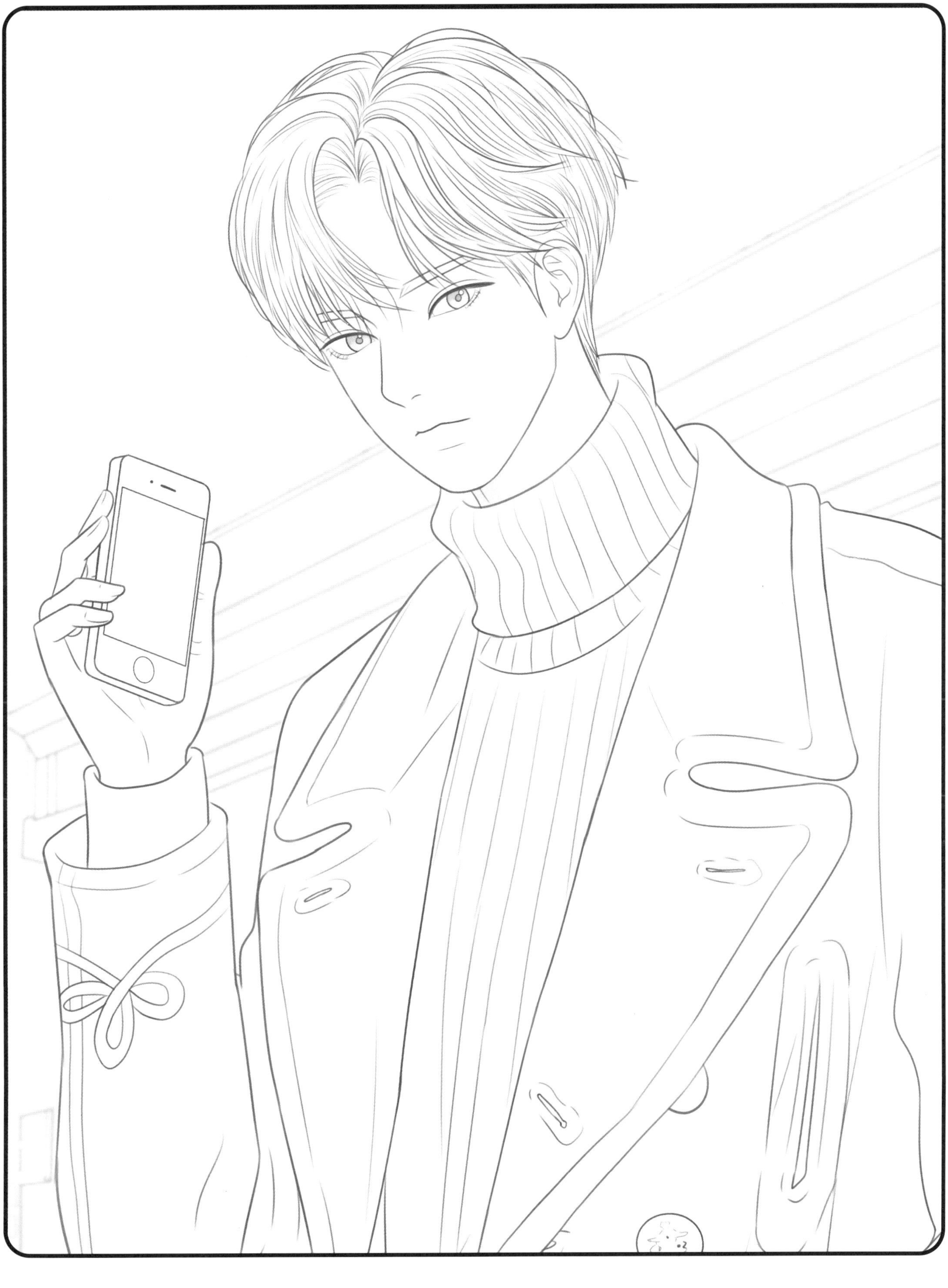

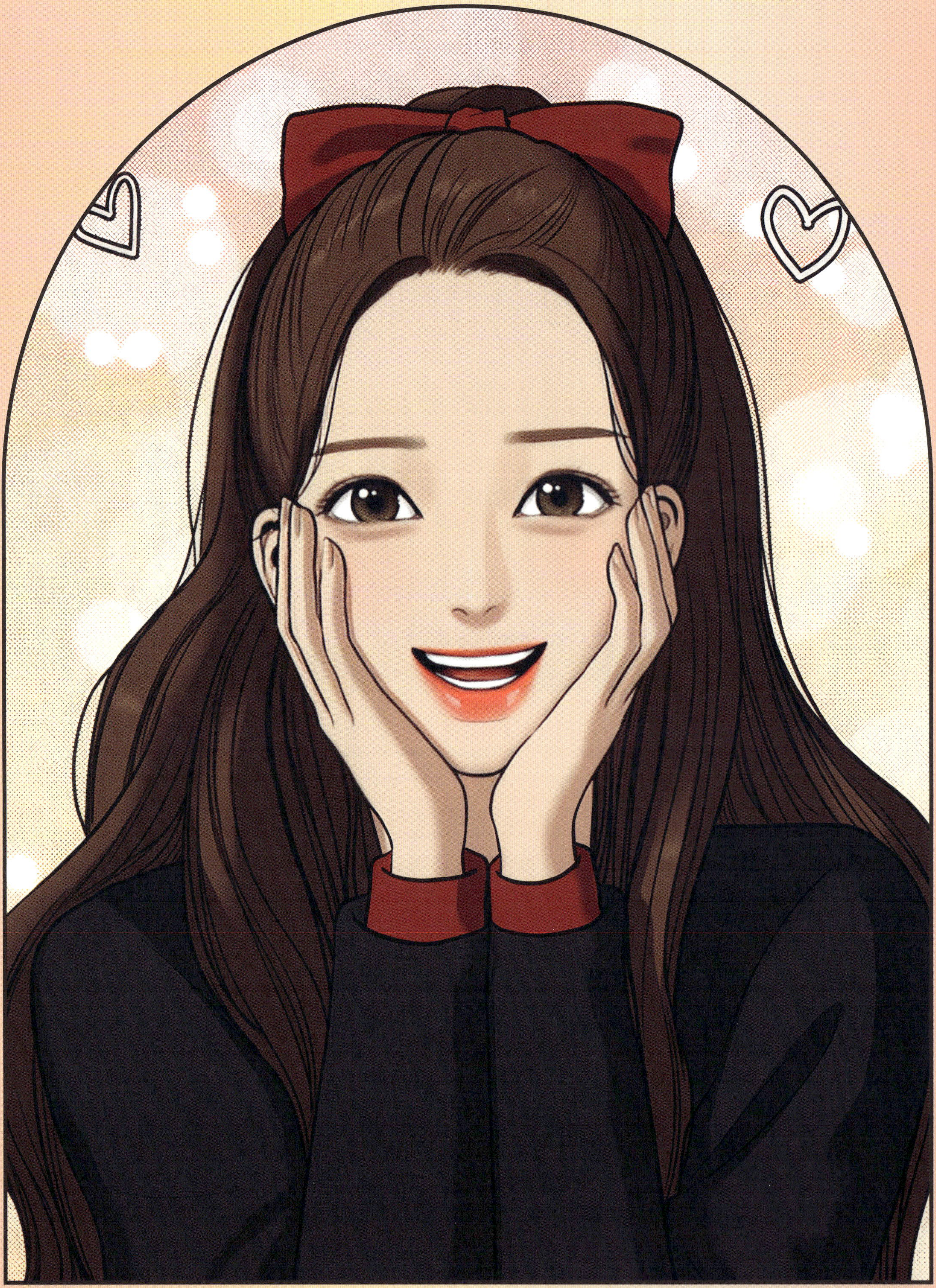

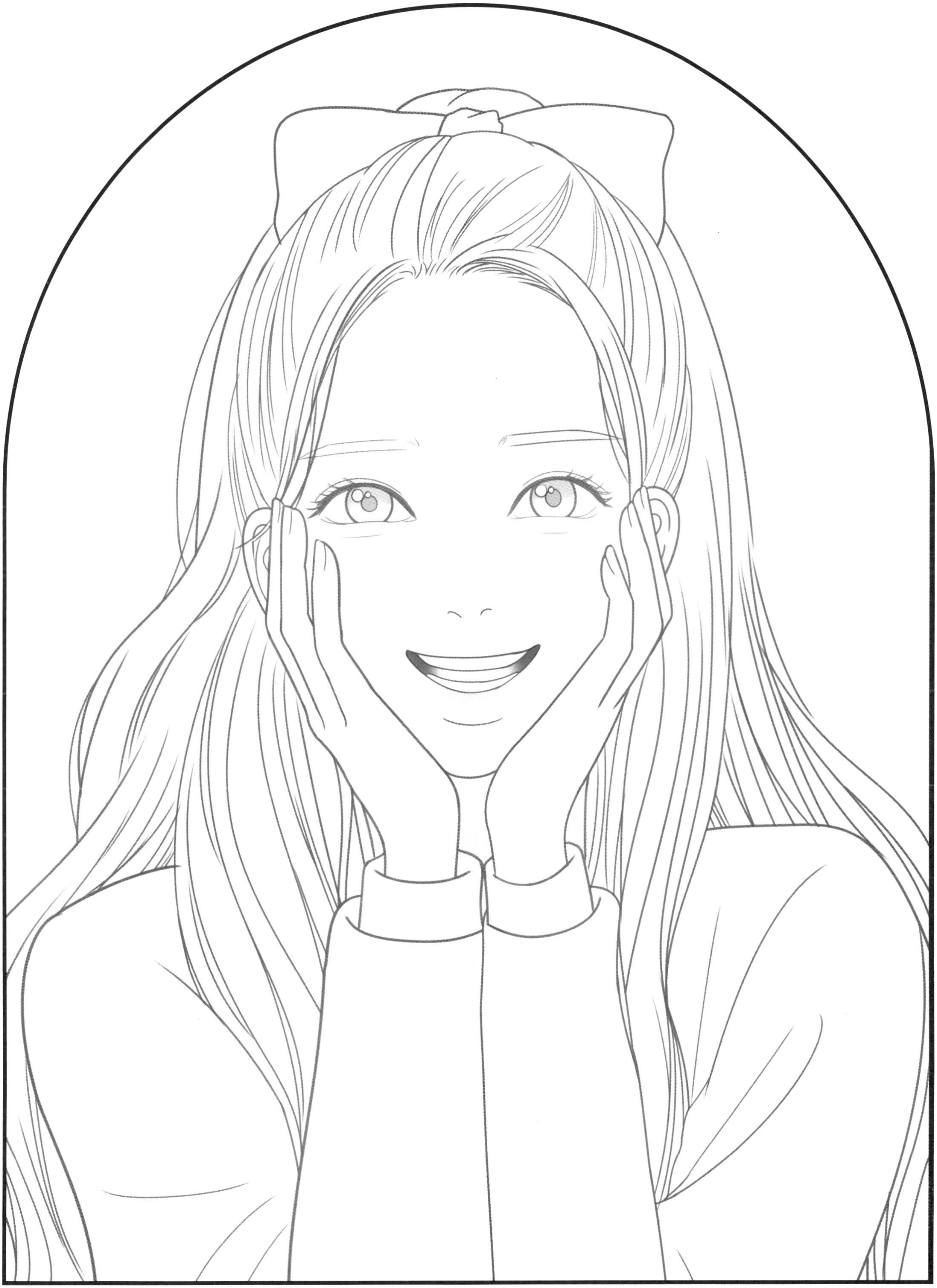

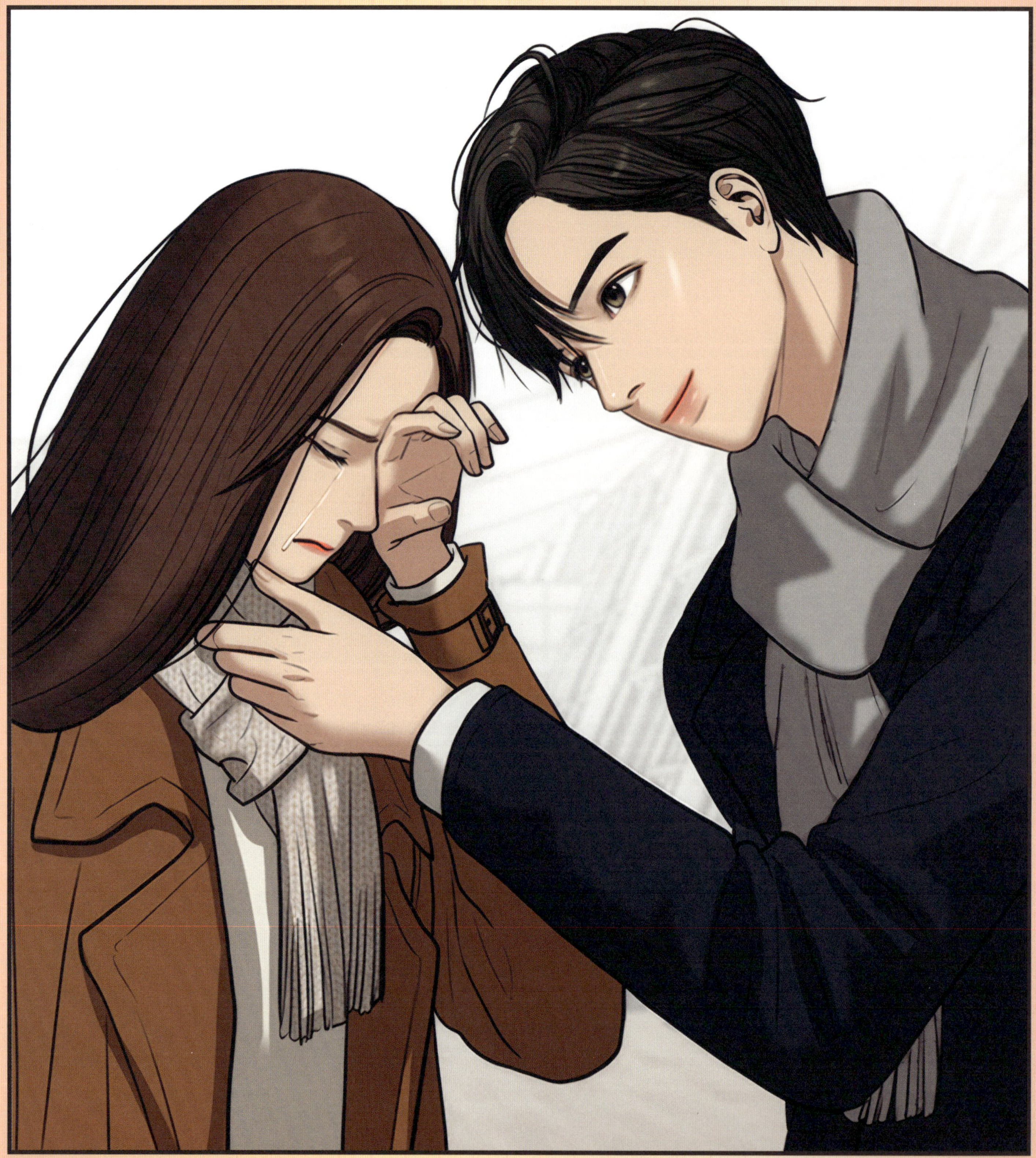

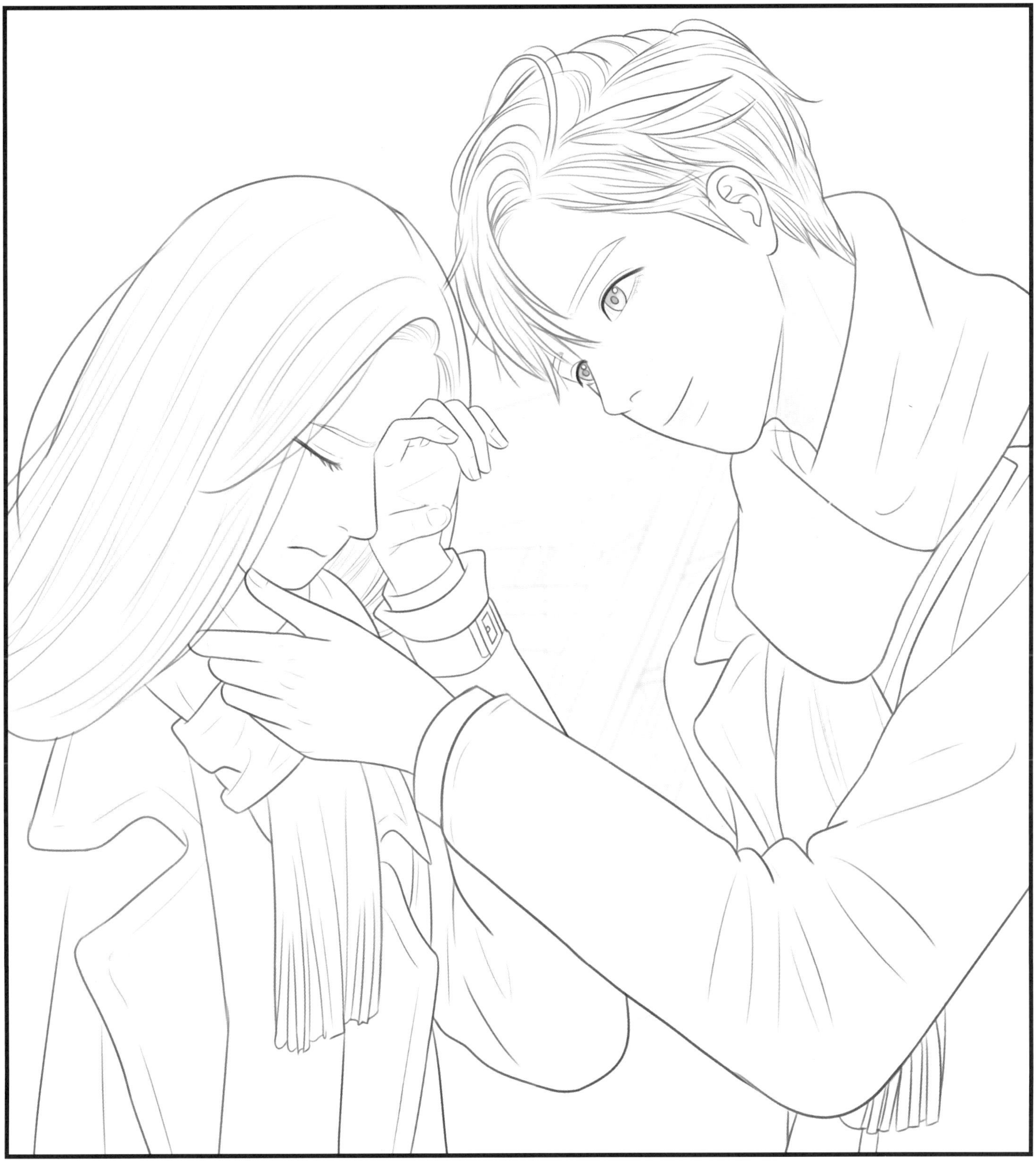

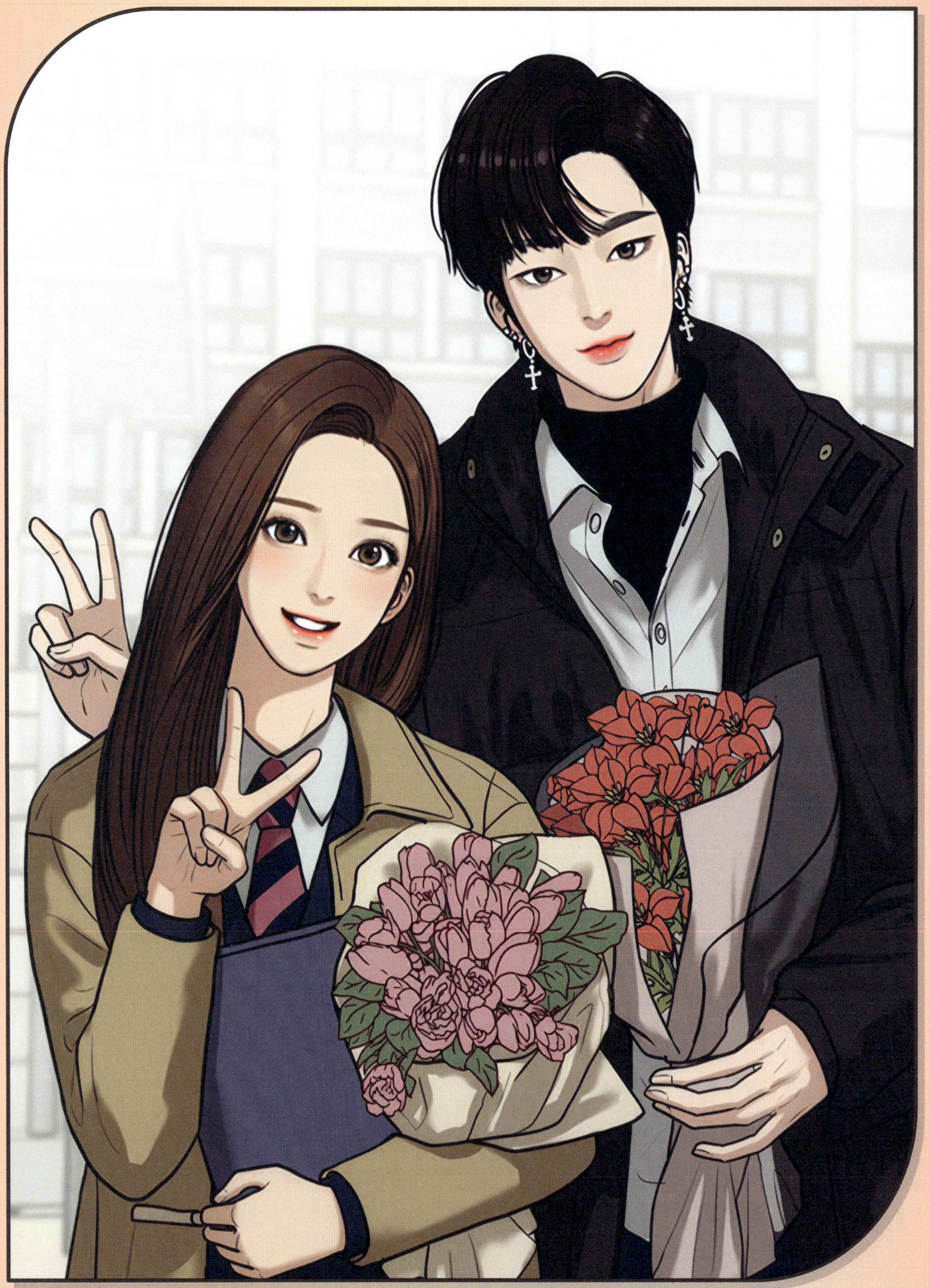

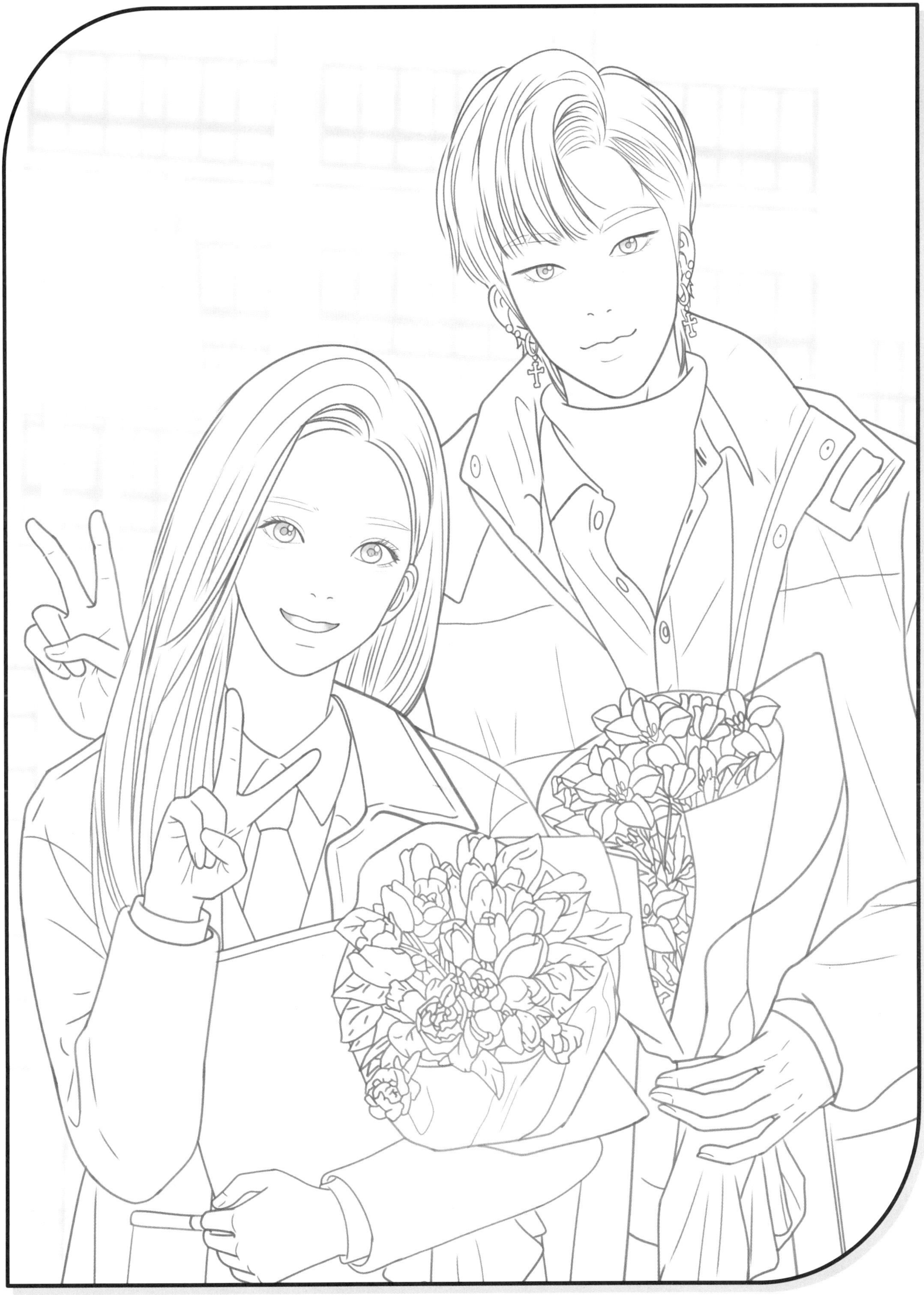

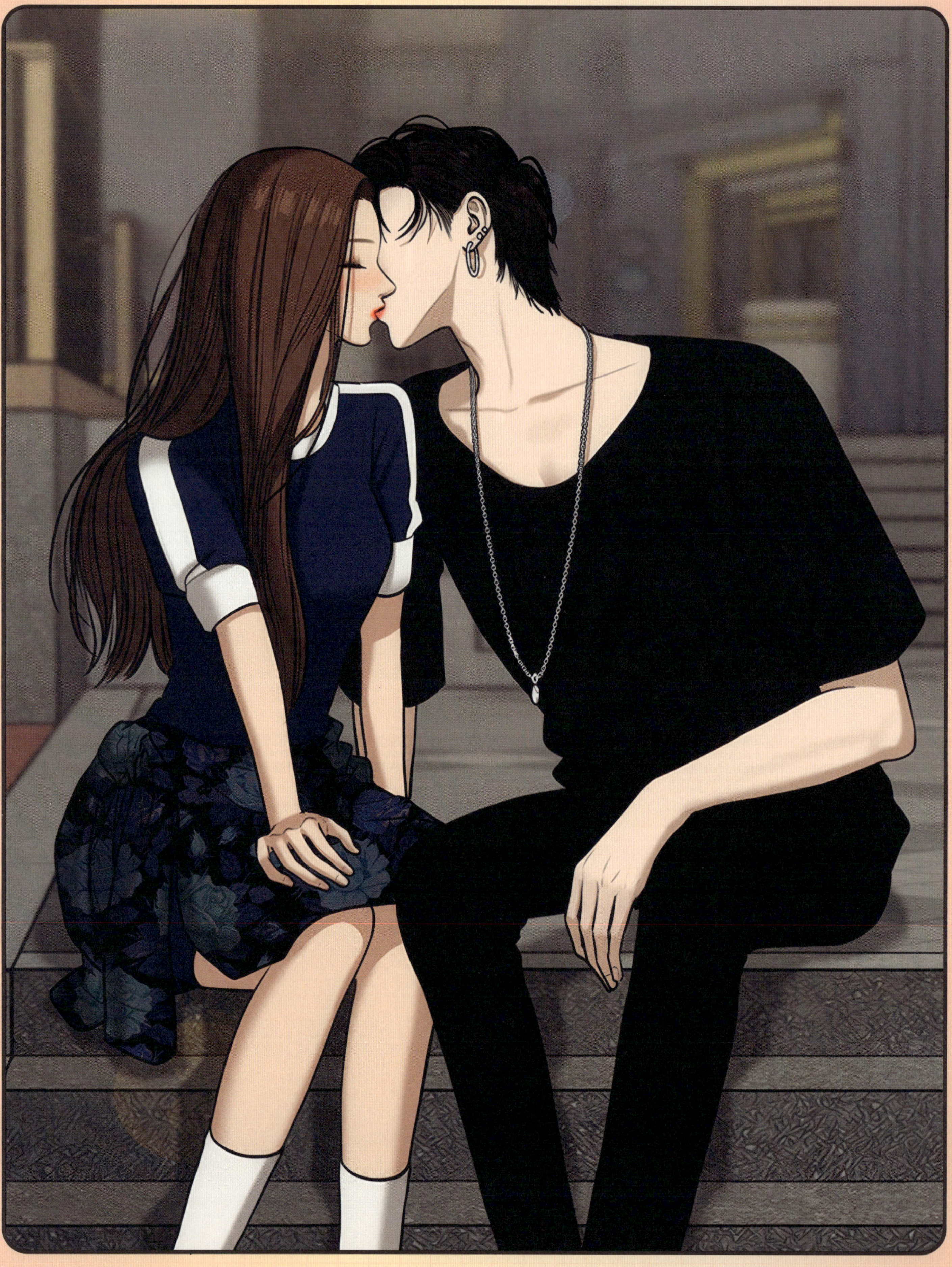

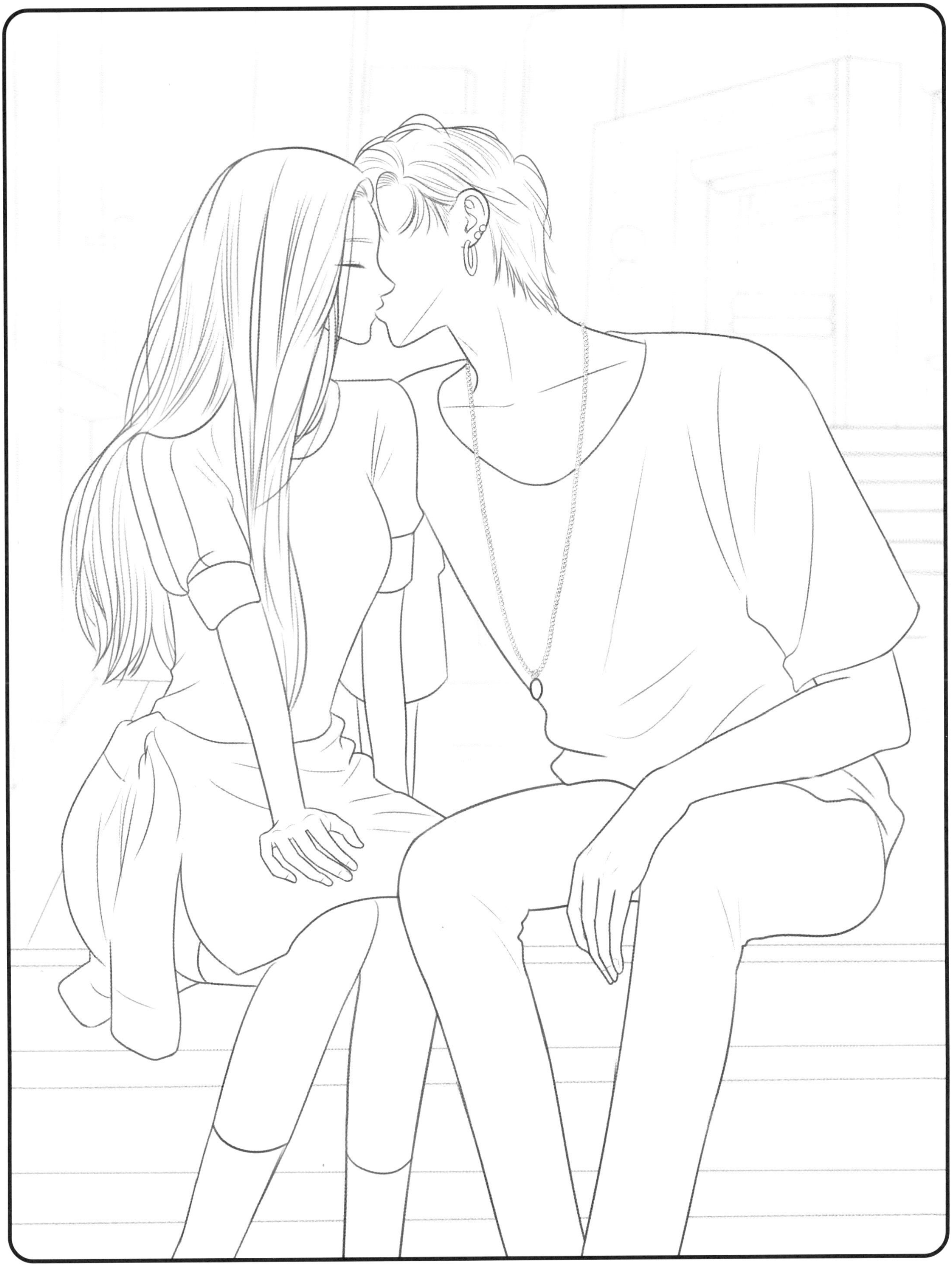

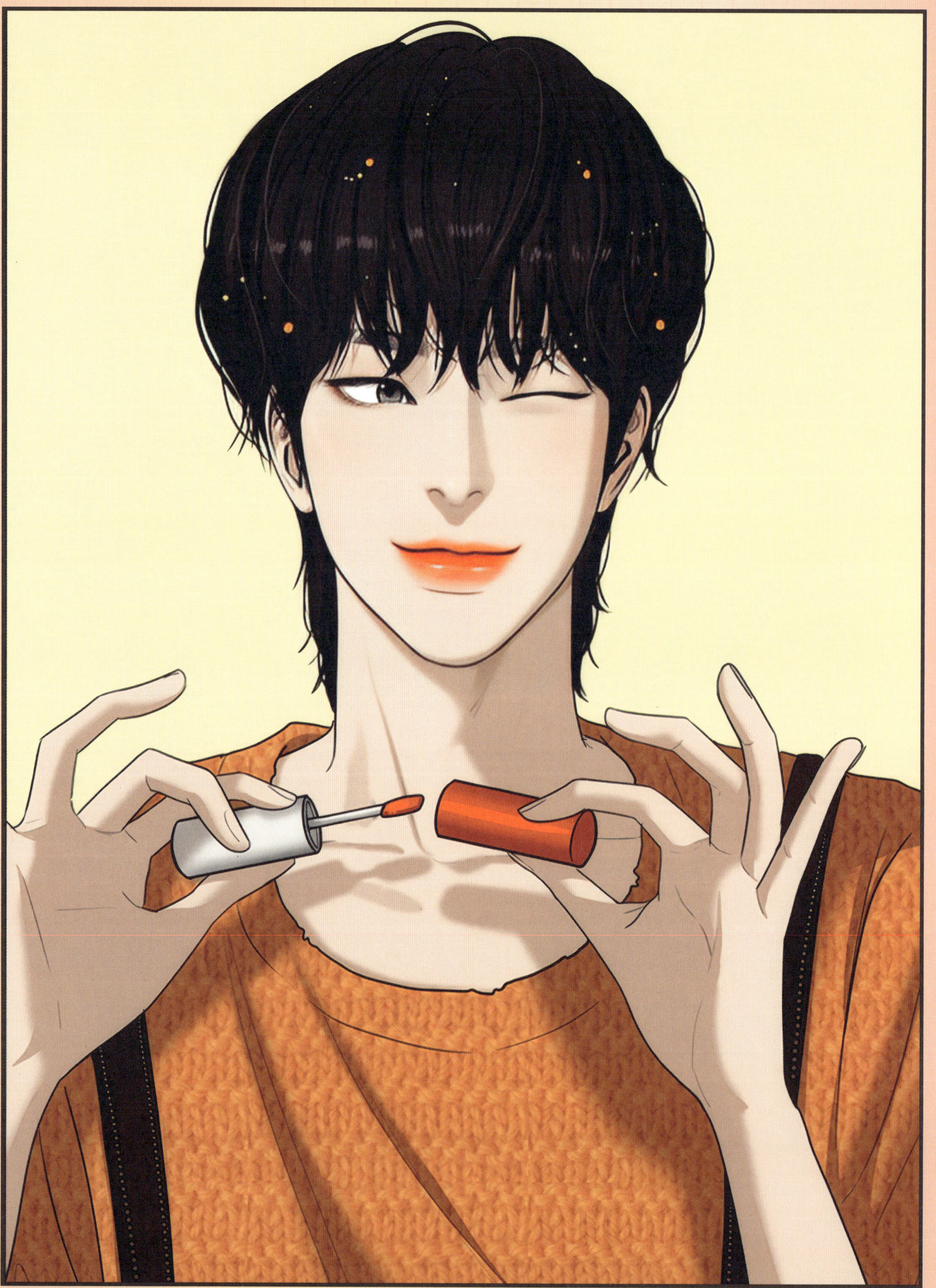

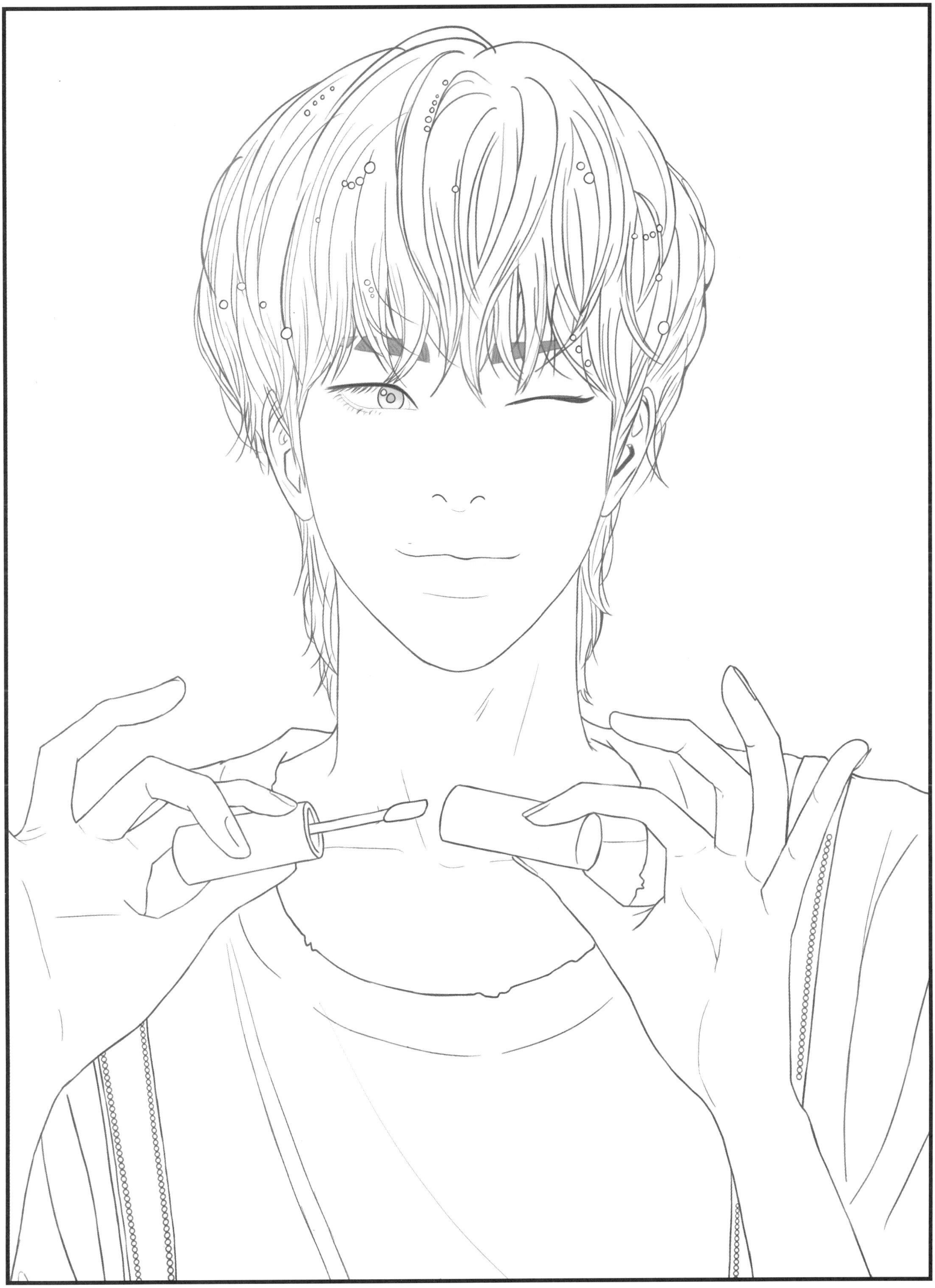

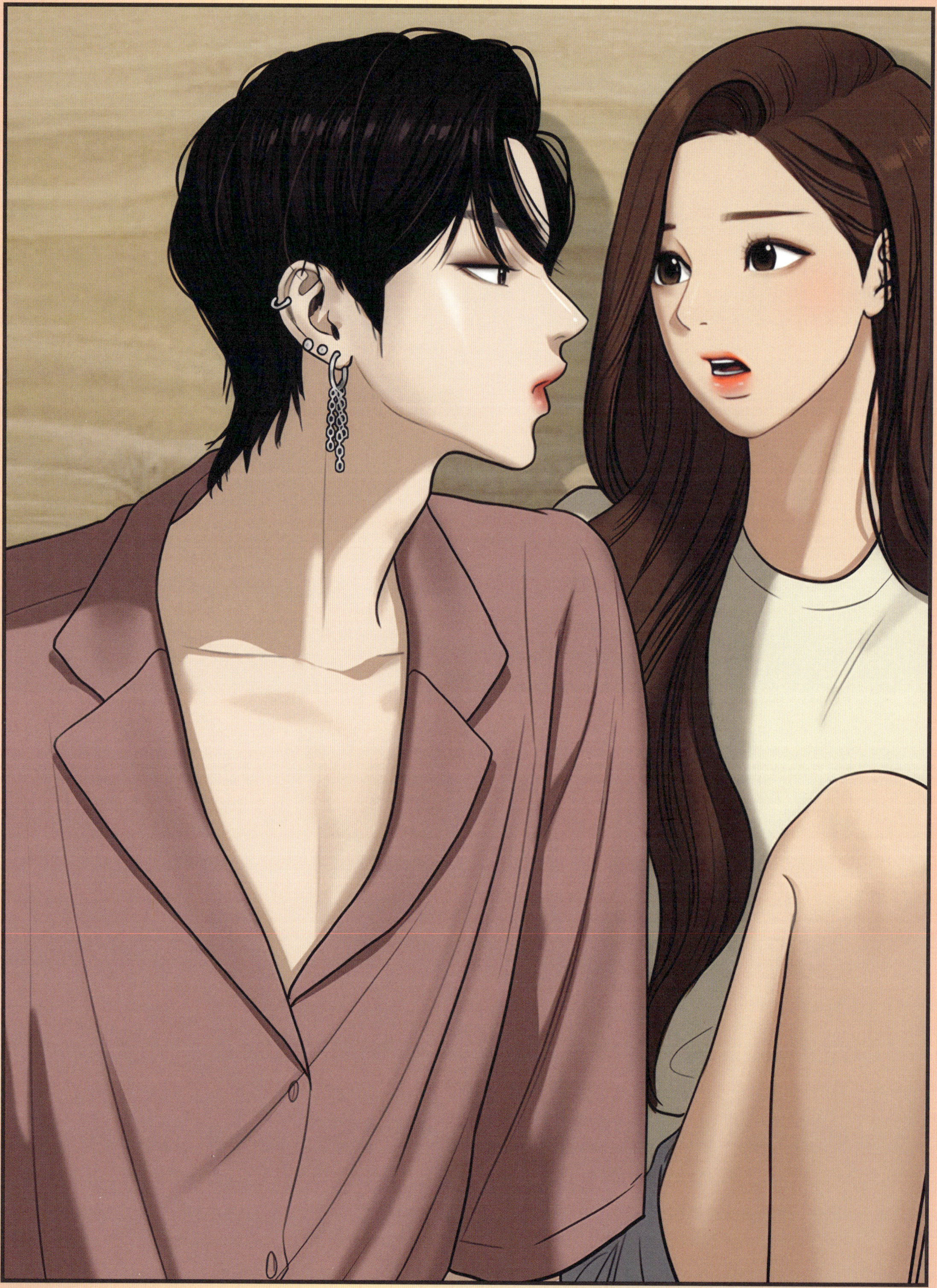

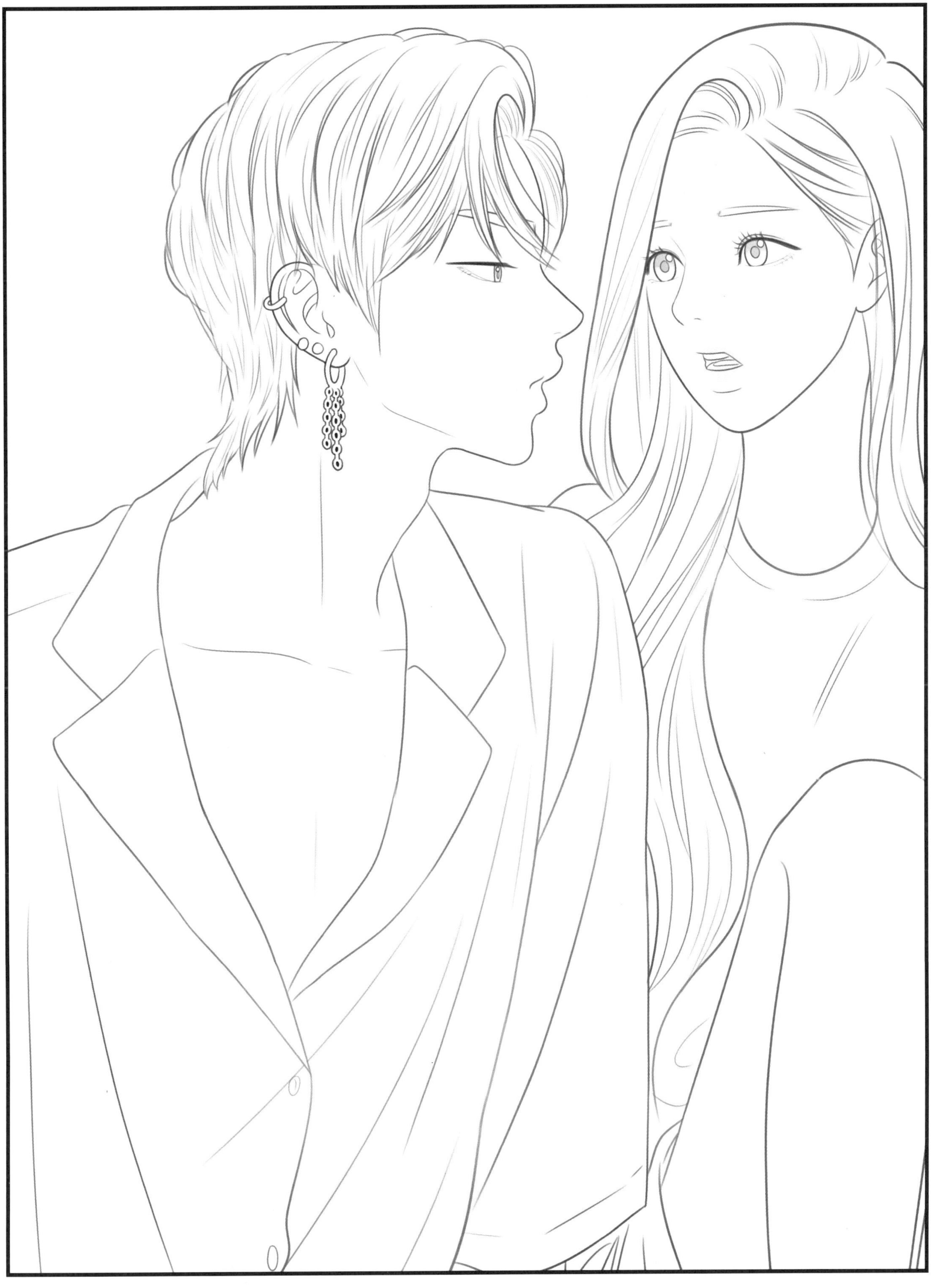

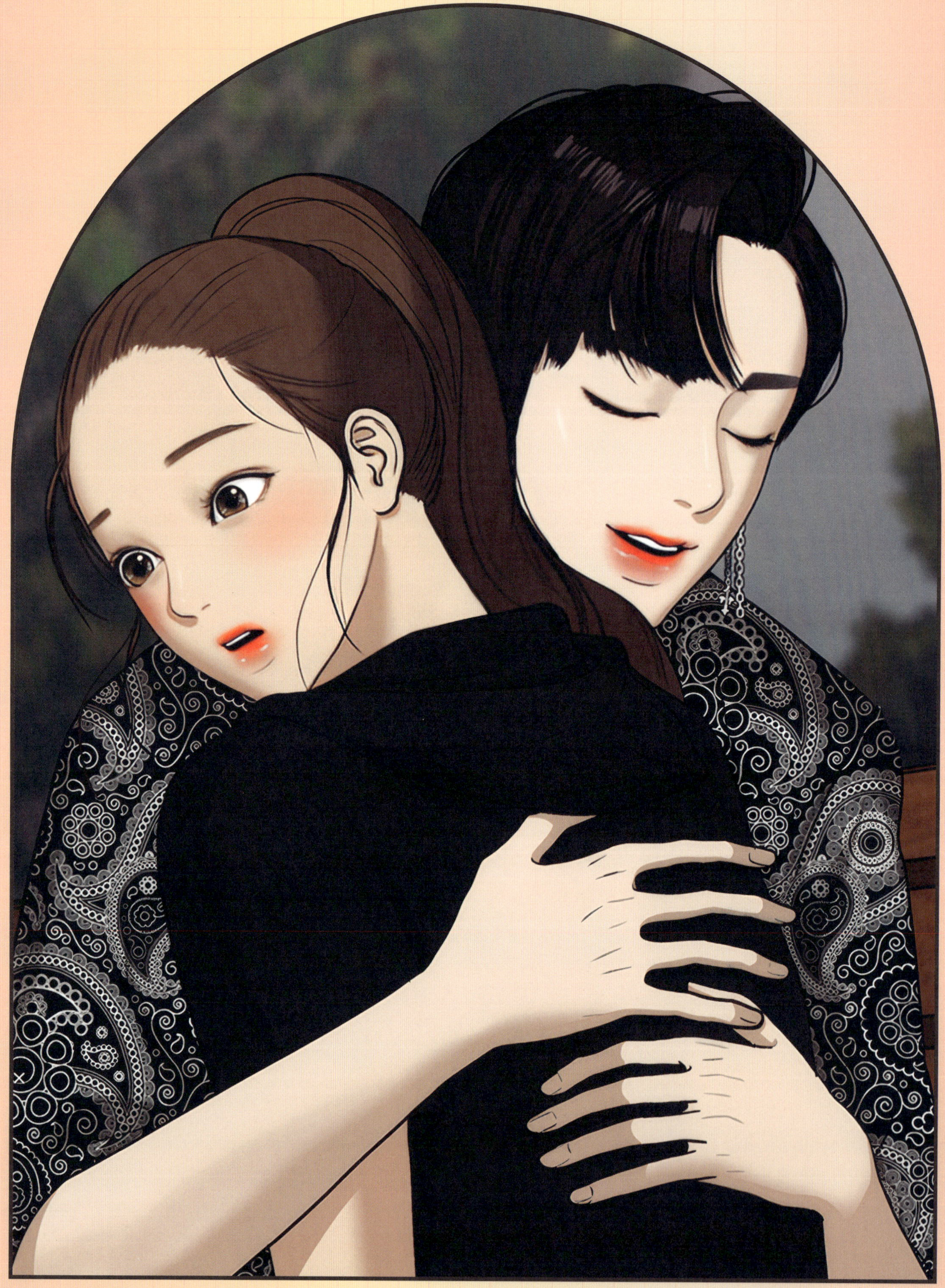

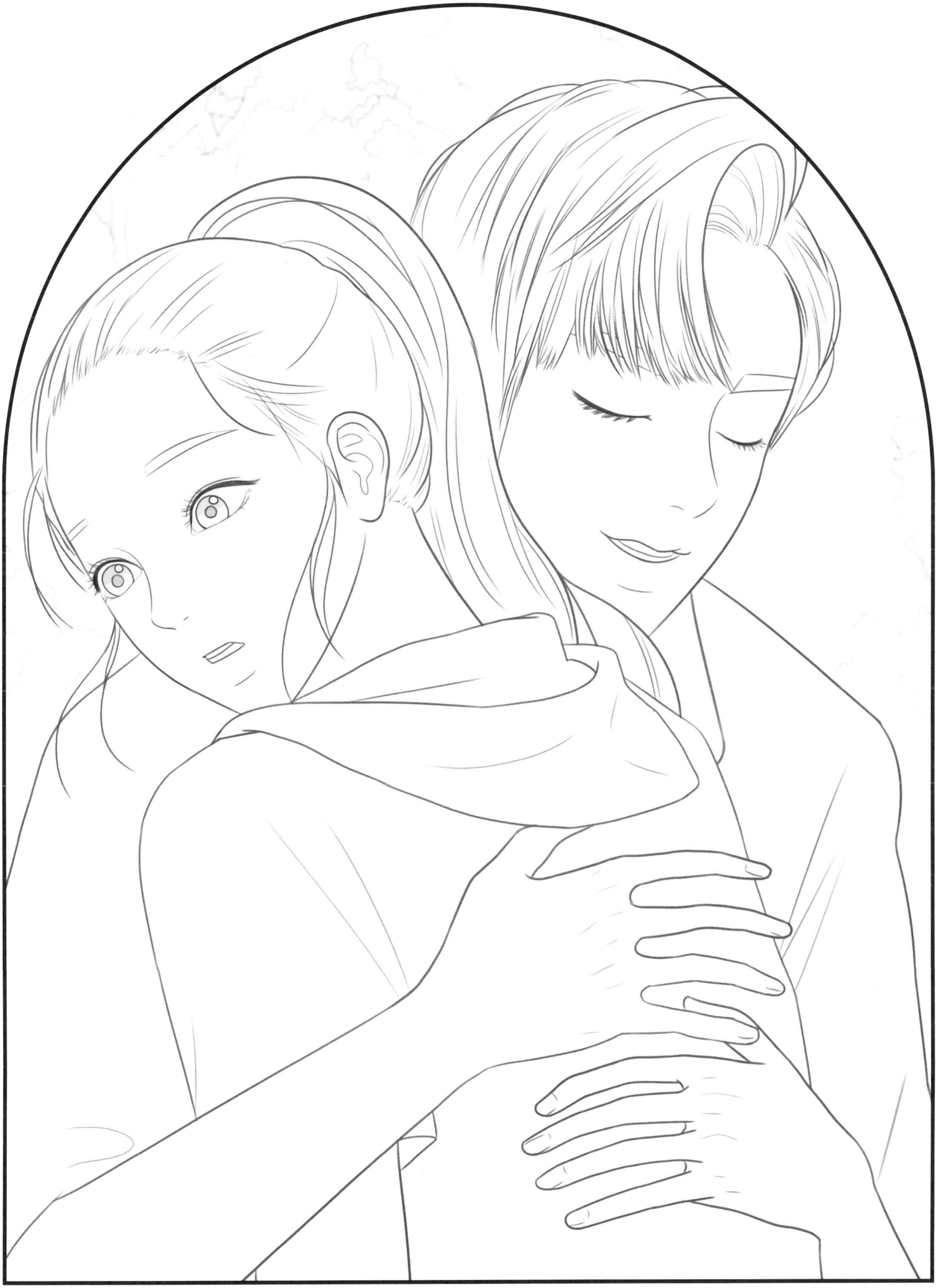

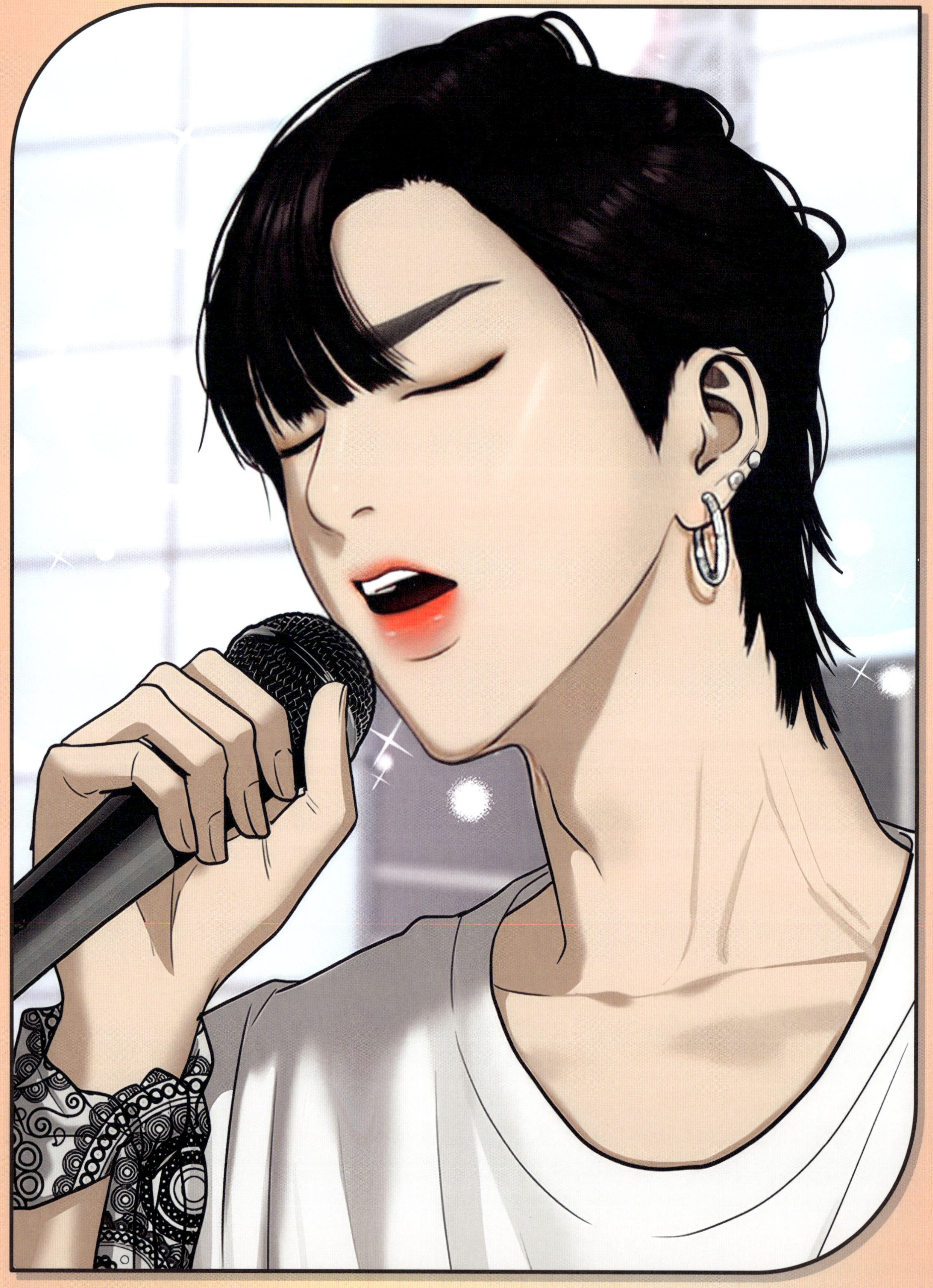

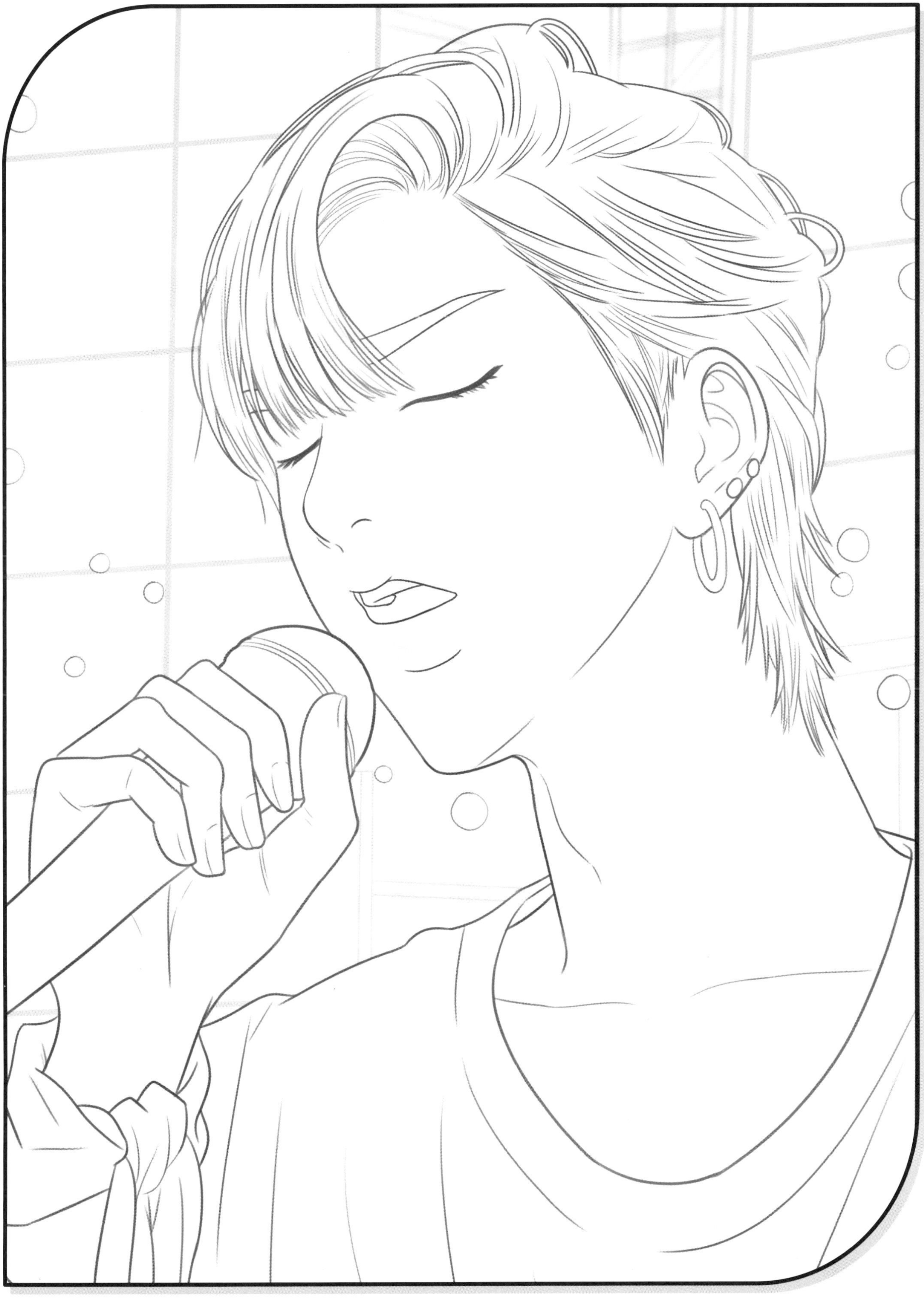

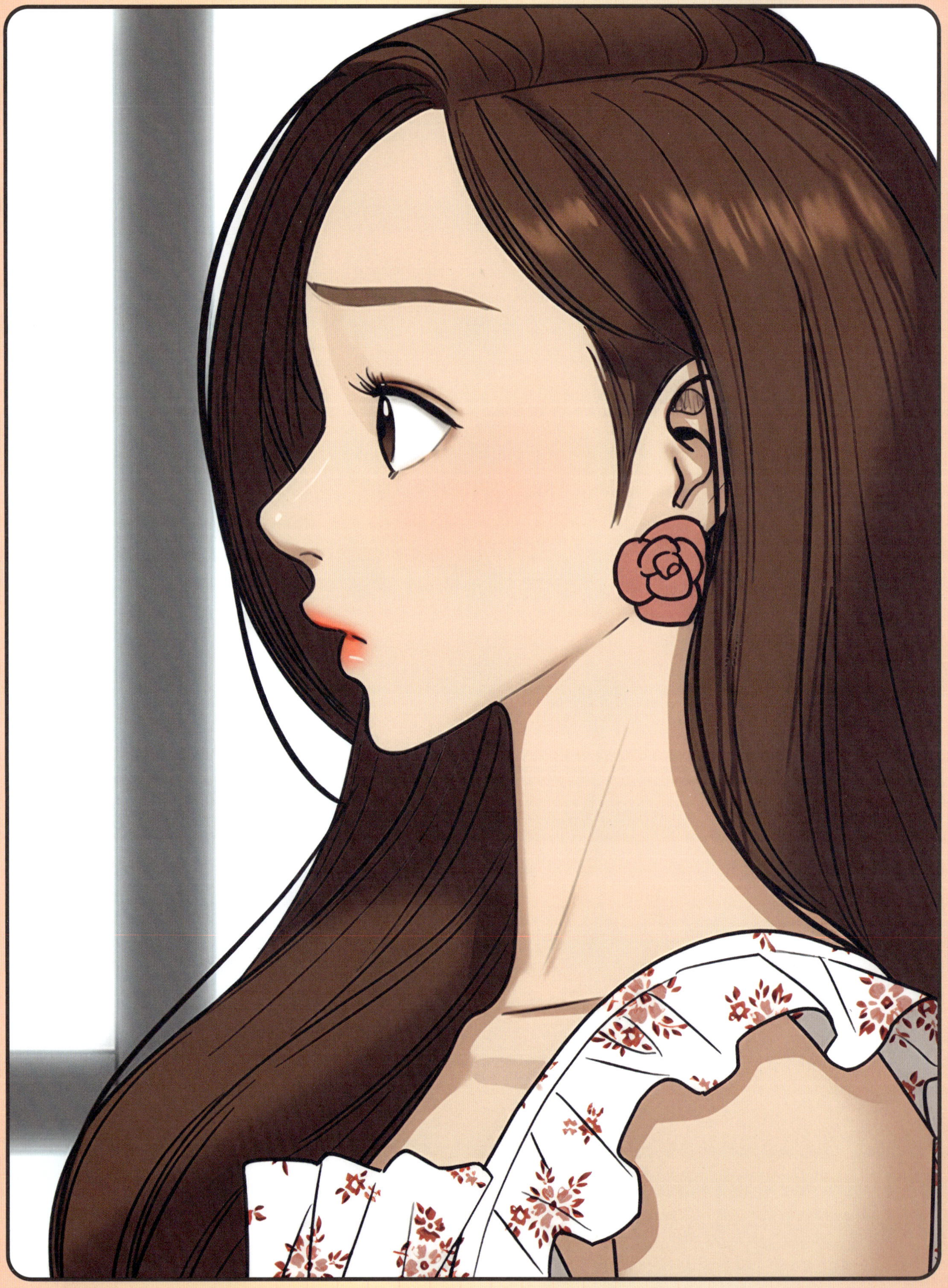

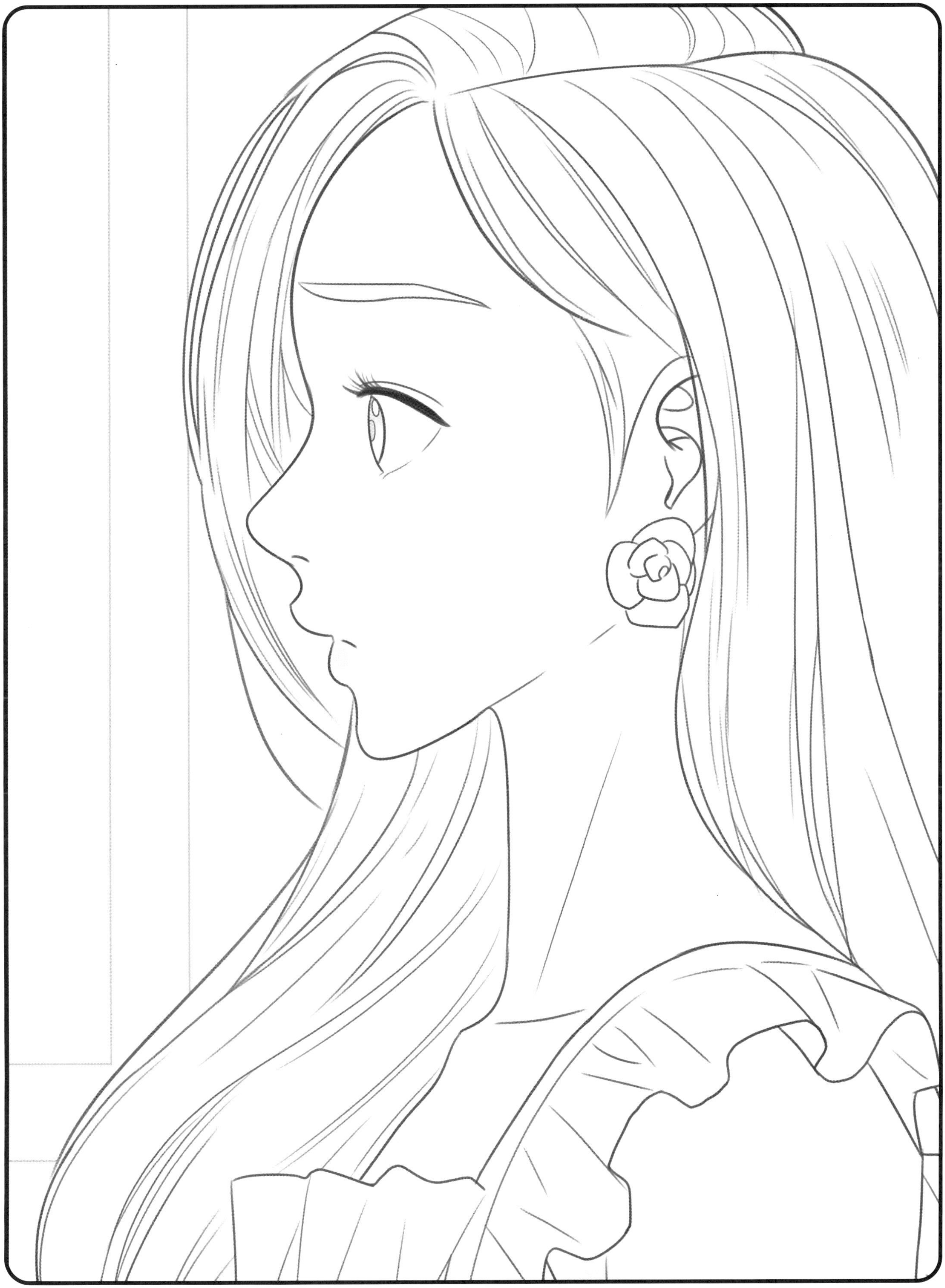

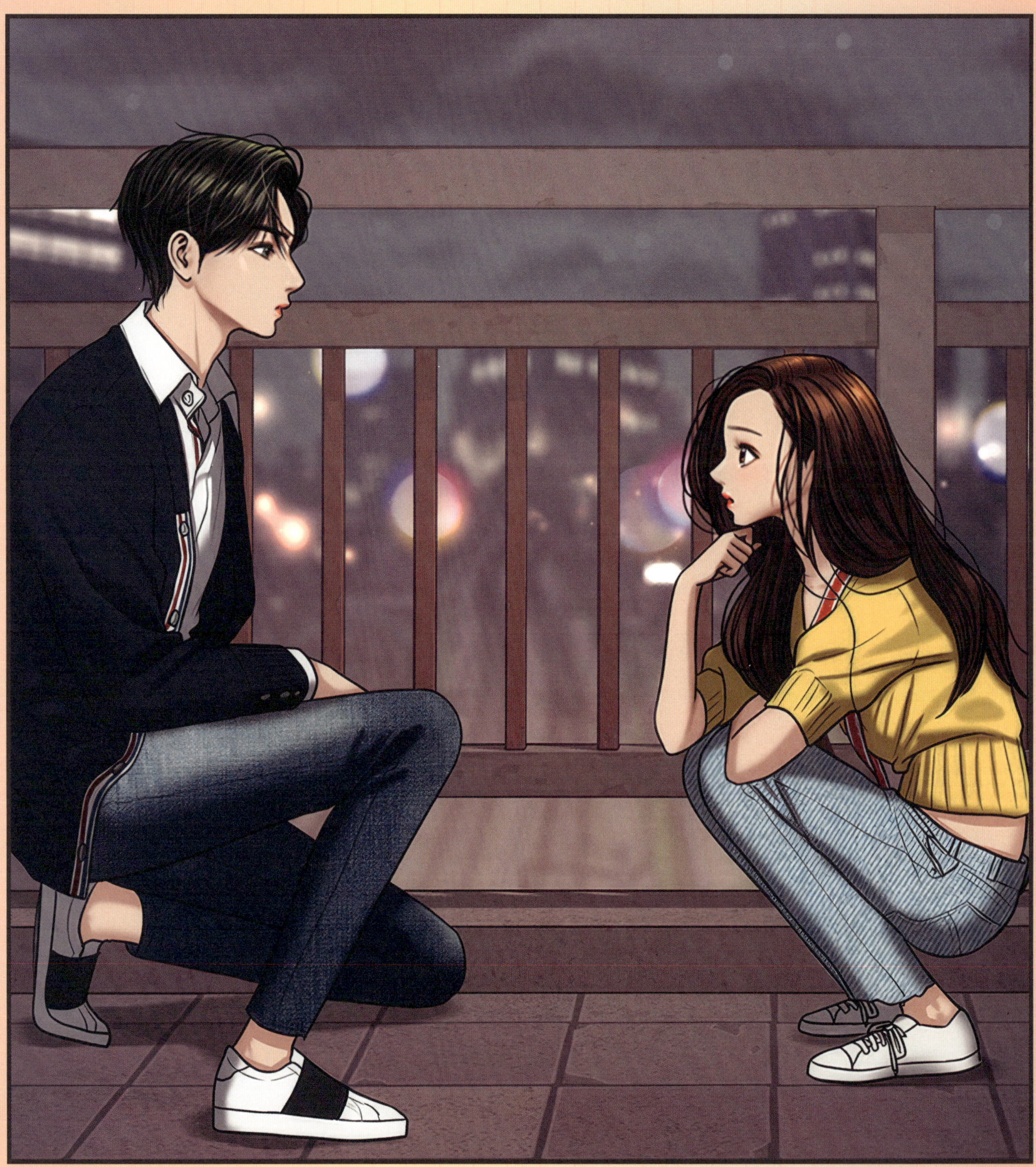

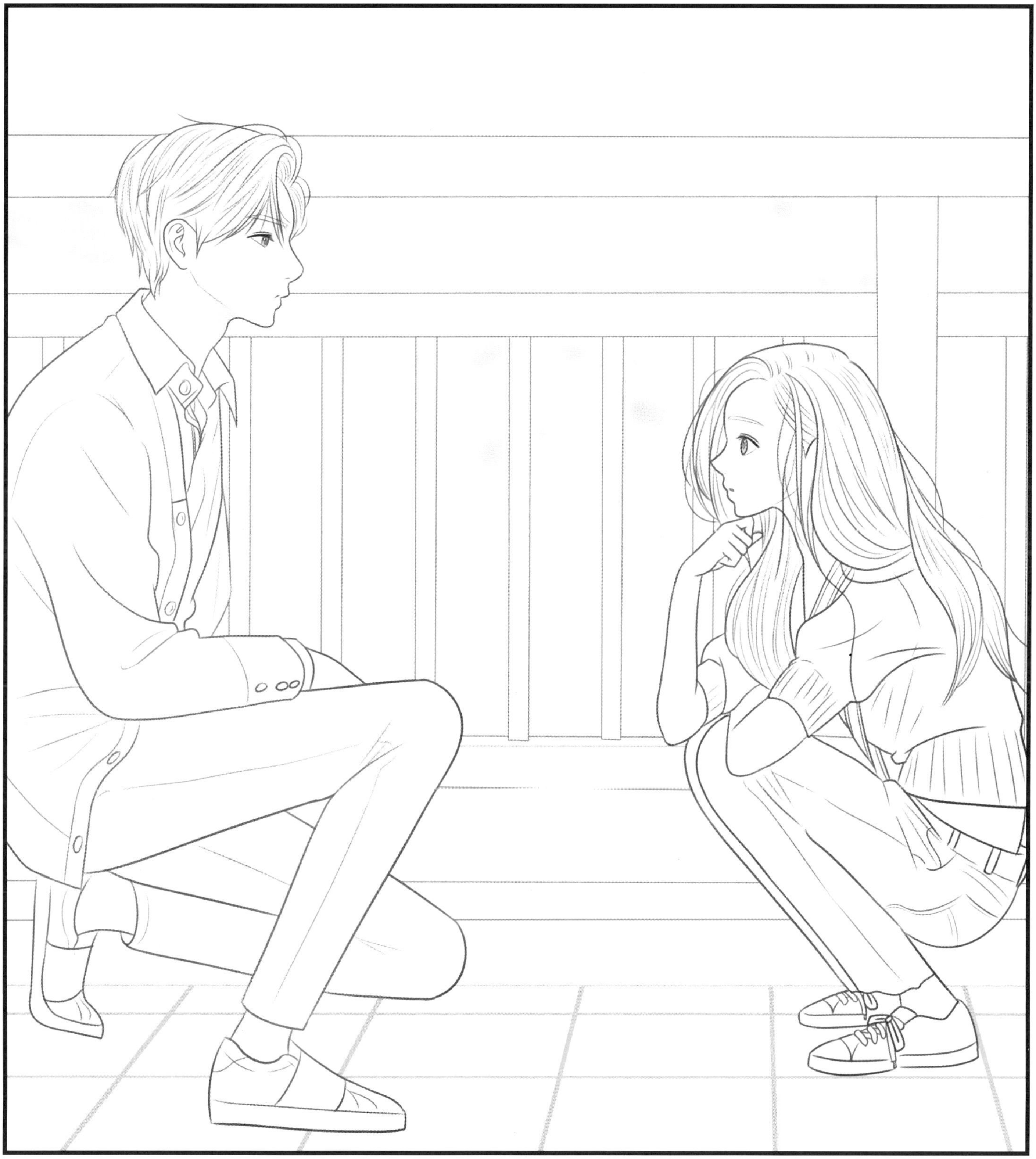

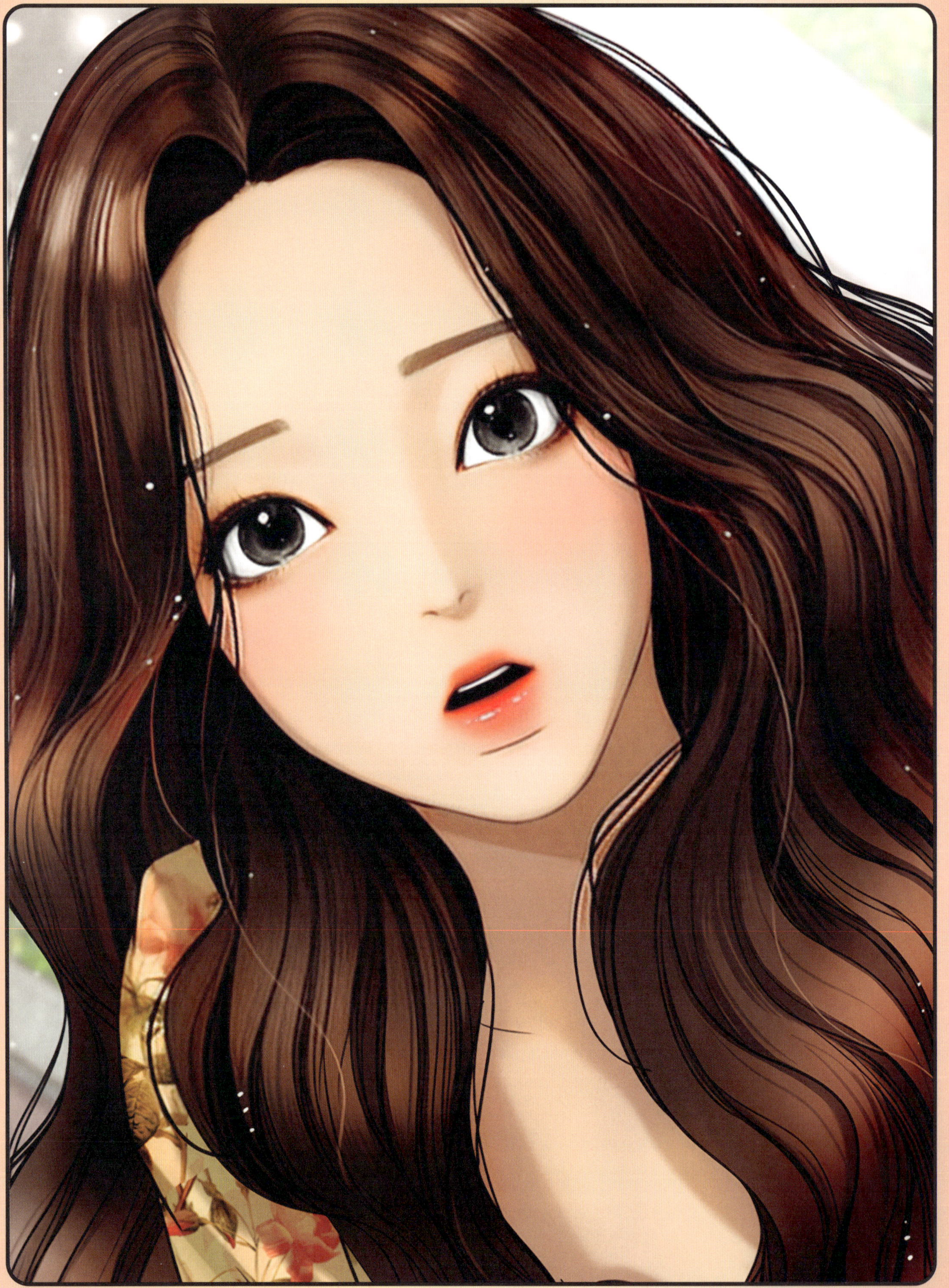

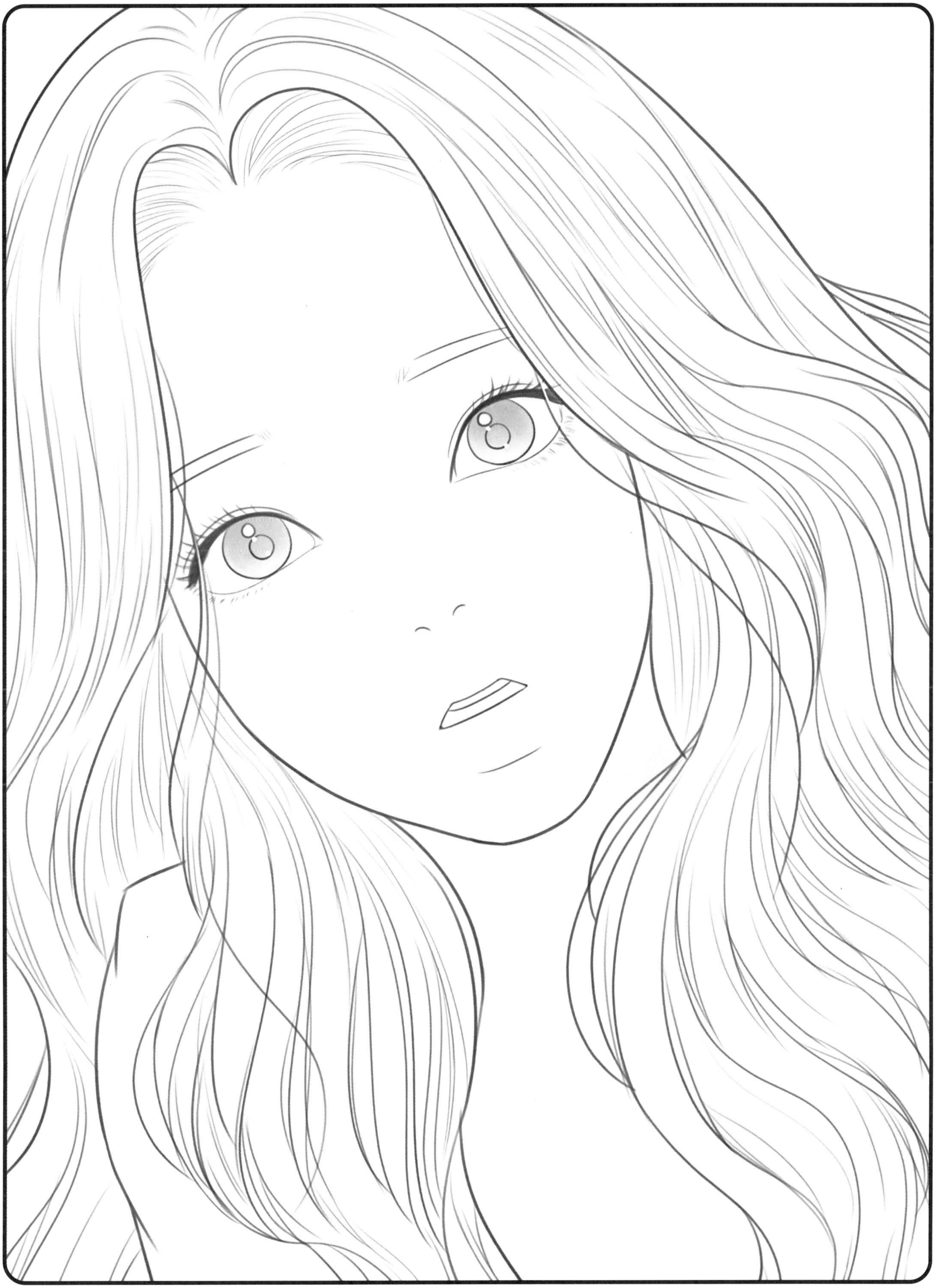

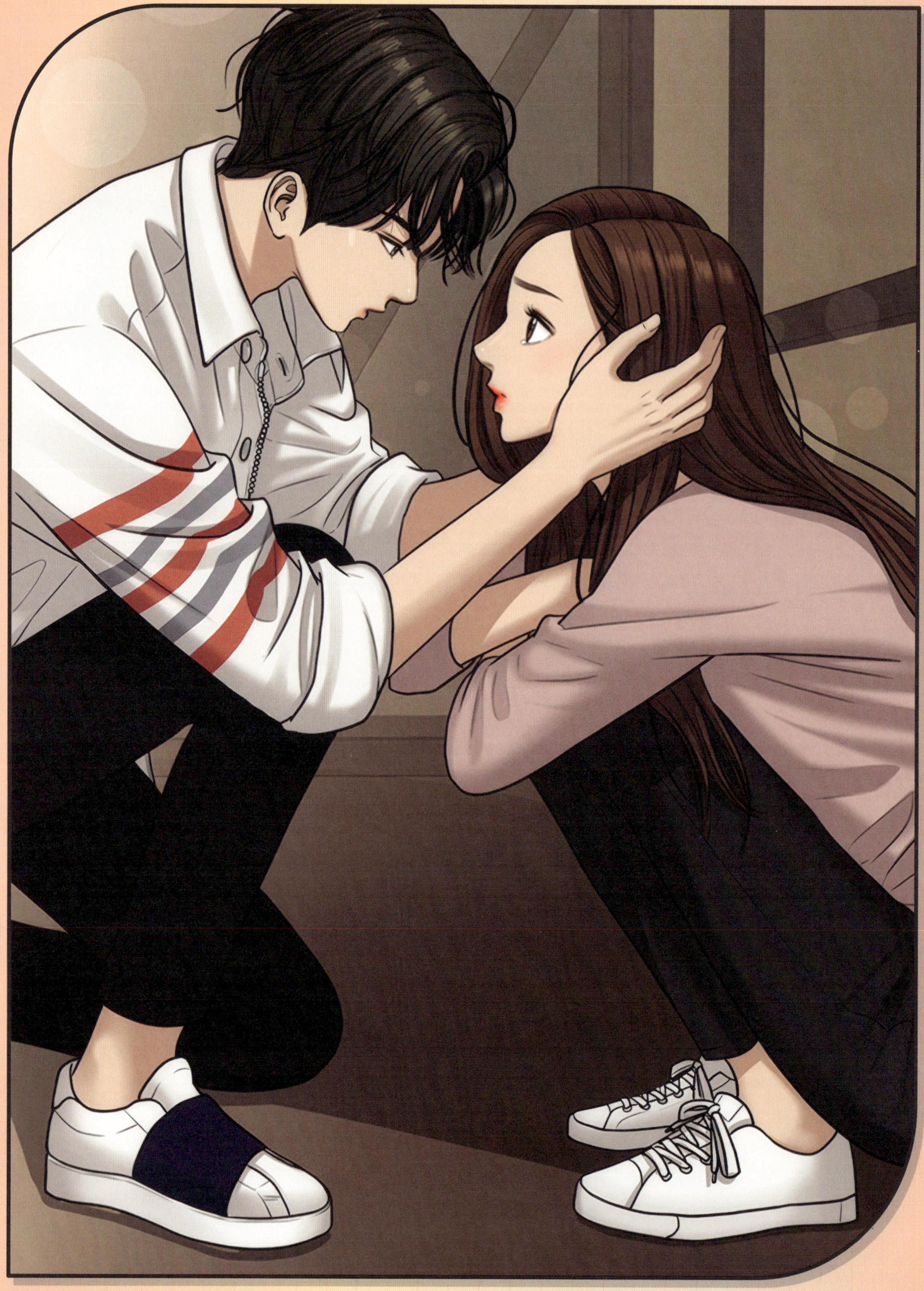

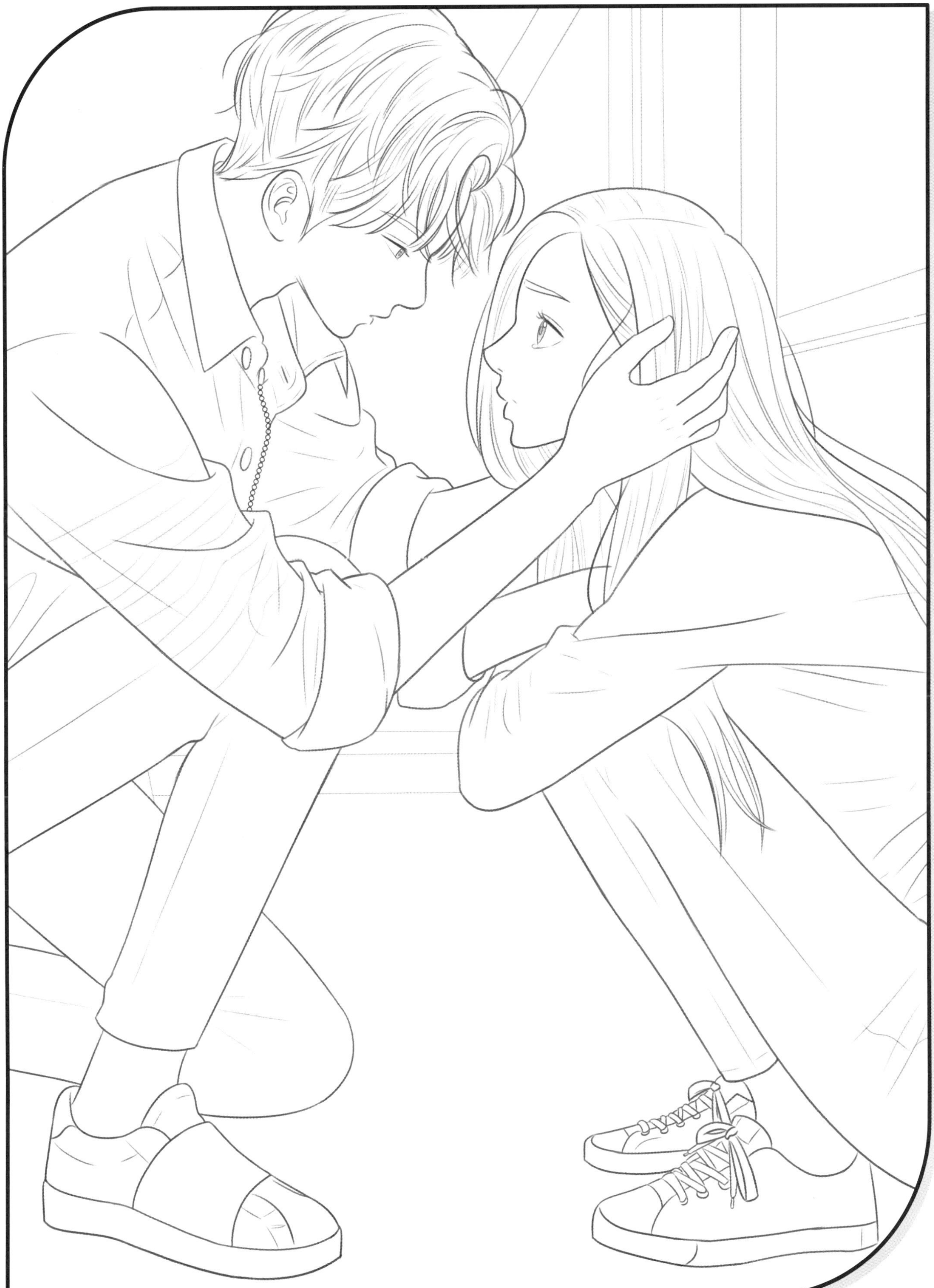

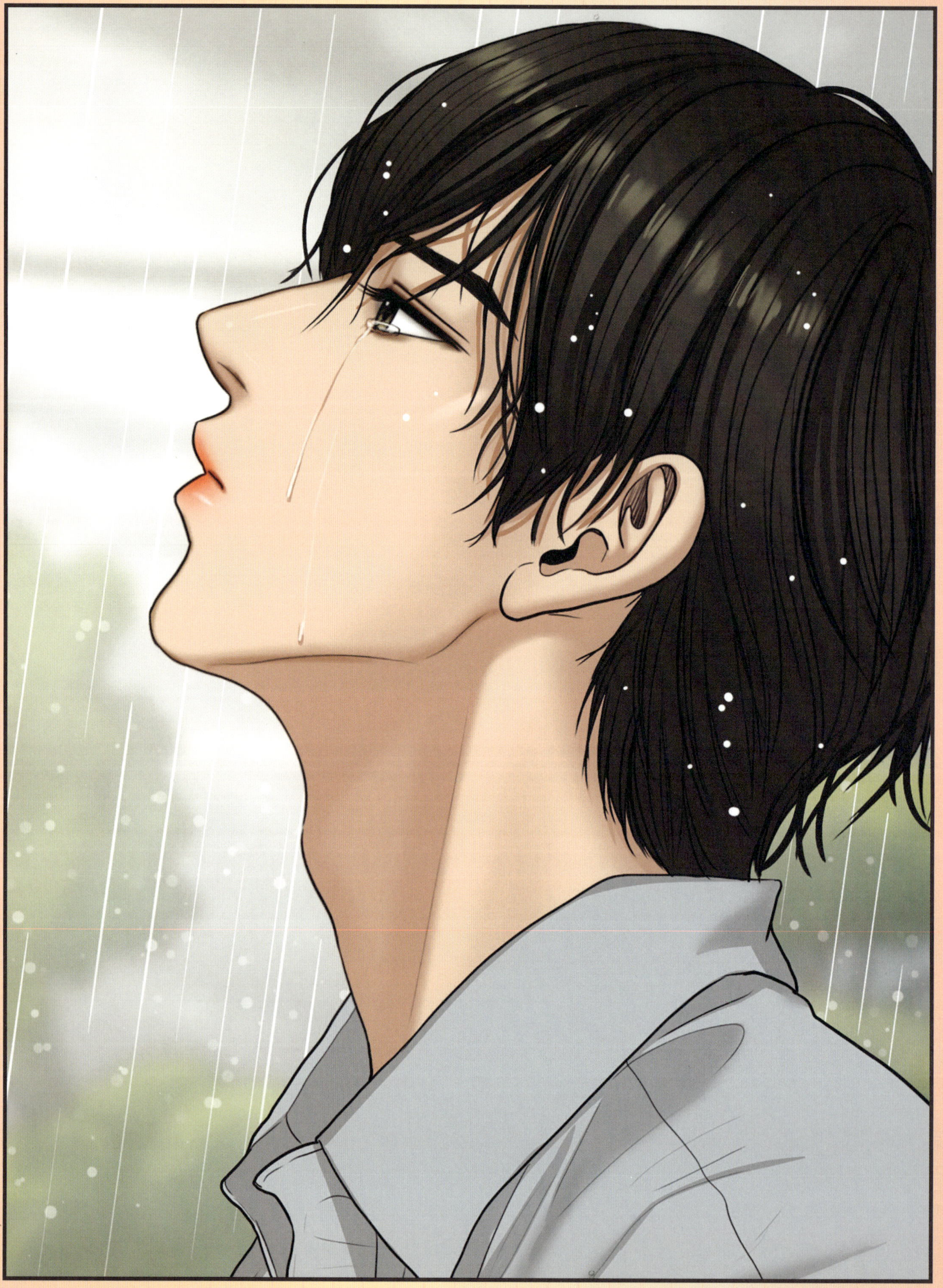

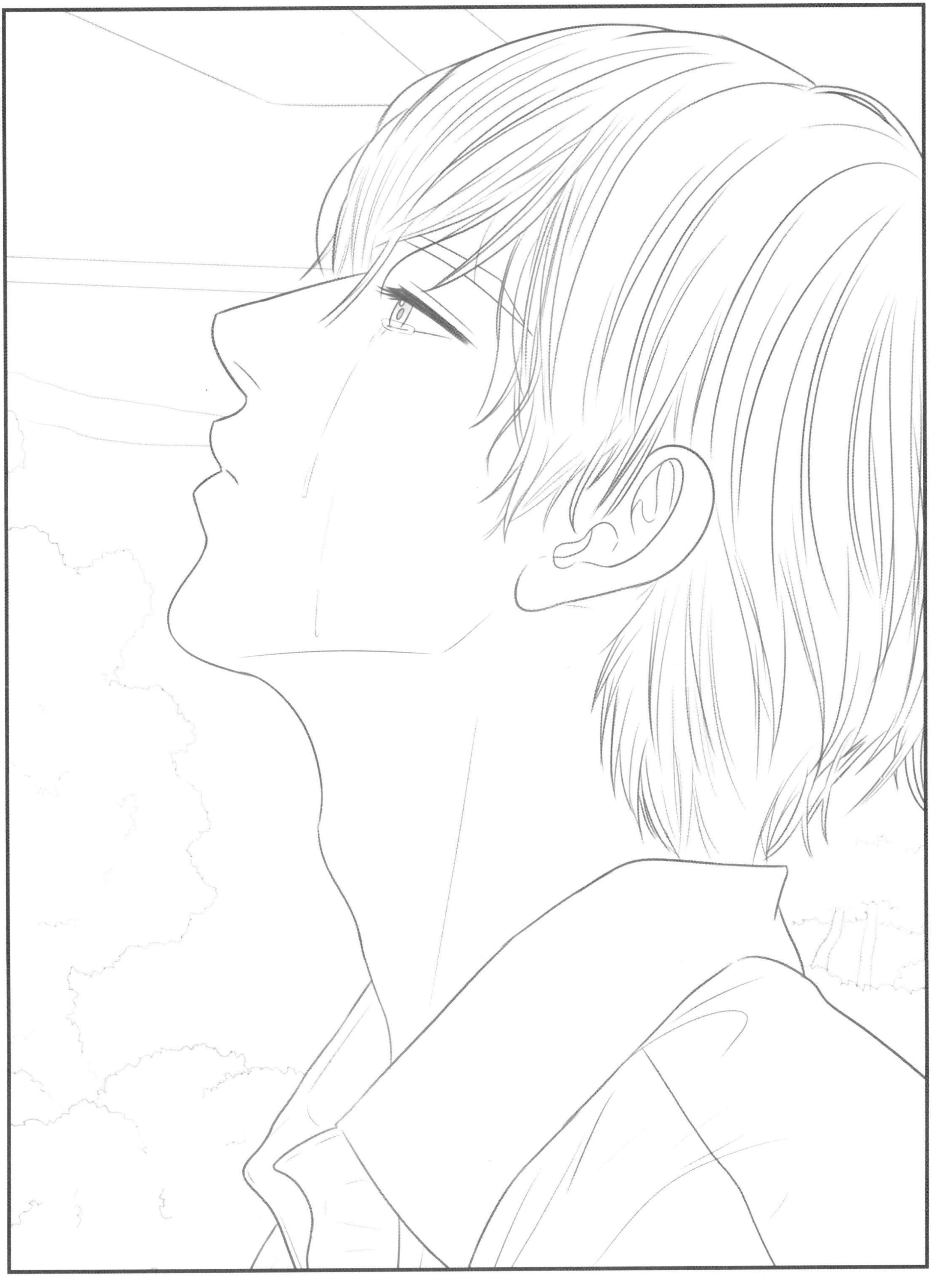

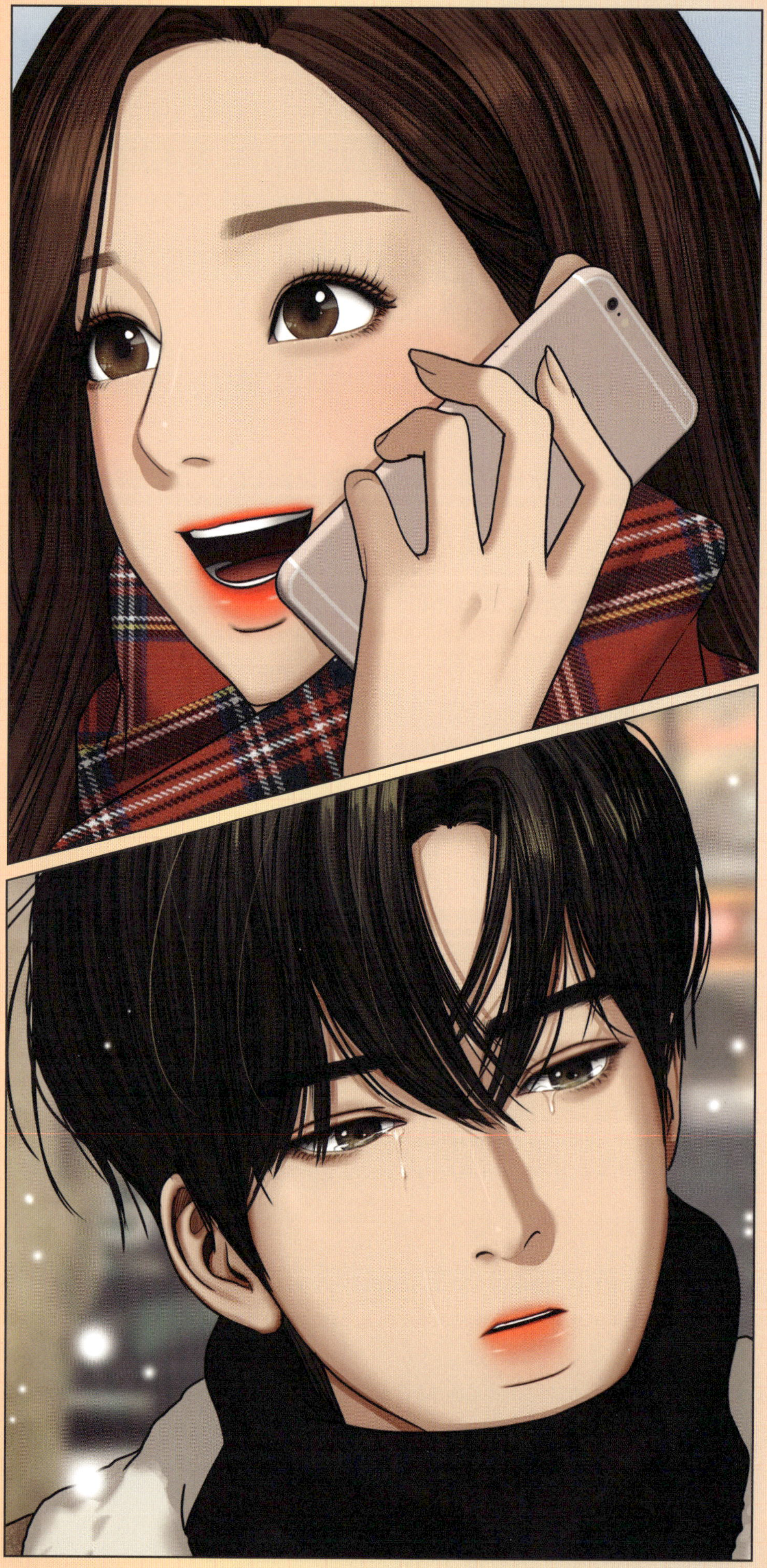

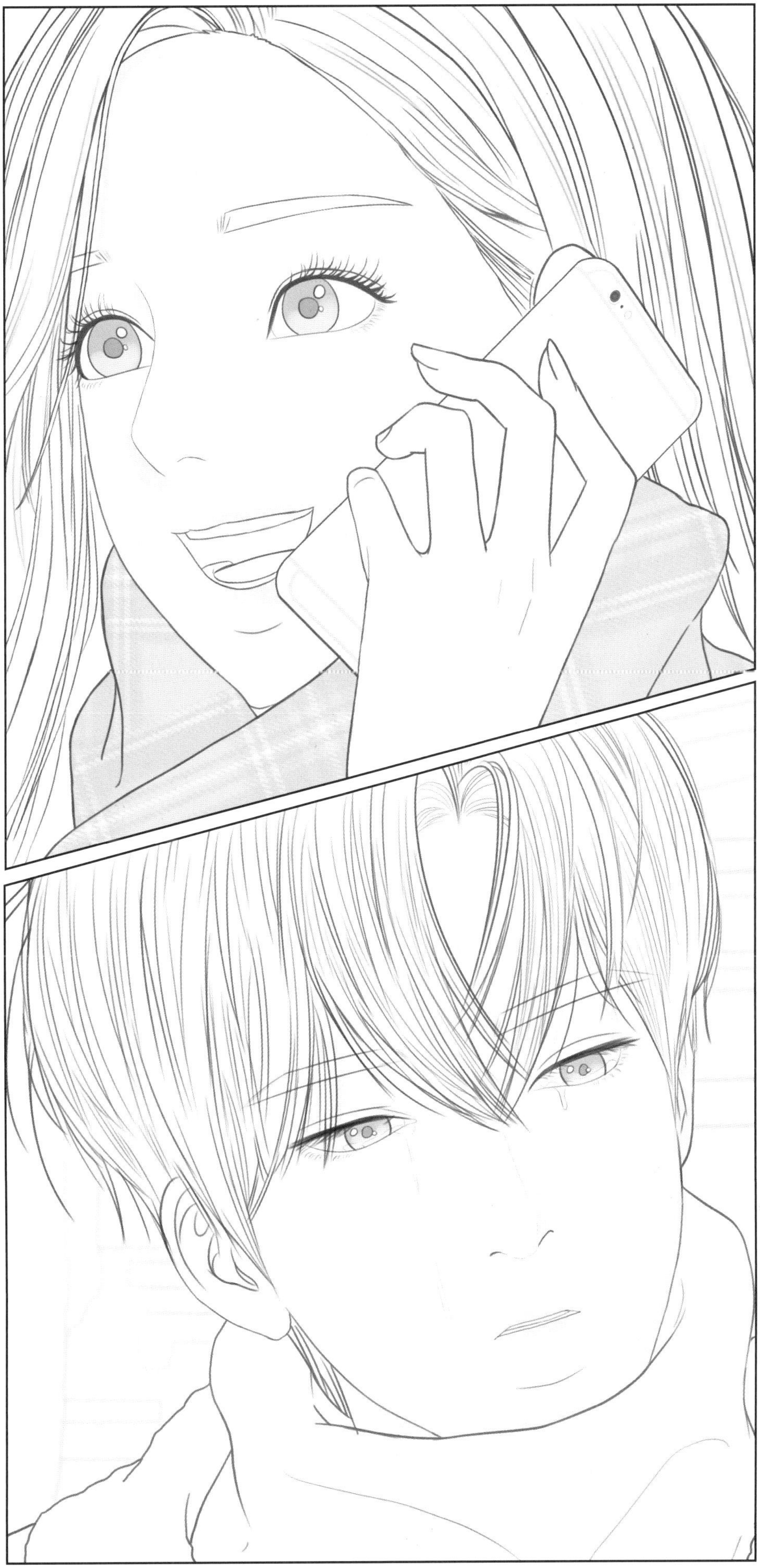

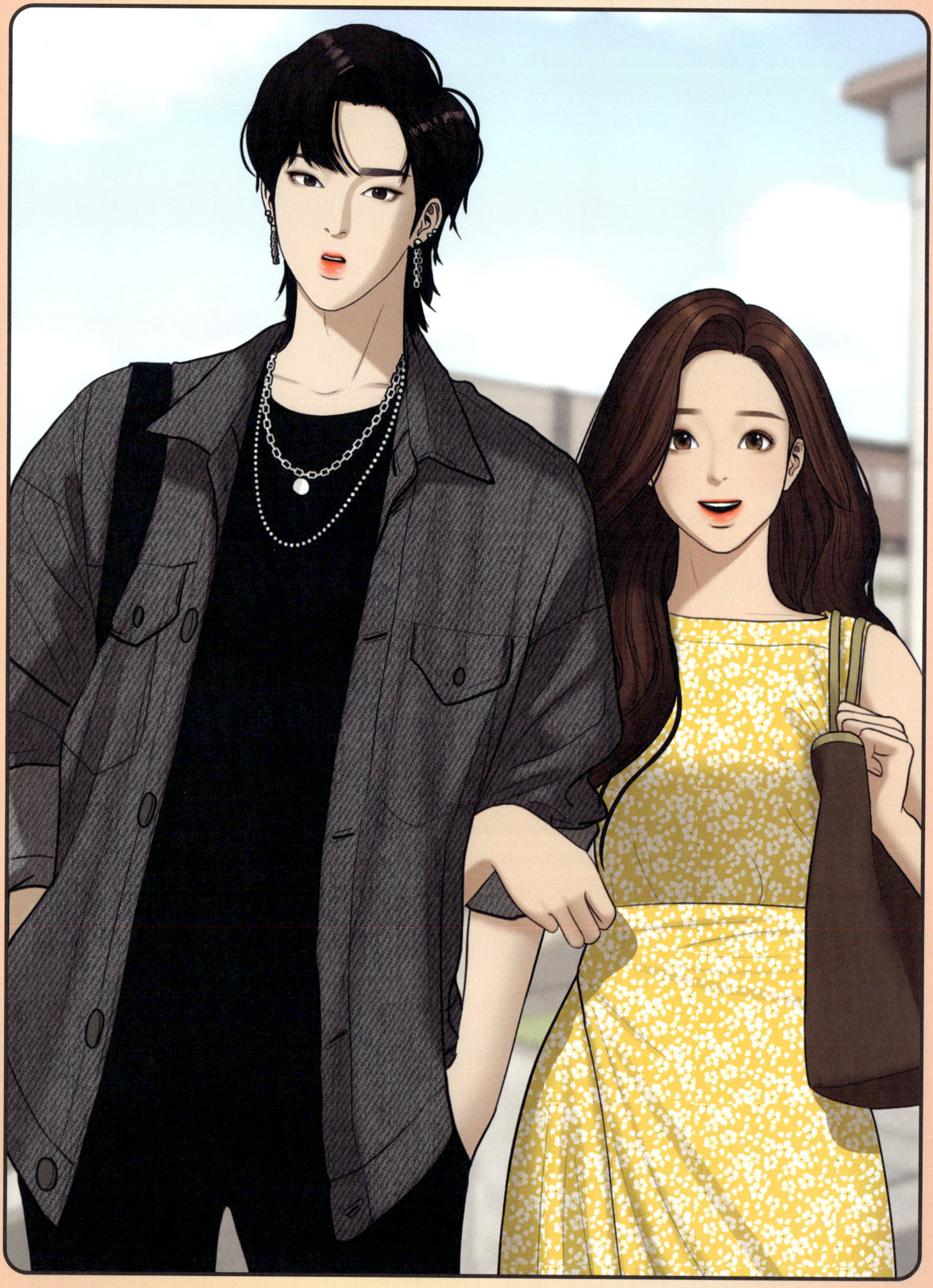

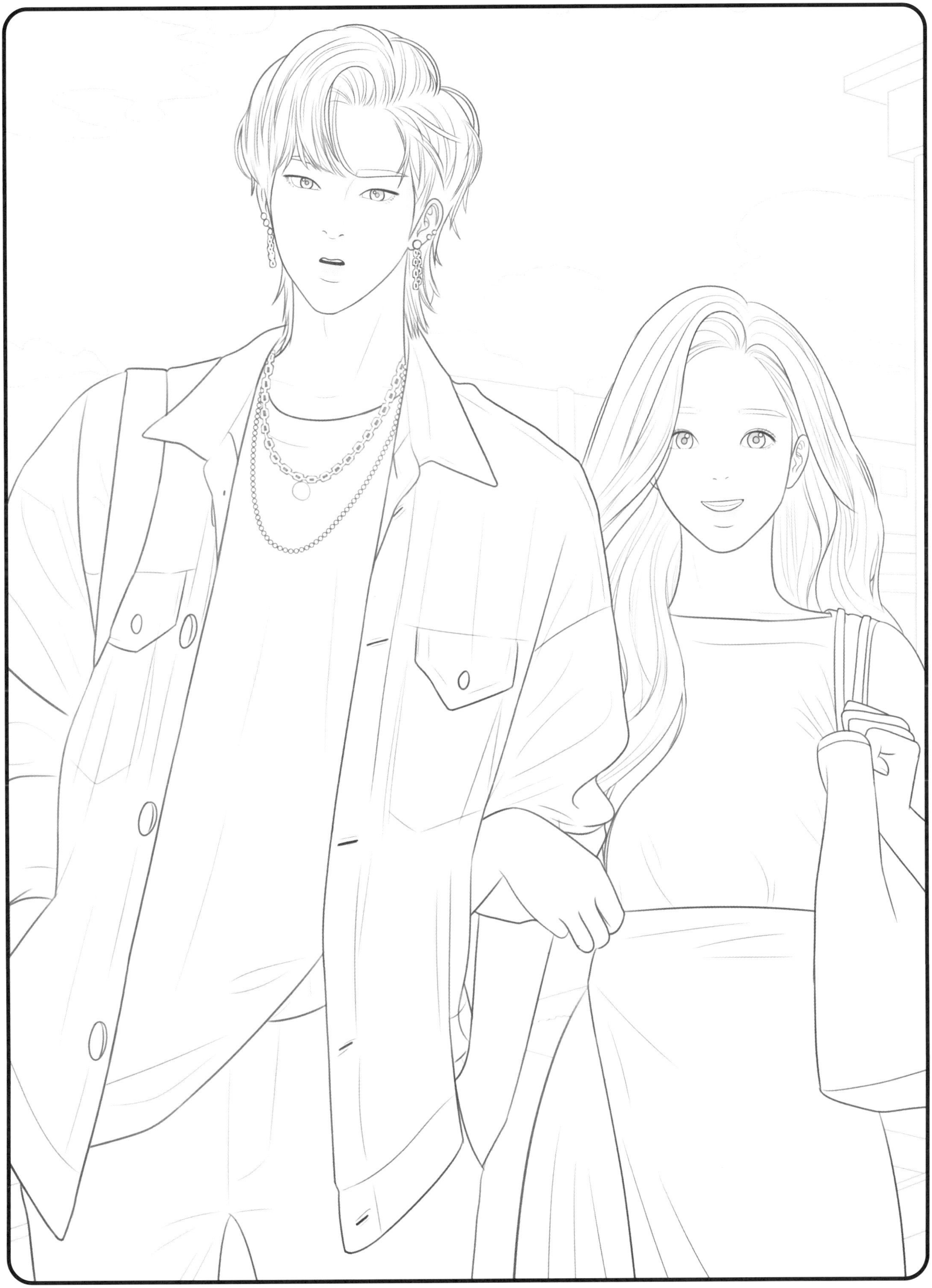

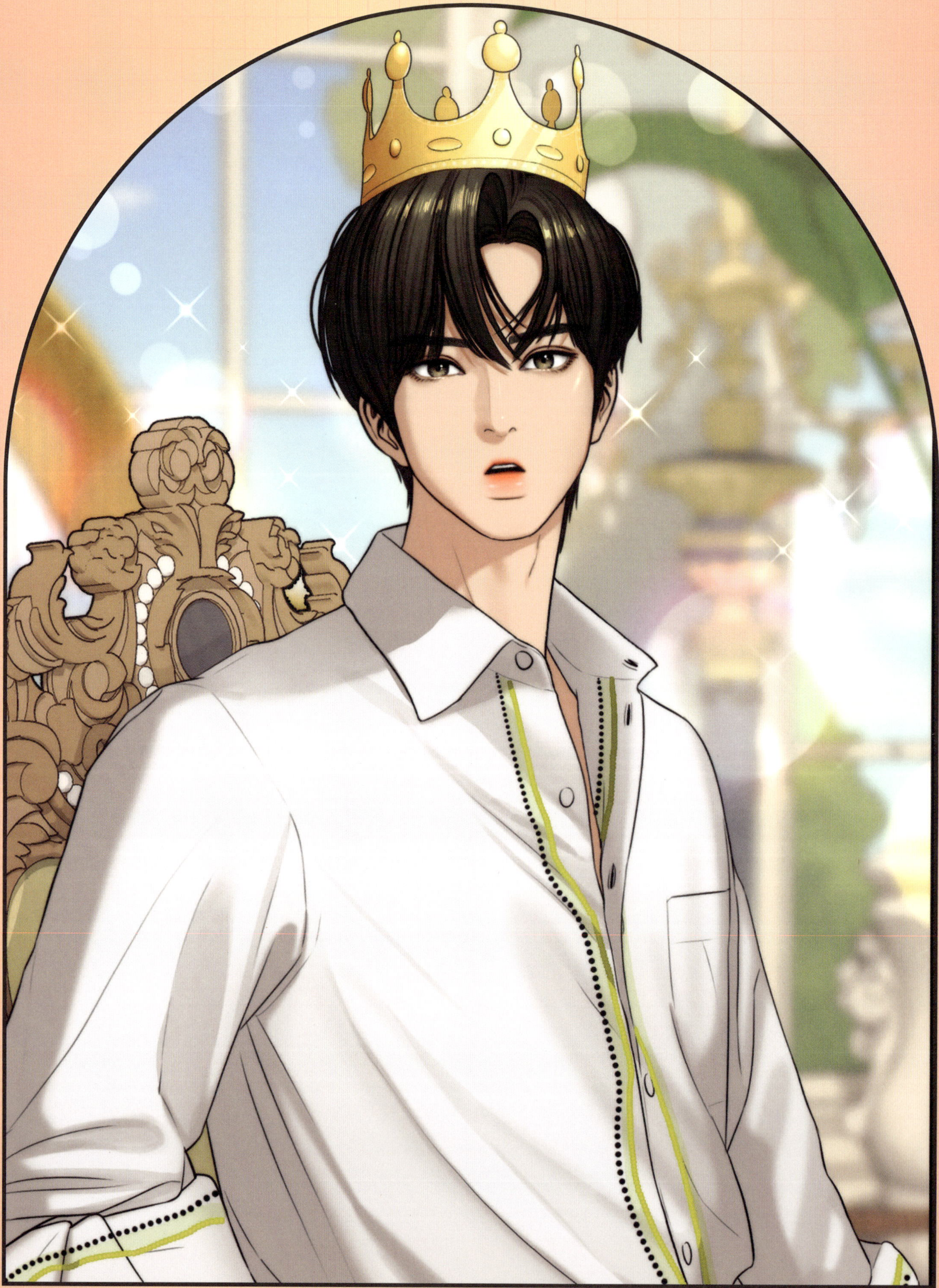

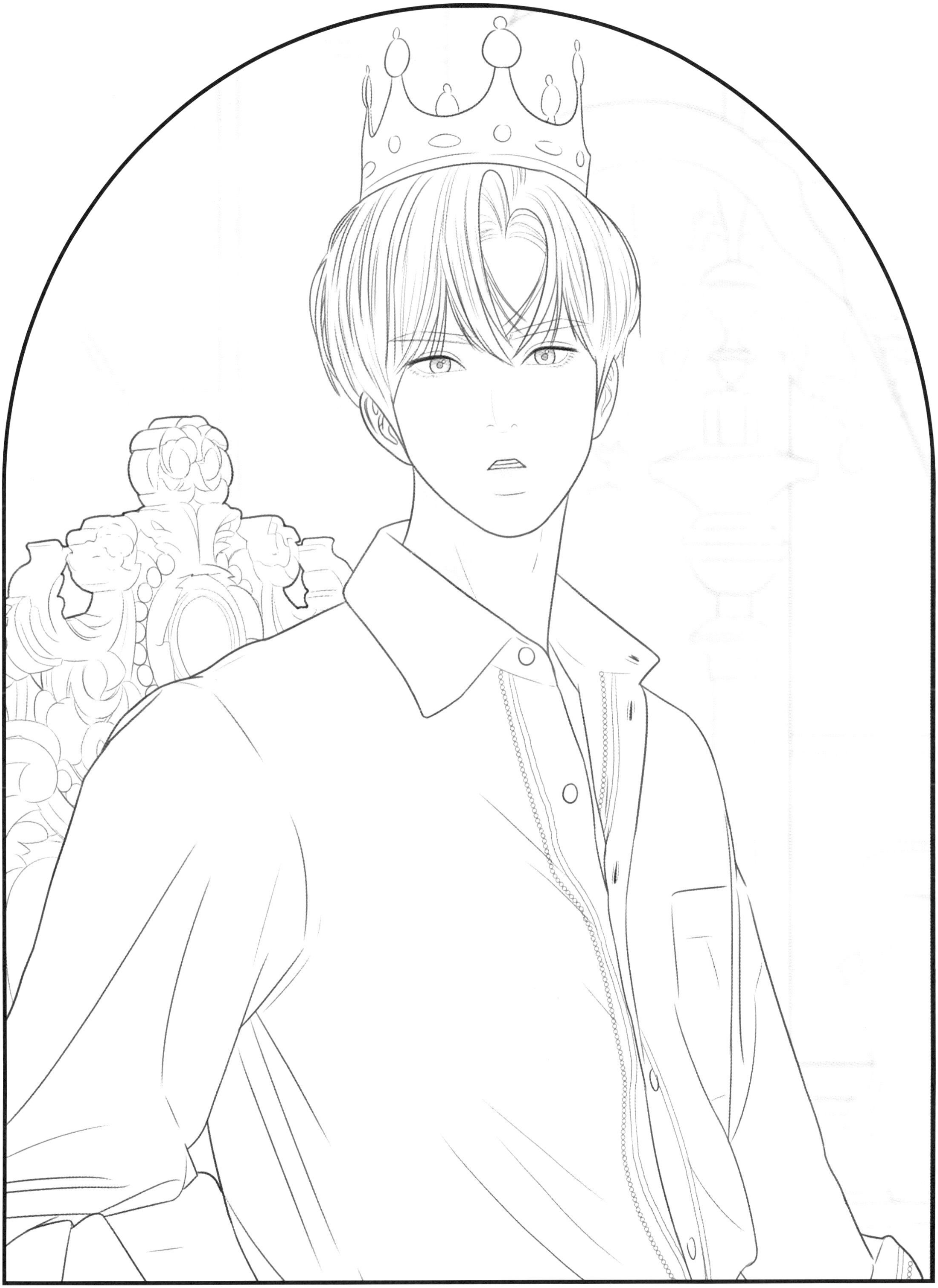

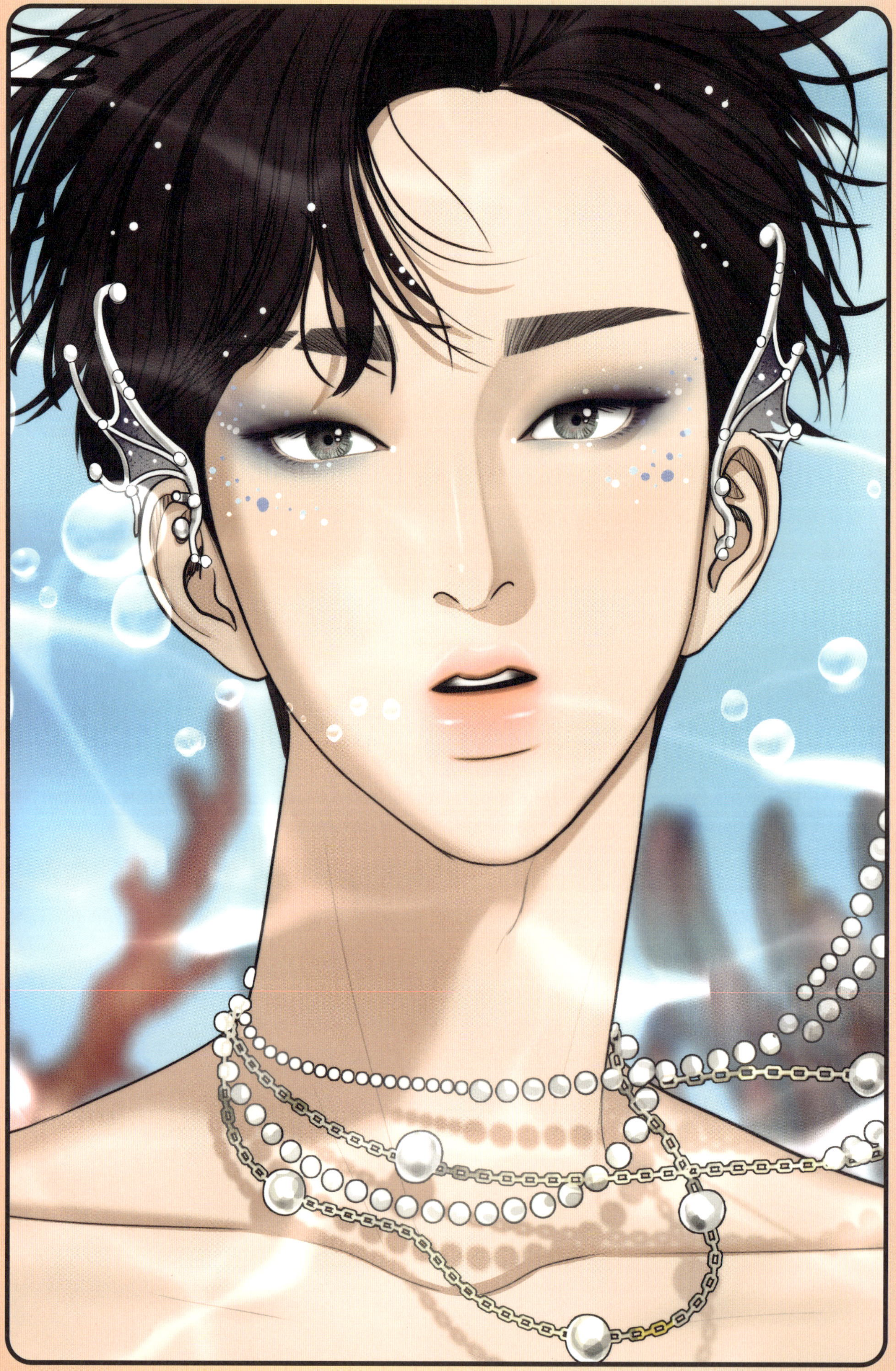

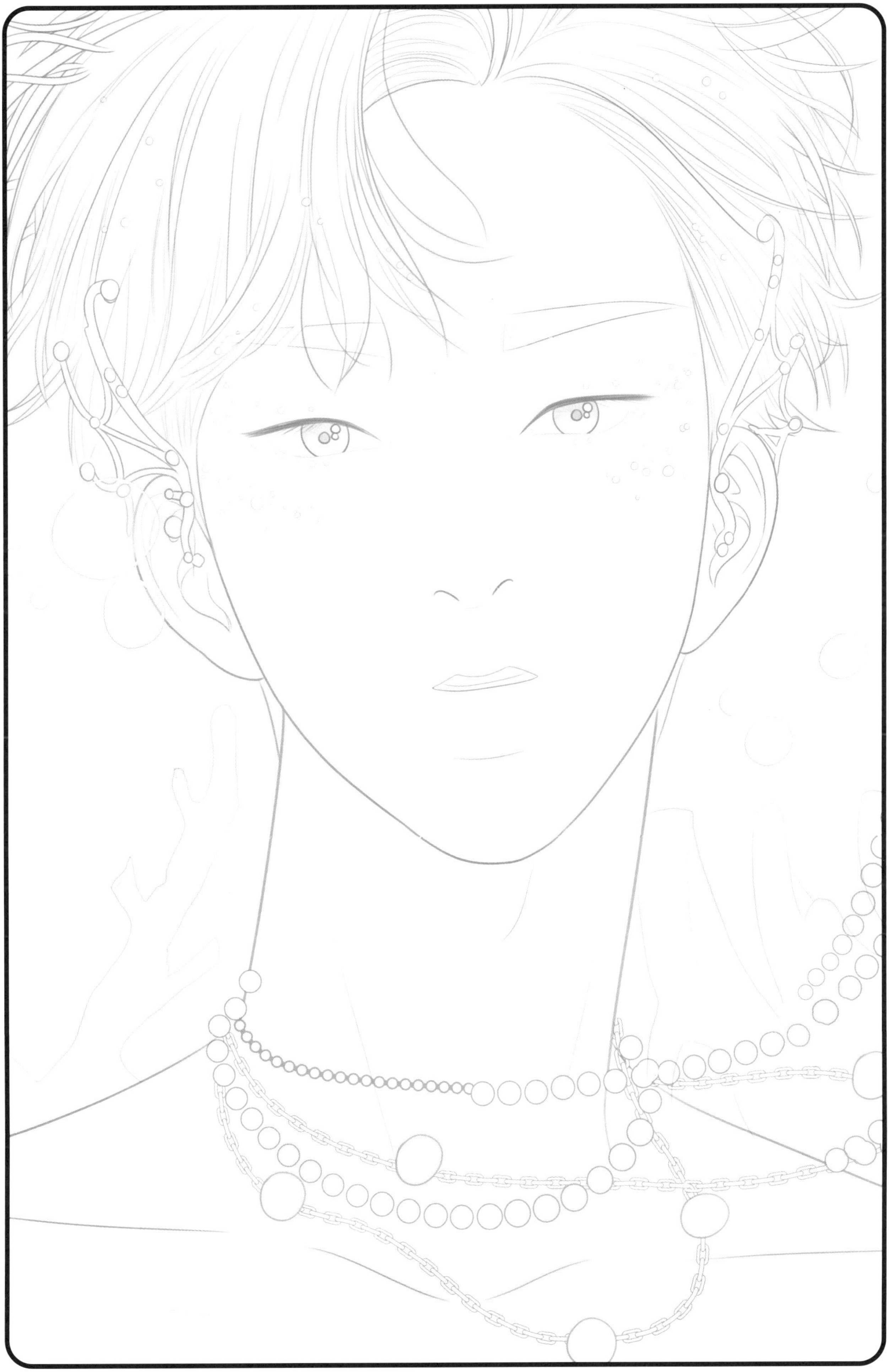

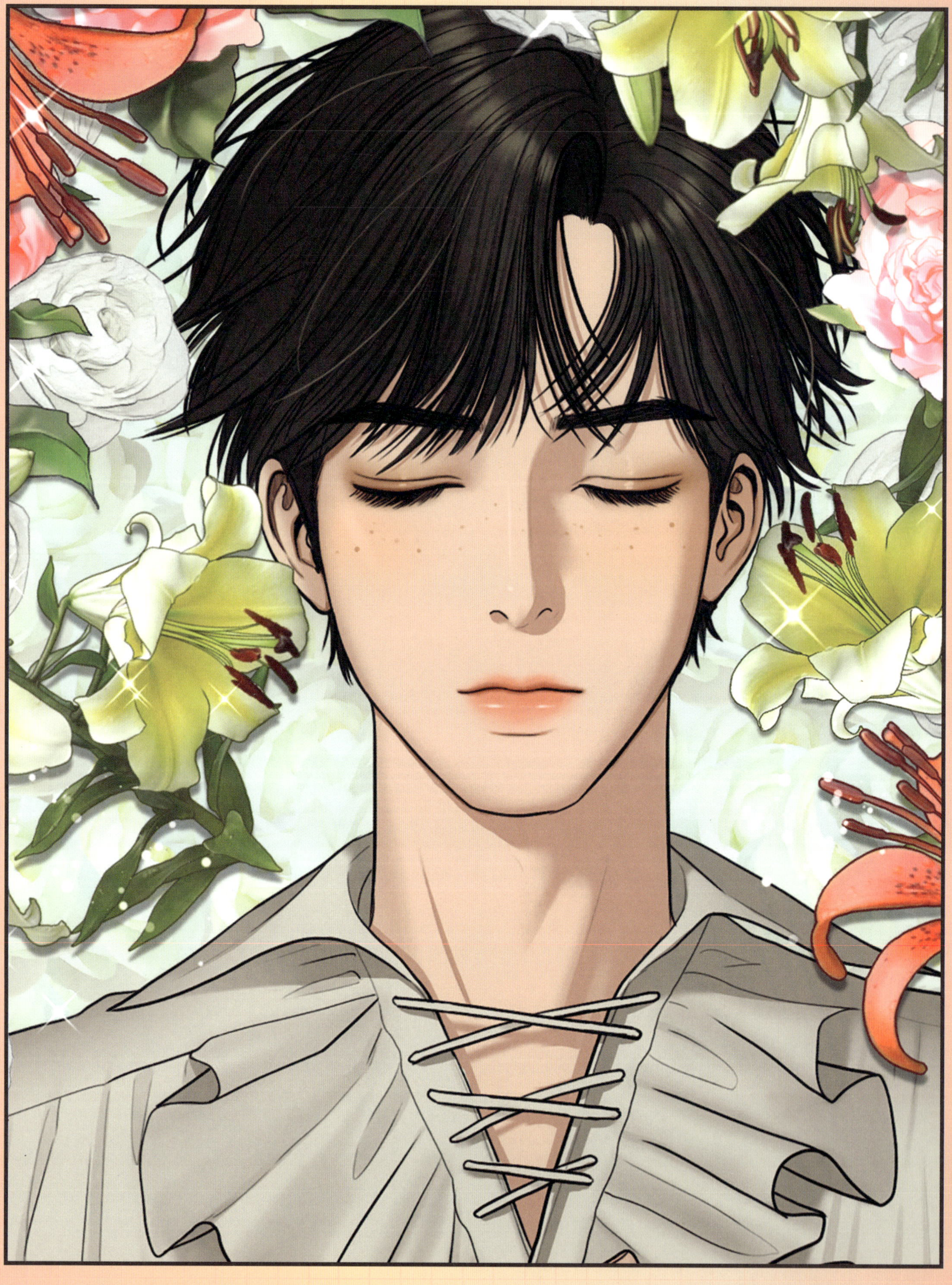

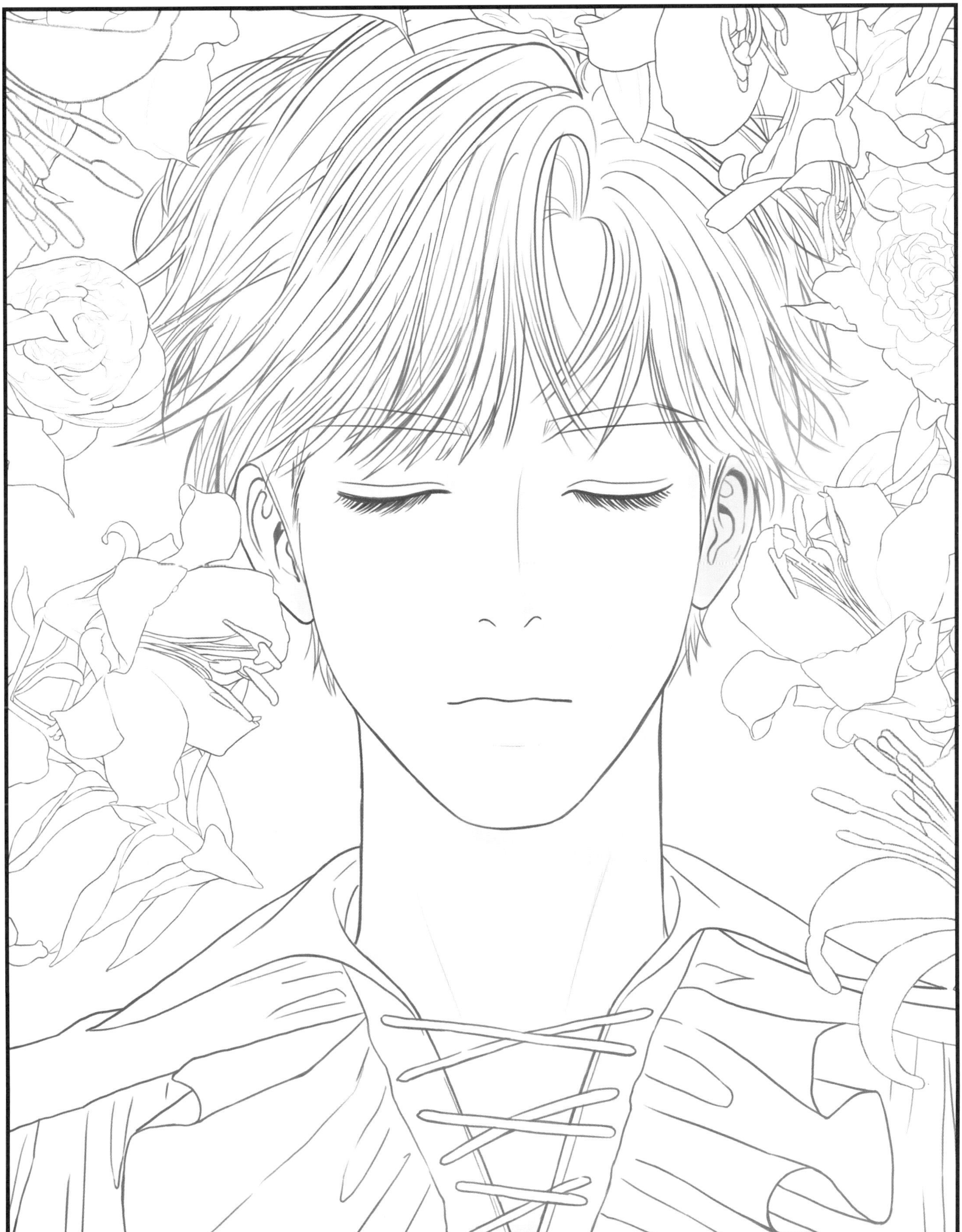

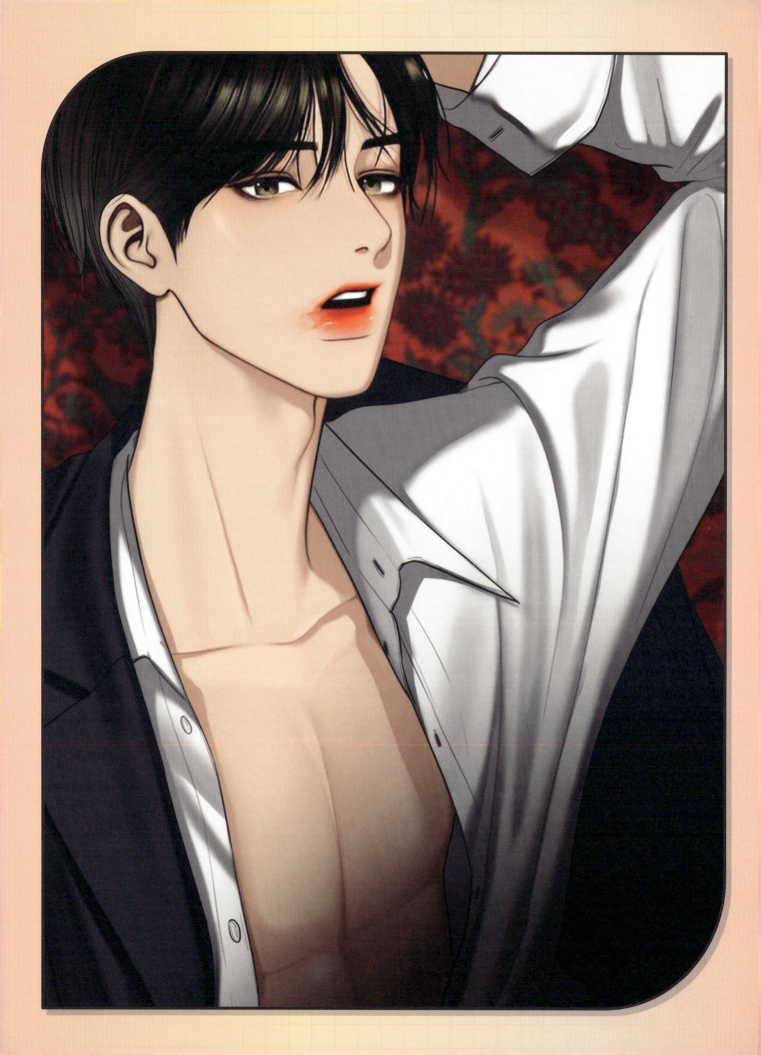

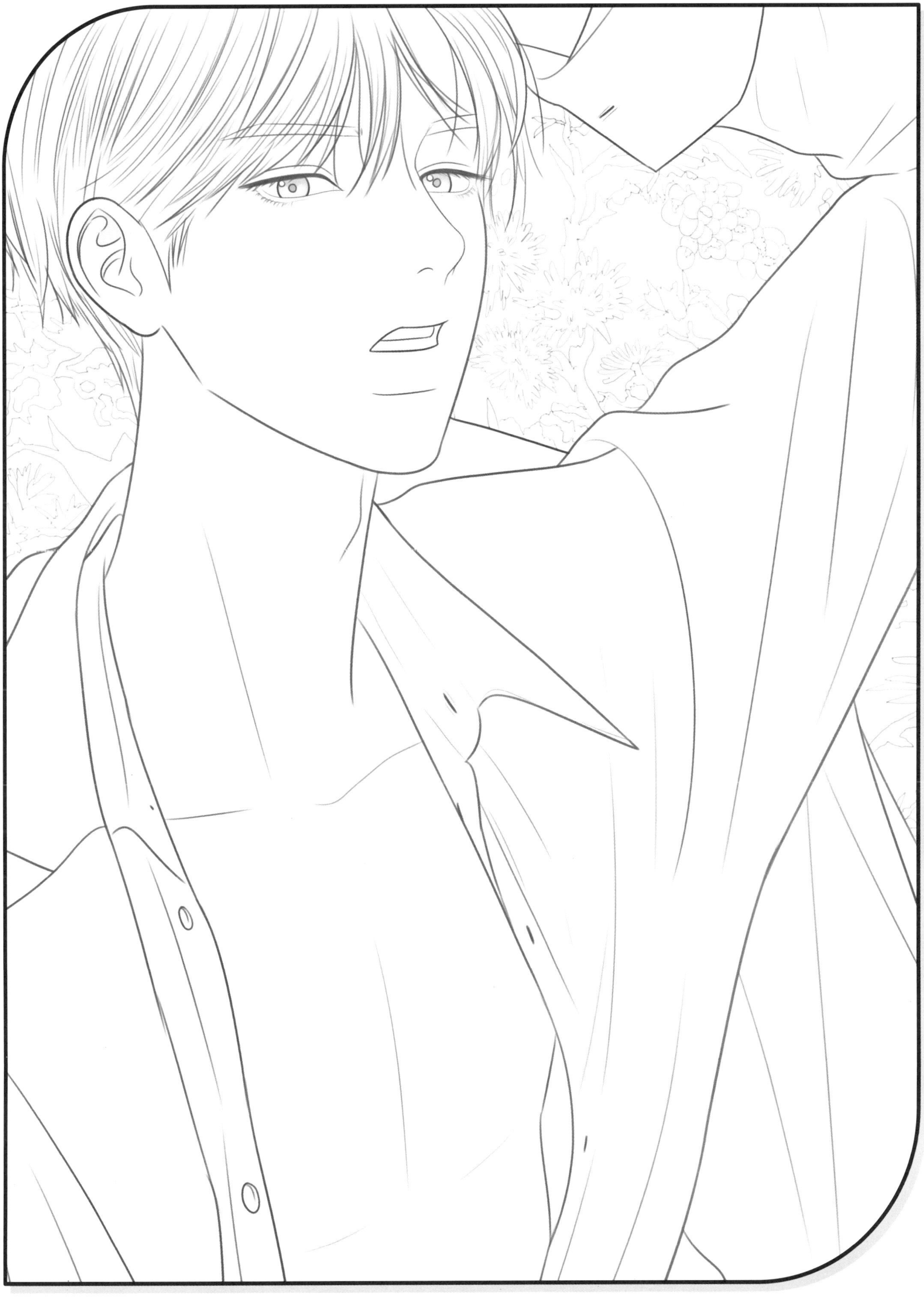

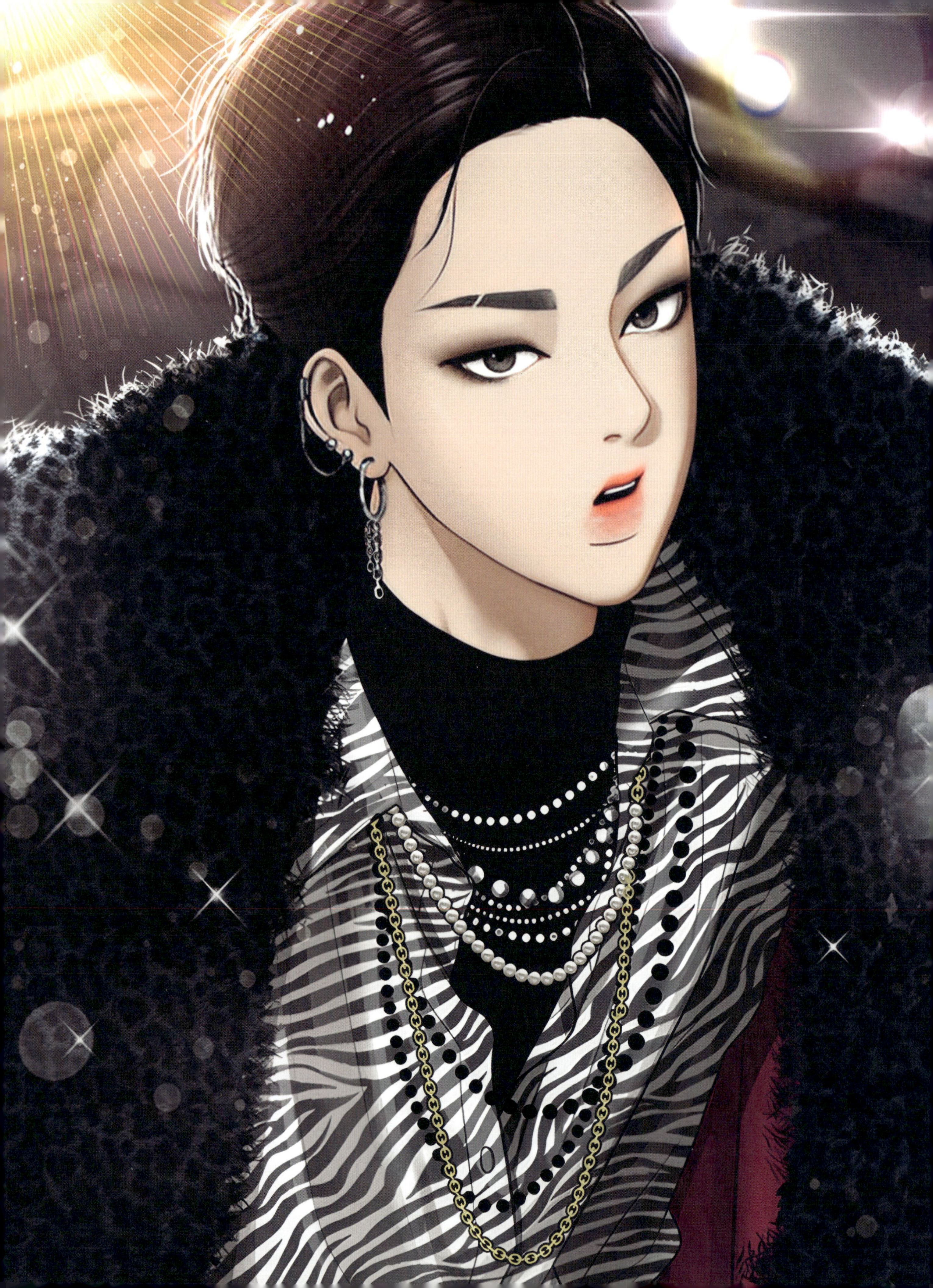

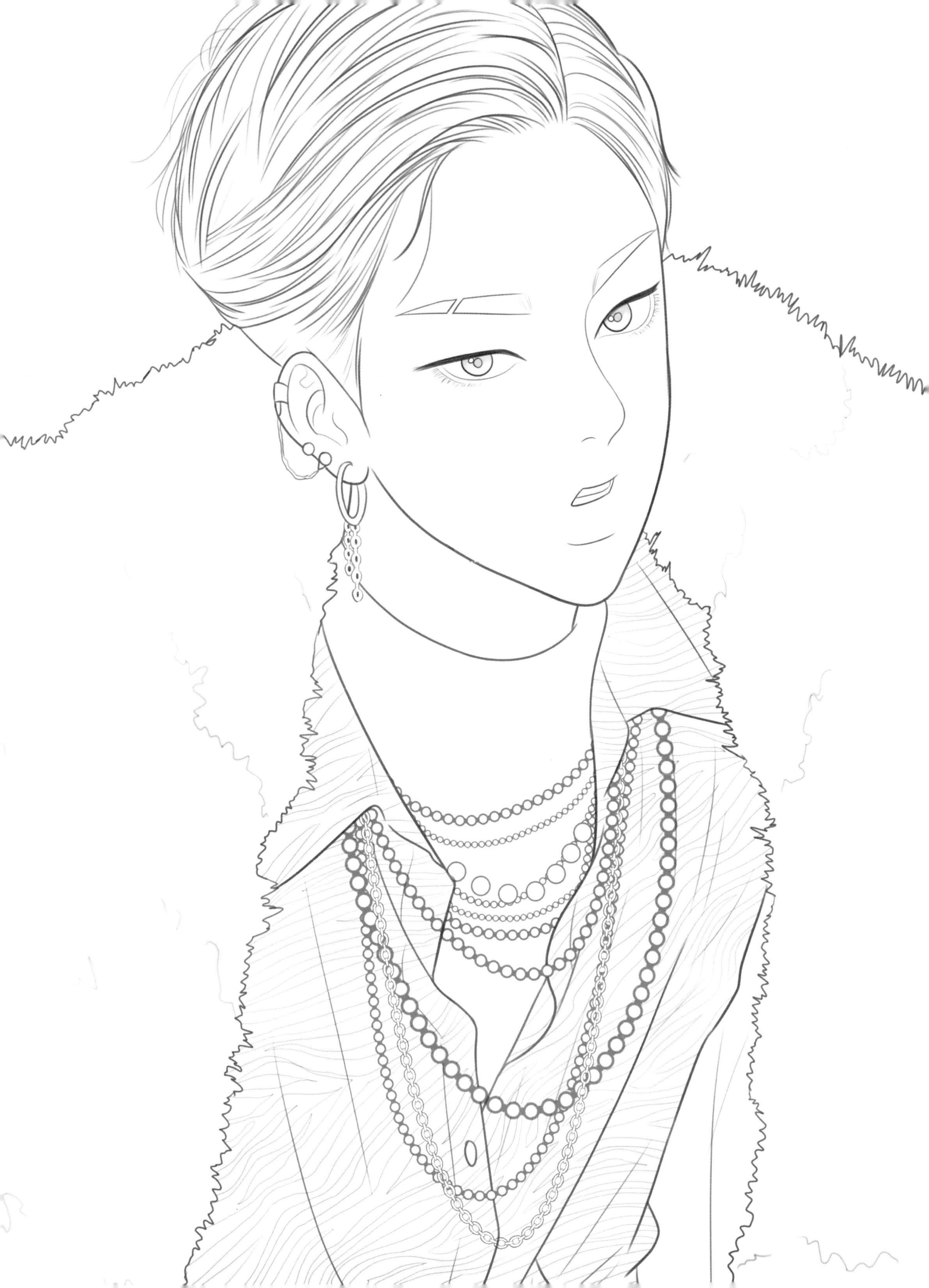

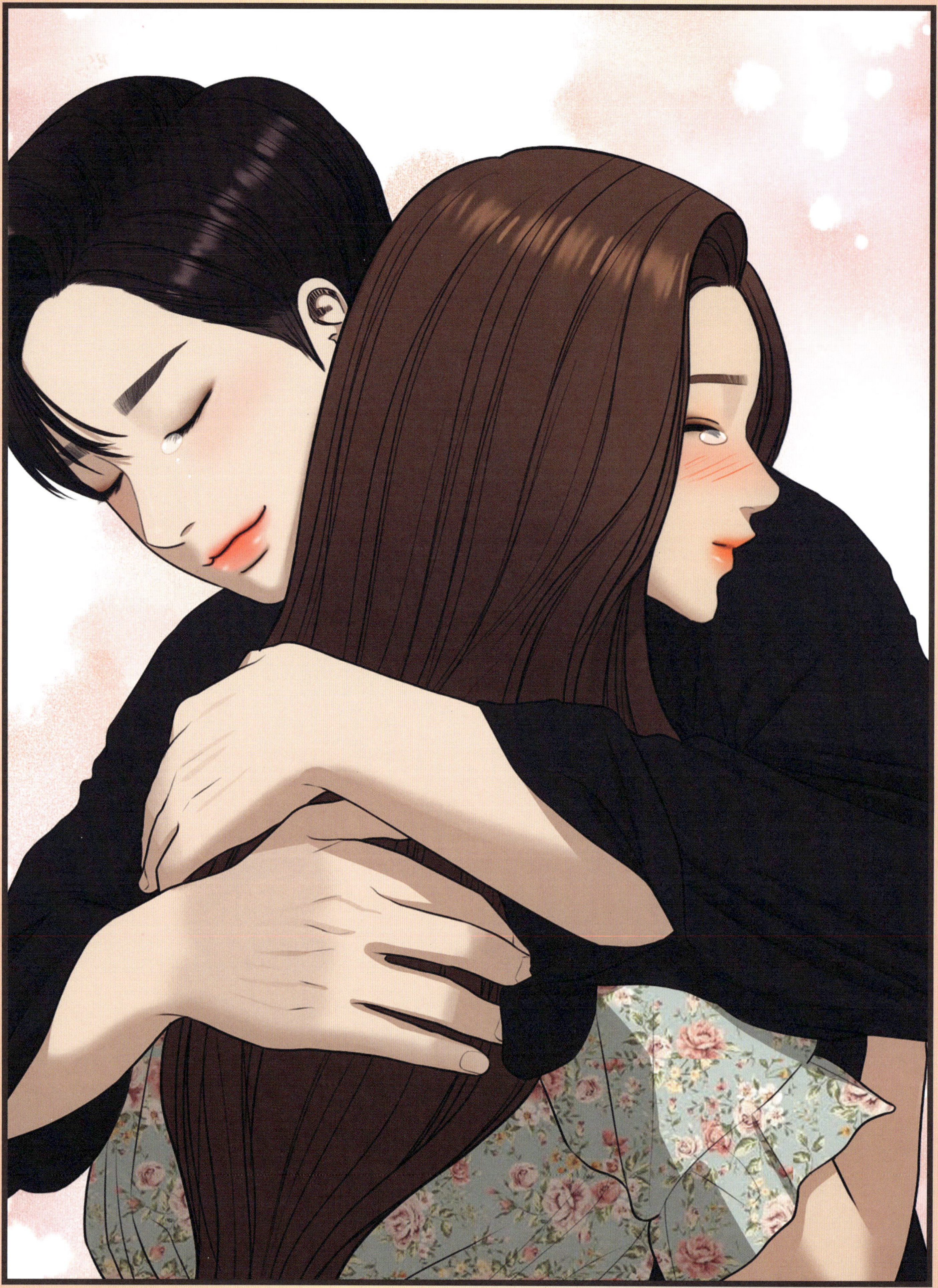

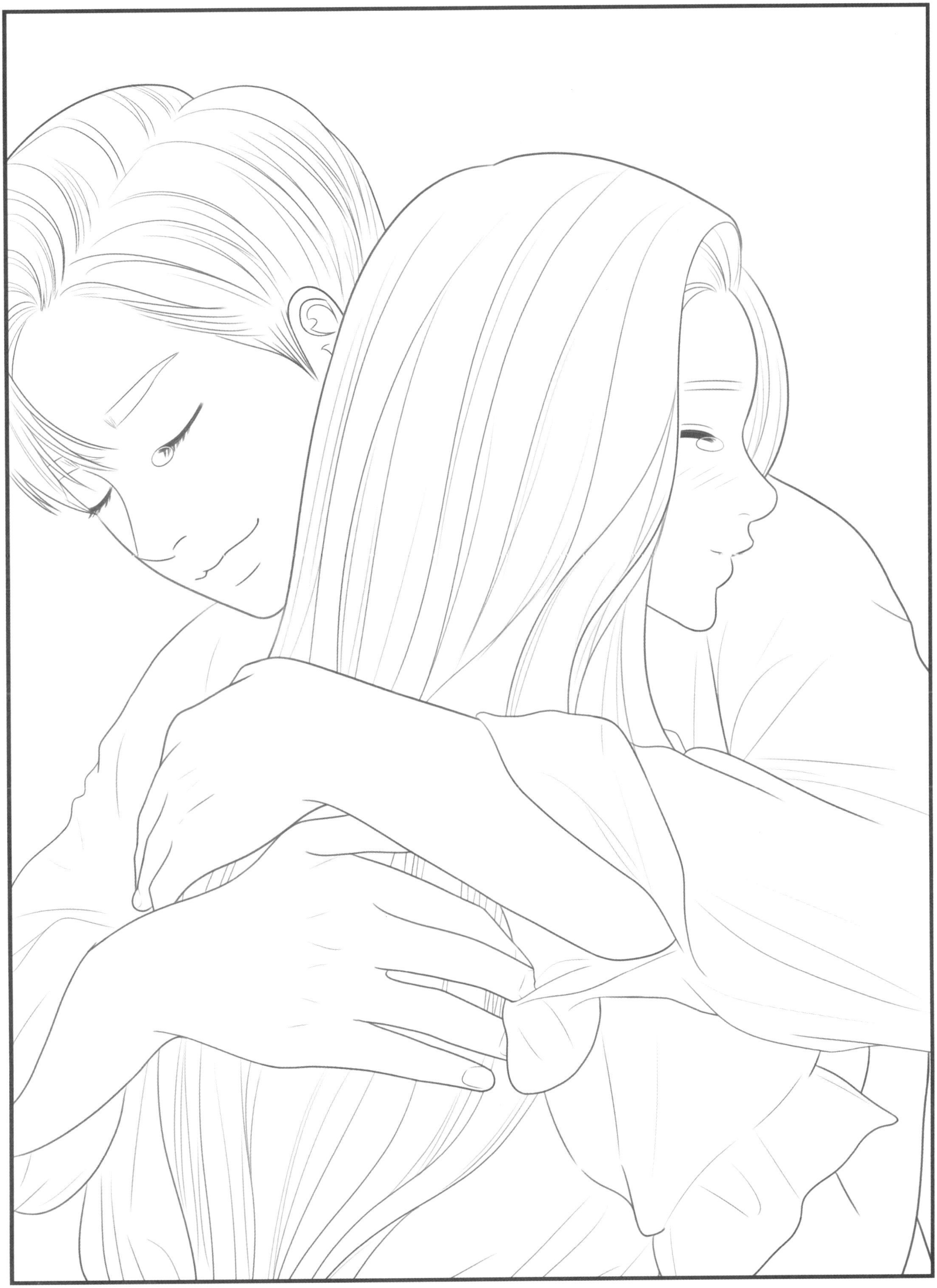

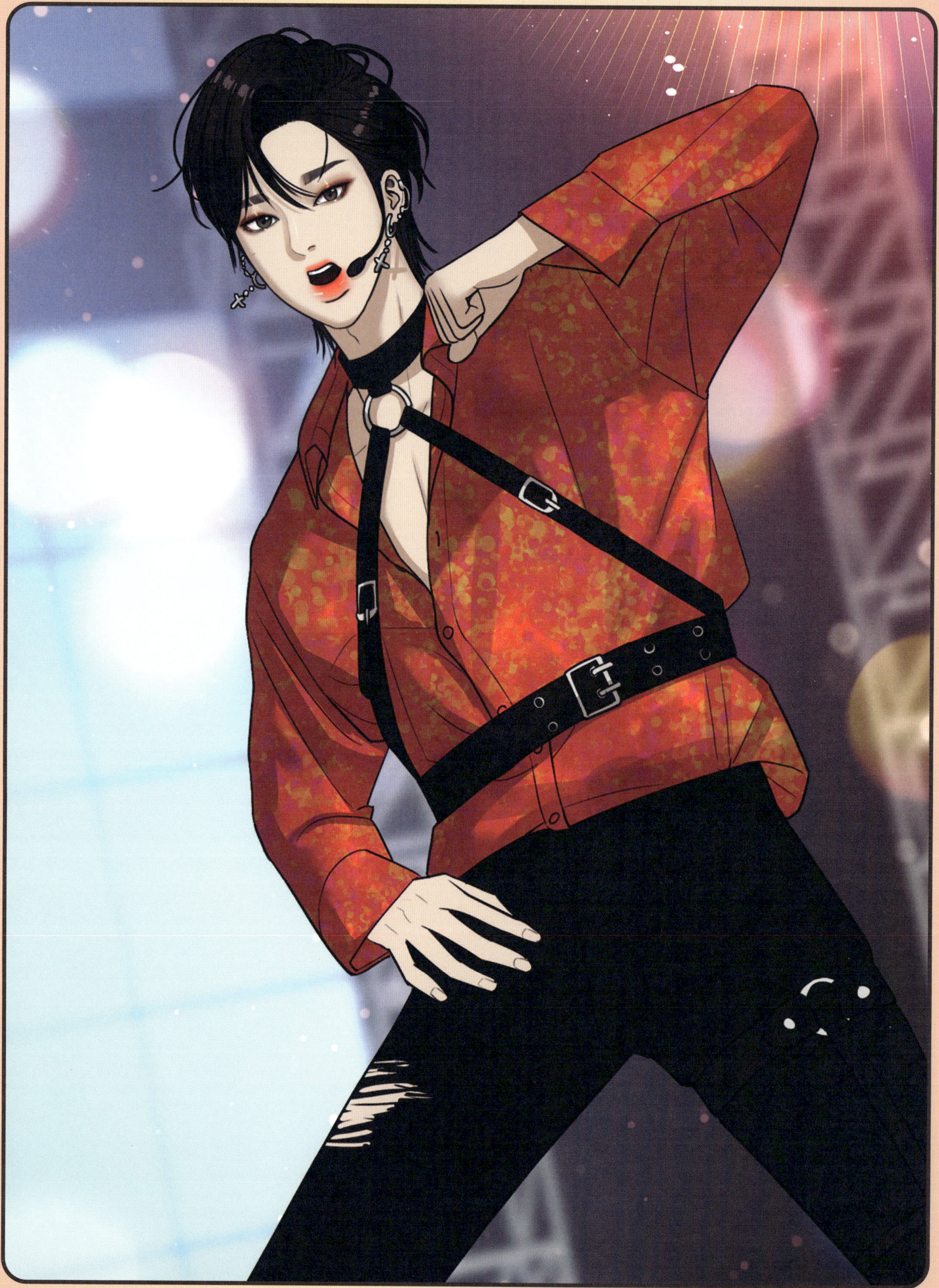

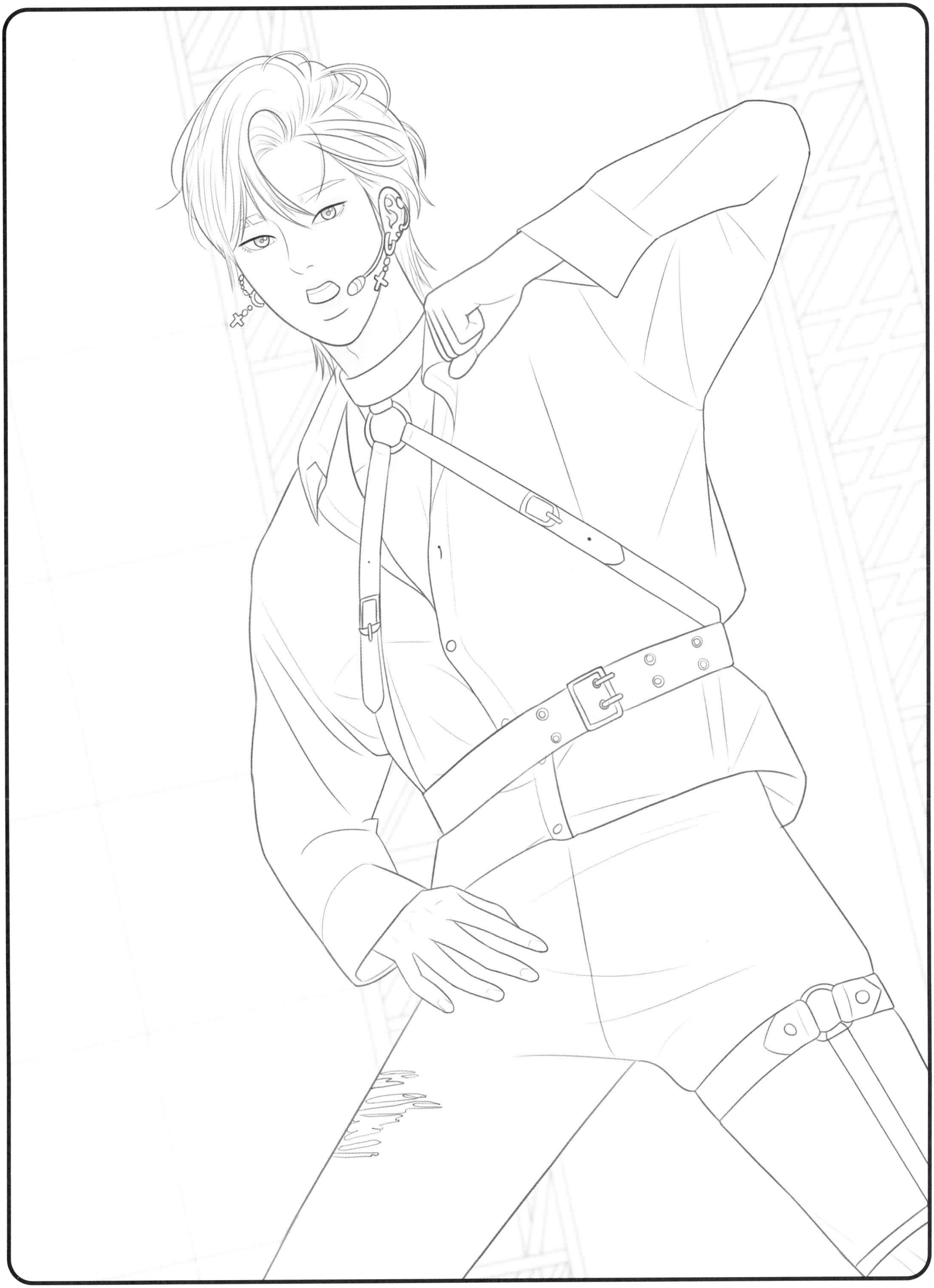

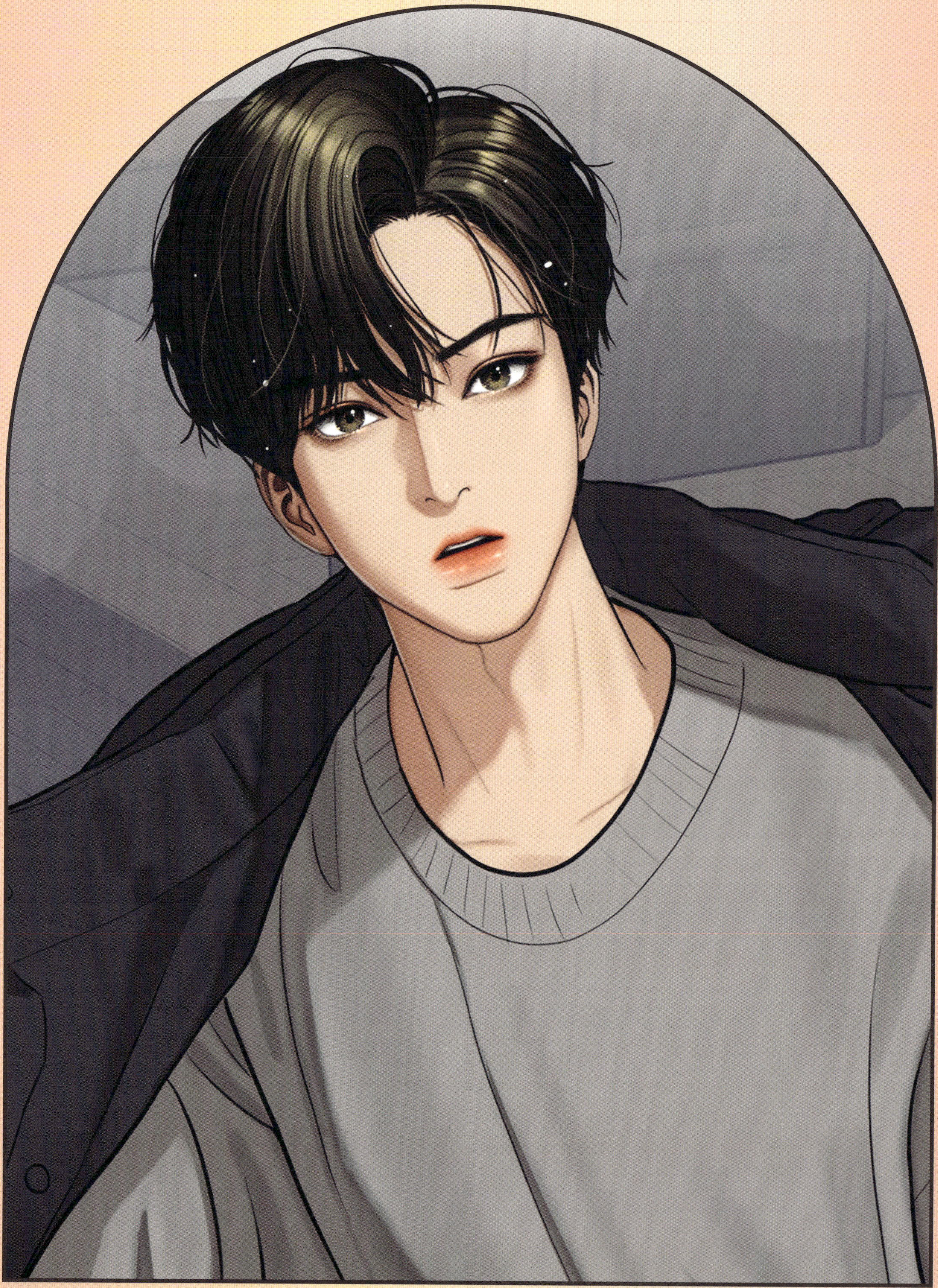

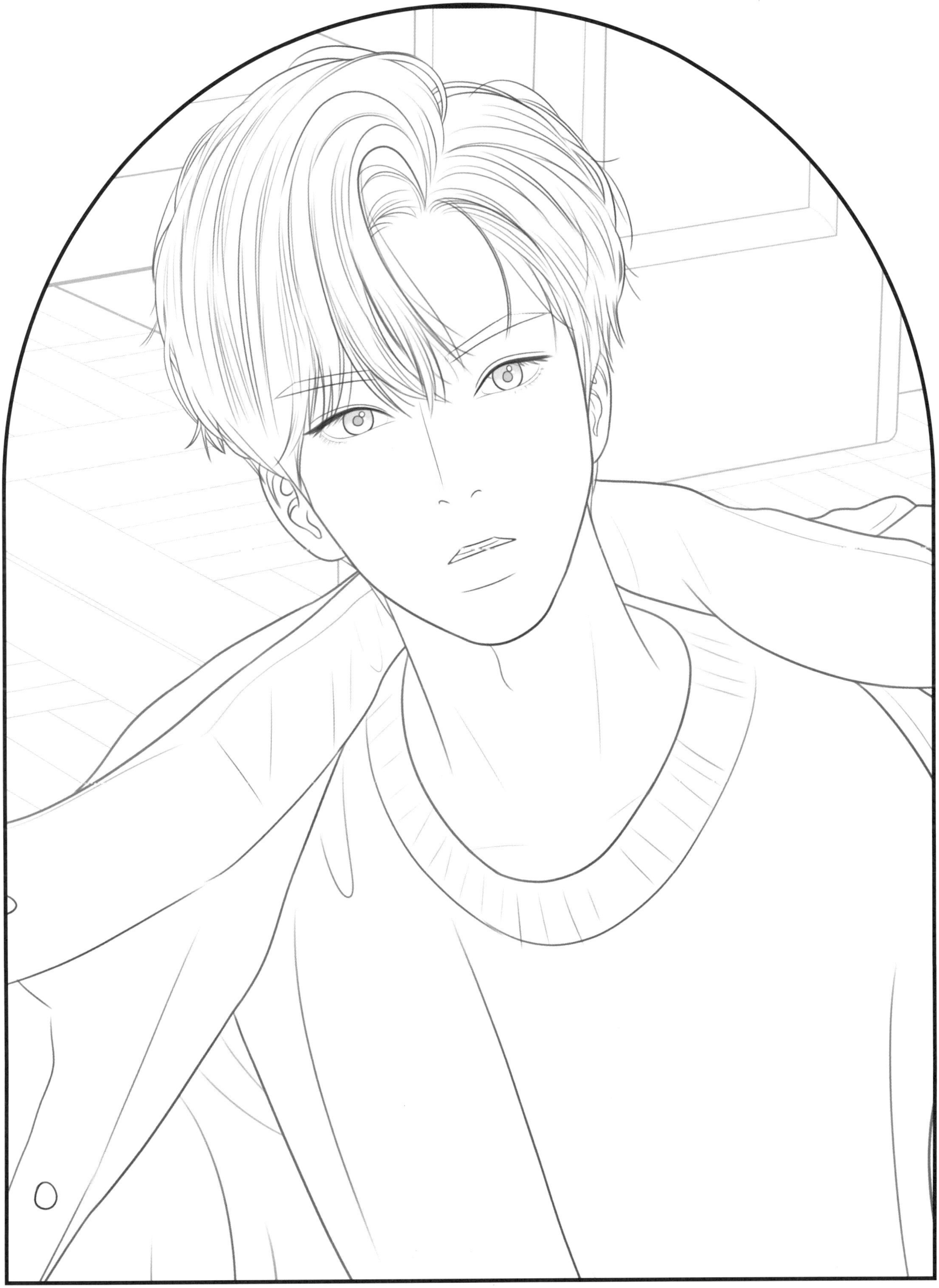

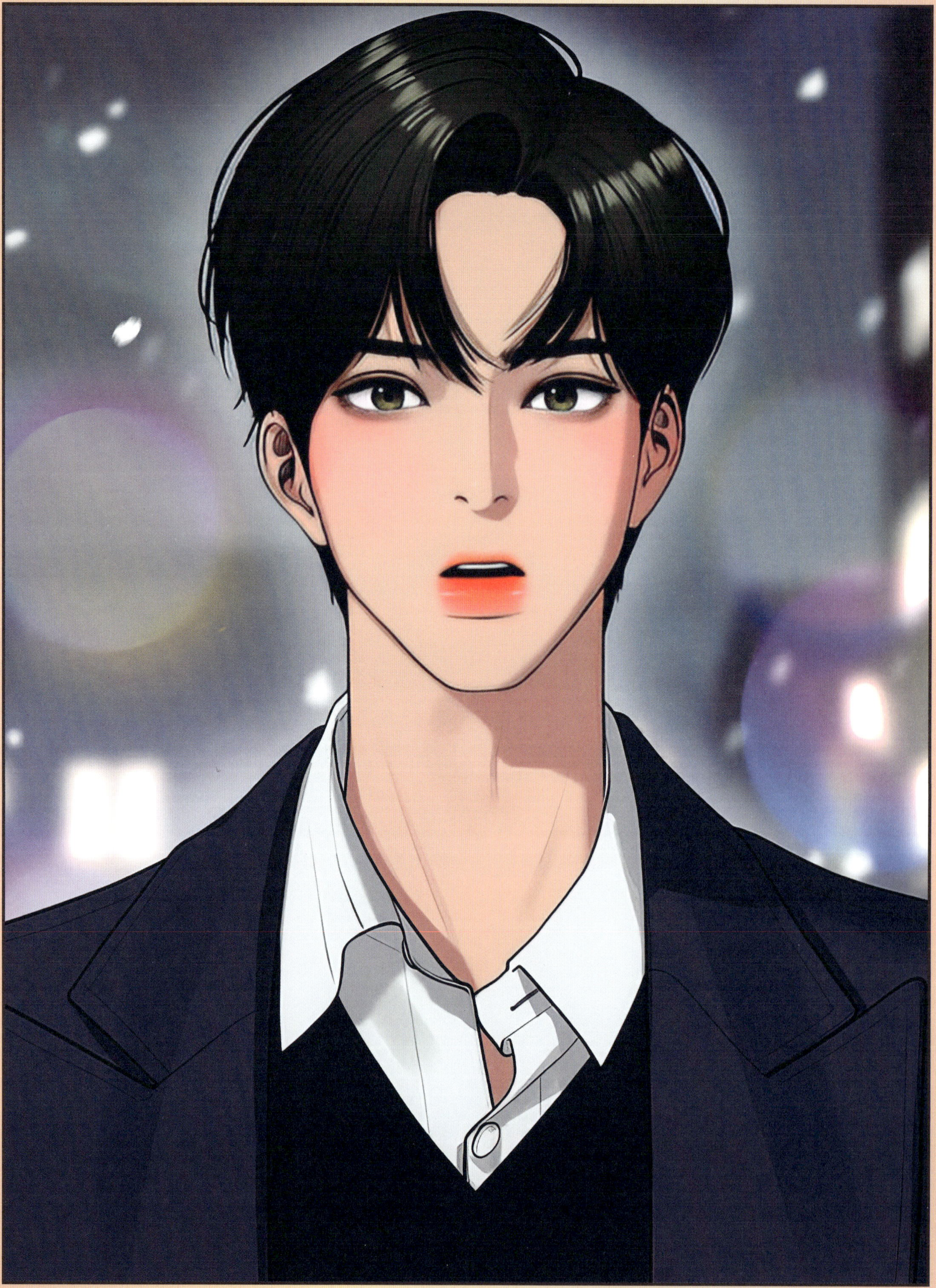

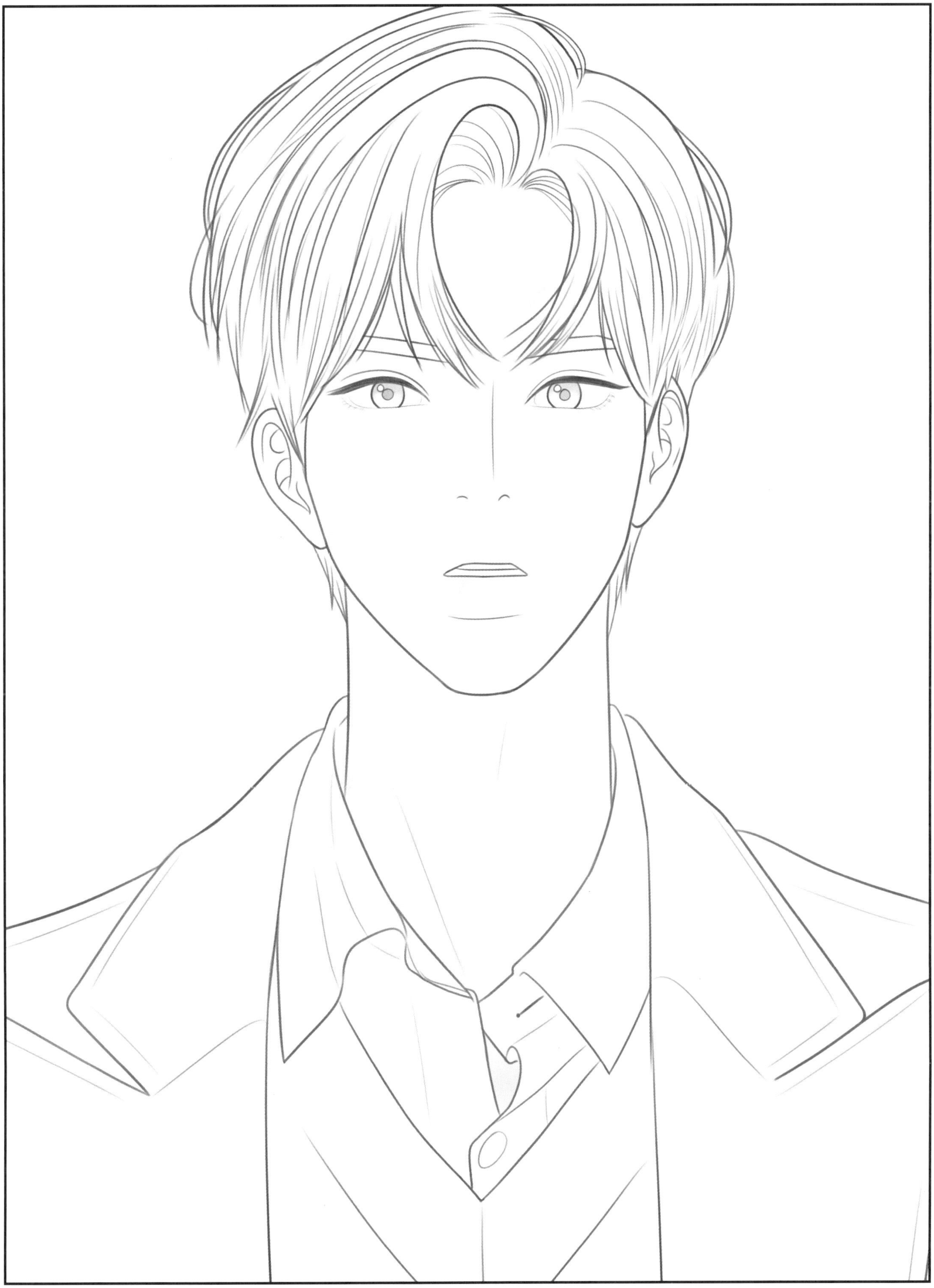

Quarto.com | WalterFoster.com

© 2024 Quarto Publishing Group USA Inc.
WEBTOON TRUE BEAUTY © Yaongyi. All rights reserved.
WEBTOON and all related trademarks are owned by WEBTOON Entertainment Inc. or its affiliates.

First Published in 2024 by Walter Foster Publishing, an imprint of The Quarto Group,
100 Cummings Center, Suite 265-D, Beverly, MA 01915, USA.
T (978) 282-9590 F (978) 283-2742

Content previously published as *True Beauty Coloring Book* (Youngjin.com, 2021).

All rights reserved. No part of this book may be reproduced in any form without written permission of the copyright owners. All images in this book have been reproduced with the knowledge and prior consent of the artists concerned, and no responsibility is accepted by producer, publisher, or printer for any infringement of copyright or otherwise, arising from the contents of this publication. Every effort has been made to ensure that credits accurately comply with information supplied. We apologize for any inaccuracies that may have occurred and will resolve inaccurate or missing information in a subsequent reprinting of the book.

Walter Foster Publishing titles are also available at discount for retail, wholesale, promotional, and bulk purchase. For details, contact the Special Sales Manager by email at specialsales@quarto.com or by mail at The Quarto Group, Attn: Special Sales Manager, 100 Cummings Center, Suite 265-D, Beverly, MA 01915, USA.

10 9 8 7 6 5 4 3 2 1

ISBN: 978-0-7603-8971-3

WEBTOON Rights and Licensing Manager: Amanda Chen

Printed in China

ABOUT THE CREATOR

Kim Na-young, better known by her nom de plume Yaongyi, is a South Korean comic artist (manhwaga), former model, and creator of True Beauty on WEBTOON.

For more from Yaongyi, check out:
Instagram: @meow91_